The Raven
By
Ann E. Eskridge

MY VISION WORKS PUBLISHING

My Vision Works Publishing
(248) 254-3847
www.myvisionworkspublishing.com

Dedication and Acknowledgements

This book is dedicated to my parents, Marguerite and Arnett, who encouraged my creativity and independence; and, I would like to thank my brothers, Arnett and Gregory, who, in their own way, have faced adversity and come out the better for it. I am so proud of both of you.

This book could not have been written without the help and advice of my friend the late Dottie Battle. My friends Donzetta Jones, and Phyllis Lodge were not only supportive, but encouraged me to continue writing...and writing...and writing

Special thanks goes to Susan Campbell Bartoletti and Spalding University's MFA Creative Writing Program and all the writers I've met there and in the future. Thank you for giving me back my muse.

I would also like to acknowledge the archivists and librarians who helped answer questions for the research on this project, The Friends of Freedom Society, The Ohio Historical Society, The University of Detroit Mercy Black Abolitionist Archives, and University of Detroit Mercy College of Liberal Arts and Education Interim Dean, Roy E. Finkenbine, who patiently answered all my questions as well as gave sound advice. I would also like to thank Dr. Willie L. Morrow for his book, *400 Years Without A Comb*, and to all those persons that I've interviewed through the years who have worked tirelessly in unearthing the history, sites, and participants in the Underground Railroad. If there are historical inaccuracies, it is solely my fault.

Special acknowledgement goes to ArtServe and the Michigan Council for Arts and Cultural Affairs, whose initial financial support made this book possible. And to the African American Studies Program at the University of Detroit Mercy.

Finally, to the abolitionists and conductors of the Underground Railroad; to those slaves who stayed on and to those who fled, thank you. In particular, I'd like to acknowledge John P. Parker, who served as inspiration for this book.

All *Raven* Poems and *Raven Songs*
written by Ann E. Eskridge

These poems and songs:
When We Are Old
Tomorrow
I Love You Dear
When Mammy Rocks Her Little One to Sleep
A Kiss
written by Thomas Alfred Anderson

Oh Worship the King hymn
written by Robert C. Grant, 1779-1838 From Psalm 104

Advisory

It is, after all, the 1850's and political correctness was not a priority. Therefore, there is the use of the "n" word, as well as other names whites called blacks, and blacks called themselves. There are also a few graphic scenes of violence meant to underscore that blacks, at that time, were not considered human and were not treated as such. We need reminders of the way things were in order not to repeat our ignoble past.

Background

The Compromise of 1850 became the turning point of the abolitionist movement, a movement to end slavery. When this act passed, some persons who had been neutral about slavery rallied to the abolitionist cause. When slave hunters began roaming into free states looking for fugitive slaves, many ordinary citizens refused to surrender the accused and fought with their fists and through the legal system to protect the fugitives. And because of this act, the Underground Railroad, the secret network of persons, both black and white, who helped fugitive slaves escape, became stronger and bolder.

...After that they all heard a big sing of wings. It was John come back, riding on a great black crow. The crow was so big that one wing rested on the morning, while the other dusted off the evening star. John lighted down and helped them, so they all mounted on, and the bird took out straight across the deep blue sea.

---Zora Neal Hurston

CHAPTER ONE

Kentucky Woods—November 1850

"*Val,*" Solomon grunted while wrestling with the frenzied slave. "... she won't stay in the coffin." Valentine turned his head and saw the two struggling. The light from the lantern cast images of Solomon and the slave woman as silhouettes against the wooded backdrop. In the dark, the trees were nothing more than black skeletons—and Solomon and the slave girl—grotesque shadow puppets. Only two weeks before the countryside was ablaze with autumnal color. The trees were a bouquet of burnt orange, goldenrod and sizzling scarlet. Then November brought with it an unseasonable cold spell that shriveled the trees, turning the landscape into murky browns.

"Val, did you hear me?" shouted Solomon, frustration putting an edge on his voice.

Valentine didn't answer immediately. He had troubles of his own. The cork black that he had used to darken and disguise his burnished, brown face itched unmercifully, causing his eyes to water. They felt like they were swelling; and in a few minutes, he might not be able to see to drive.

"I heard you. And keep your voice down. Tell her if she doesn't get in the coffin, we'll take off without her, and she and her baby can be caught by patrollers," Valentine snapped back.

"You tell her," Solomon grunted angrily, struggling to pull the frightened woman toward the coffin.

"You're white. She understands threats from a white man," Valentine yelled back. He was trying to tie the soiled head rag to the grayish-black wig he was wearing, while keeping the horse steady,

"Yeah, but you're older," Solomon persisted.

"By four years," Valentine retorted. Valentine heard Solomon repeat the threat about the patrollers, but the woman continued to struggle.

"Damn!" Solomon cried out, "She bit me."

Valentine threw down the reins and climbed over the wagon seat. He made his way gingerly to the back, lifting the tattered dress he wore to keep from tripping. Solomon and the woman were still wrestling among the coffins that were stacked haphazardly three high, in two rows. The lantern resting on top of a coffin lid was threatening to tip over. Valentine pitched his voice slightly higher than normal, as if age had shriveled his vocal cords. He spoke to the young woman in the raspy tone of an old woman.

"Der...der...girlie. Ya don't have no worries. Dis here good white man gonna save your life. He and me gonna take you ta freedom. Ain't nobody gonna harm ya."

The slave woman calmed down somewhat. She clutched her baby tightly in one arm as she pointed to the top coffin with the other. "But dat der mean death," she croaked breathlessly.

"Better ta play dead, den *be* dead. Dat dere ya passage to a new life. What do dey call ya?"

"Ruth," she said rocking the fretting baby as it flailed weakly in her arms.

"Now, Ruth, we gotta go. We gots another one to pick up. Den we gonna head to de Ohio. Your baby cain't be makin' noise, so gib your baby some dis here Valerian root. Bitter taste, but it put da lamb ta sleep. And maybe you take a little too," Valentine gave the woman the vial.

"Now you place a drop on your finger and put it in de baby's mouth for it to suck and go ta sleep, so's it don't wake up if we get stopped. You do the same, if you want. Now, climb on in," Valentine urged, taking the child into his arms while the woman stepped into the coffin. He gave the baby back to its mother and made sure that she gave the child the oil. Solomon closed the lid, leaving a small space for mother and baby to breathe.

"Thanks for your help," Solomon said, holding up the lantern. By lamp light, Solomon stared at Valentine in wig, cork face, with puffy red eyes.

"My God, you look hideous."

"That's the point, isn't it?" Valentine responded as he and Solomon jumped off the back of the wagon and made their way to the front. Valentine whipped the old mare, and the wagon with stacked coffins, bumped down the dirt road.

ଔ

Kentucky Woods—same night

Jesse Frye was saddle sore and chilled to the bone. The only thing he was going to catch was his death. The frost came on quickly, and most folk swore it would be a bitter winter. Jesse's ears and nose were raw from the wind. He rubbed his cold hand over his patchy stubble. What he wouldn't give for a decent shave. His boyish face was nicked and scarred from too many mornings of cold water and a dull razor. He had decided to grow a beard, but that was a failure. Light stubble grew in patches across his chin, and it itched like crazy.

"No nigger-stealers comin' tonight," Jesse said to his horse as it snorted steam from its nostrils and stomped the ground irritably.

"Yep, I feel the same dang way. Waste of time." He scratched his chest through the itchy heavy wool of his frock coat and hacked a wad of tobacco onto the frosty ground, wiping off the juice before it stuck to his face. Jesse shook his head vigorously to keep awake and let out a gurgling yawn.

Five nights in a row he had patrolled the road two miles outside of town that led to the river. And five nights in a row there was nothing to arouse his suspicions. But the night sounds played havoc with his imagination. Every rustle of dead leaves or snap of a twig made him flinch.

To Jesse, the talk of nigger stealers was foolish. No one was that smart to go up against the law. The countryside was swarming with constables, deputies and any gadabout with a gun willing to earn a few dollars using darkies as target practice. Just the other day two boys wandered in half-starved and ready to kill just to get a meal in their bellies. Jack and Harry were their names, Jesse recalled, and about the two dumbest boys Jesse had ever met. But they were put on patrol and given authority to capture or kill anyone trying to help slaves escape.

Every stream was being watched, and every boat, searched. Patrollers were riding constant vigil and each one of them had a reward poster offering five thousand dollars for the Raven's capture—dead or alive.

Slaves were being whisked from under their owners' noses. At least four in three months. And all escapes were attributed to The Raven; his telltale black feather left as a taunting gesture.

The problem was nobody really knew what he looked like. That reward would sure be something, Jesse thought to himself, as he smeared the snot from his dripping nose and hacked up the rest of the tobacco he'd been chewing.

Jesse wasn't a volunteer. He was earning a few dollars for each mile he patrolled. It was his job. The local sheriff hired him because he needed more men to patrol the northern Kentucky border. Too many fugitives had been escaping.

Puffs of smoke expelled from Jesse's mouth. He shivered against the wind. He was tired and he knew that those two loafers, Jack and Harry, had built themselves a fire and bedded down for the night. *It wasn't fair.* No one would blame him for going home early. He'd done his duty and earned his money. Anyway, talk of the Raven being loose was just that—talk. If it were up to him, he'd just let 'um go. Hell, no pay, bad food, back breaking work. He didn't blame the niggers for runnin' away. Still, he had a job to do.

Jesse let his horse lead while he burrowed inside his coat, drew his hat down, and closed his eyes, hoping to get some sleep.

ભ

Down the road, the wagon rolled on through the darkness with only the lantern's dim circle of yellow light guiding the way. Valentine's eyes were almost swollen shut. His nose was running and the wind that whipped through his threadbare dress felt like hundreds of needle points stabbing his chest. He was miserable, but he knew that the rescue was worth it. *One more soul to safety*, he repeated to himself, and to the rhythm of the rolling wagon.

Above and to the rear he heard Solomon softly snoring. *To be young and foolish*, Valentine thought. *No, to be young, foolish, and white*, he corrected himself.

"Solomon," he whispered loudly, "Wake up we're almost there." Valentine heard Solomon stir and jump down off the wagon. Then Valentine spurred the mare on, hoping the old girl would make it to the river before she collapsed from the exertion.

Cℬ

Jesse didn't know how long he had napped. The screech of an animal woke him. He looked around, but the clouds partially obscured the moon. All he was able to make out in the darkness was the skeletal outlines of trees with their dying leaves rustling in answer to the chilling wind. Jesse reined his horse to a stop and listened.

He heard the sound of a wagon coming toward him. Muscles tensed, Jesse fumbled for his unlit lantern, but dropped it on the ground. It was lost in the darkness. Wagon wheels creaked up ahead. Jesse straightened up and spurred his horse on toward the sound.

The wagon's lantern cast a faint, eerie circle of light around it. An old black woman sat on the wagon pulled by a horse that should have been dead, as old as it looked. Jesse jumped down from his horse and stood in the middle of the road, one hand raised, signaling a halt to the wagon. He walked closer as the wagon approached.

"Old Auntie, whatcha doin' out this time a night?" he called out.

The old woman had gray frizzled hair peeking out from her dirty head rag. She smiled a ragged grin on a face that was tar black and pitted.

"I goin' ta the graveyard, Massa. Ta the graveyard," the woman said, stopping the wagon in front of Jesse. "I got me some peoples need ta be put ta rest, suh." Her voice was as ancient as her face and sounded like flint on iron.

"Who says you kin be out this late, Auntie? You know there's a curfew," Jesse said, grabbing the bridle of the mare to steady the animal.

"Oh, ah knows, ah knows. But deese hyeah folks cain't wait." She gestured toward the back of the wagon with a slight turn of her head.

"Gimme your lantern, Auntie. Let me see what you got back there." Jesse grabbed the light without waiting for a reply. He casually strolled to the back of the wagon and held the lantern high. The light illuminated six pine coffins piled on top of each other. With the light in one hand, he used his other to pry the top open.

"You do dat Massa, you let out de devil," the old woman called after him.

"Stop talkin' in riddles old woman. I gotta see what you got in these here coffins. I got to know how come you choosin' to break the law."

Jesse's hand slid underneath the coffin top. He leaned over with the light to see better.

"You do that sir, you lettin' out de devil cholera. These'm people done died from it. They gots ta be buried soon's I get dem to de grave. Da devil cholera gonna grab ya tonight, put yer in de grave tomorrow. Make you run at both ends like the rushin' river," she cackled.

Jesse froze. He snatched his hand back from the coffin and backed away, bumping into his horse.

Cholera. There had been an outbreak in a town close to the Mississippi, and another one in Cincinnati. Five months before that, President Taylor had succumbed to the disease, dying in his own vomit and feces. Nobody knew what caused it, but if you got it, you would surely die within a day.

"Why you didn't tell me, old woman? You tryin' to kill me?" His anger sliced through the darkness.

"I done tol' you, Massa. Got ta get dem to de graveyard foe sun up. Let dere spirits rest in peace, so dah devil cholera won't git ter nobody else."

Jesse thrust the lantern at the woman, grabbed the reins of his horse, and guided it away from the wagon. "Get on with ya then, and don't you stop. Anybody stops you, you tell 'um right away what you got in them coffins. You hear me old woman?"

By this time the woman had already started moving down the road before he could finish scolding her. He heard her gravelly voice break out in what he thought was mumble jumble. Half-singing, half-muttering, she headed the wagon toward the pauper's graveyard that overlooked the river's edge.

> *His soul is black, as black as night,*
> *A good luck omen to those in flight,*
> *For he has come to set them free.*

Jesse Frye mounted his horse and galloped away. He no longer thought of the cold, only that he needed to put distance between him and the dreaded disease. So, he didn't hear when another voice joined in lustily with that of the old woman's as they sang the remaining stanzas:

> *And in the darkness he doth roam,*
> *A spirit sent to lead them home,*
> *Where freedom waits for them.*
> *Who is this trickster, this dark knight?*
> *This spirit guide, this demon bright?*
> *They whisper Raven on the wind.*

ᘓ

CHAPTER TWO

Kentucky— Mercer Plantation—same night

"You cold, George?" Leona asked as she and her brother sat in the frigid air on a fallen log. They were just beyond sight of the main house and slave cabins.

"I'm fine for right now, but soon we'll have to use the shed. It's gonna be too cold in a little while to sit outside." George wrapped his arms around himself to keep warm.

"Take my shawl and put it 'round ya." Leona took the shawl from her head and gave it to her brother, then moved closer so he could get some of her body warmth.

She wished she could see him in daylight, to see how much he'd grown and filled out, but it was forbidden by order of Dr. Fowler, her master. If she wanted to see George, she had to sneak out after dark. It seemed that each time she met him, he'd grown inches taller. His chin stubble brushed against her face and tickled when they hugged. He was growing a beard like he threatened.

"Here, here's some of the pie I made. It's apple. I put raisins 'n pecans in it."

"Ya know I don' like no raisins." George made a face.

"Yeah, but Dr. Fowler do; and Mrs. Fowler likes what Dr. Fowler likes," she said, handing him the napkin with the huge chunk of pie.

"Just pick the things out or give it back, don't make me no difference," she grumbled.

He put his arm around his sister and leaned close to her.

"I ain't lettin' this pie go to waste, Le-le," he said, using his childhood name for her because as a baby he couldn't say Leona. "You can bet on that. Shoot, I ain't had nothin' this good since the last time you wuz here." He bit a piece off and hummed his approval.

"I swear you kin cook. Them Fowlers should be glad they got you. Master Mercer got the worse cook in the world. Shoot, even I kin cook better'n she kin. An' he think she the best thing that ever come 'long. Her cornbread taste like rocks. Like you got ta drink a pitcher of water jest to soften it up. I kin take her cornbread and throw it at one of dem pigs and knock 'um dead with one blow," he laughed and pretended to squeal like a pig in agony.

Leona listened to her brother's laughter. It had been a long time since she'd heard him laugh. "So, everythin' all right wit you? You doin' all right?"

He shrugged. "Doin' the best I kin. Ain't nothin' to get joyful about. Still the same thing up before the sun and in the fields. Gets a break by noon; 'n back to work until it git too dark to work," he sighed. "Le-le," he said quietly. "I heard that some of us gonna try and get to Ohio. It ain't that far. Maybe a few days walk and if they lucky, they can walk across if the river done hardened."

"Don't talk like that. You scare me when you talk like that," she said anxiously. "You don't know what them ab'litions do to ya. I hear they just try and sweet talk you into bein' put on a boat back to Africa...and you be eaten by de African niggers. And...and if they don't do dat, then they sell you again."

"Who told you that?" George asked angrily.

"Doctor Fowler say so. He say, them people like the Raven only out ta get they selves some free nigger labor or worse...he say they got ab'litions doctors who skin de black off de slave and sells it for leather and feeds de meat to the pigs."

"What? And you believe him? Huh? You believe all he say?" asked George. "Girl, you ain't got good sense. Why you think he say that?" But George didn't wait for an answer. "He say that 'cause he wanna keep you stupid and doin' what he say. He wanna keep you as his slave. He don't want you ta know what freedom's like. You think livin' with the Fowlers is livin' high on the hog? You crazy girl," he scolded. "That man ain't good for nothin'. He livin' off his wife's money and he ain't much of a doctor, truth be told. All he know how to do is bleed people dry 'n lie," George said emphatically.

"Don't matter," she said angrily. "Don't matter what he is. He still treat me okay; and she don't mess with me—not really. So I got me a warm bed and a place to stay. I'll be all right. I don't need to be runnin'," she shot back defiantly. Then she remembered about the other day. She had been washing clothes, and Dr. Fowler had demanded that she stop what she was doing to come and assist him.

෨

"Leona, I need you," she heard Dr. Nathanial Fowler's voice carry on the wind. Leona shielded her eyes from the bright sun and saw her master standing in the doorway. His shirtsleeves were rolled to his elbows, and a pair of scissors glinted in his hand. Leona looked down at her wash. The bubbling lye water seared her nose as the steam rose to meet the frosty air. Crows overhead glided in lazy circles, and caught the updraft. Their black bodies were silhouettes against the sky. Several were perched on the bare branches of trees, and cawed to their soaring mates.

Leona glanced up at the birds and wished she were that carefree. *To be a bird, to soar, to glide, to fly away.* Instead, she wiped the sweat from her forehead with her rough brown hand. She could not ignore her master.

"Dr. Fowler sir, I'm doin' de wash," Leona yelled back.

"Forget the wash, girl. This is more important. Come inside," he ordered. He then abruptly turned and went back inside, closing the office door against the cold wind before she could protest any further. Leona grabbed the long wooden stick and stabbed the sheets in the boiling wash. She knew that he had chosen this time to interrupt her housekeeping chores because Mrs. Fowler was upstairs in her darkened bedroom after having taken ill with another one of her sick headaches.

Leona laid down the stick and dried her hands on her chintz housedress. Her bishop sleeves and bodice had gotten wet from the wash water, and were spotted from the fresh blood that soaked the linens.

Every Monday was washday. He knew that. For several weeks Dr. Fowler interrupted her chores with some urgency that—he claimed—only she could help him with. The "urgency" always corresponded to his wife's sick spells. Because he was too cheap to buy another servant, seventeen-year old Leona tended to the housework as well as the doctor's office.

Leona brushed away stray curly strands of hair that matted her forehead, wondering how long she could delay before trying his patience. She looked up at the bedroom window where Mrs. Fowler lay, pretending to be asleep. She got no help from the mistress of the house. Mrs. Fowler, who barely took any interest in her husband's profession, did not interfere; but that did not stop her from lurking in the hallways and spying on Leona's every move.

On Mondays, the doctor's linens had to be washed separately from the household linens. Those were Mrs. Fowler's orders. Not one blood stained sheet was permitted to touch the house linens.

Leona had to lug the heavy washtub from out of the barn. She would dig a hole, build a fire and set the tub over the fire. Then she would fill the washtub with water from the pump and wait until the water was hot. Then she washed the clothes with soap so strong it made her gasp for air.

After Leona hung the clothes on the line, Mrs. Fowler would come out and inspect the wash. If there was one speck of blood or dirt on any of the sheets, Leona would have to wash the clothes again. Once the wash finally met with Mrs. Fowler's approval, Leona would then dump the dirty wash water and lug the washtub back to the barn. It was an all day affair, and any delay meant that she could end up outside, late at night, trying to finish the wash.

Dr. Fowler always kept a clean set of clothing in his office. Leona caught him several times with his pants off behind a screen. Though he feigned modesty, she knew he timed his change of clothes to coincide with her office cleaning.

Once again the office door was flung open. "Leona!" he bellowed. The anger and impatience in his voice betrayed him. She had waited long enough. She left the wash to bubble on the fire and ran across the blanket of leaves to enter his office.

"What kept you so long?" he said, as he plopped down in his chair, his long legs stretched out on a hassock. The scissors, comb and brush were arranged on the table beside him. He had draped his jacket over another chair. He was lying almost prone, vest unbuttoned and shirtsleeves rolled up—a position befitting a man in the bedroom, rather than the office.

A full-length mirror that he used to guide him when operating on patients, was placed at just the right angle so he could see her as she worked.

"Dr. Fowler," Leona said meekly, with head down and rough

hands hidden behind the folds of her skirt. "You know I got to do the wash. I cain't be in two places at the same time," she protested feebly.

He waved away her protest. "There will always be dirty linens. I need my hair trimmed. I'm not paying a barber to do something that I know you can do quite well. He laid his head back on the chair and closed his eyes.

Leona glanced around the room. She noticed that one of the doors to the medicine cabinet was open. A clear glass bottle was missing. She saw it lying on the surgical table. She bent over and sniffed near Dr. Fowler. He sometimes took his own medicine and when he did that, he went into alternative fits of laughing and crying. She did not smell the odor of the medicine on him, only his rank body odor. She also noticed that the door leading to the living quarters was closed. There would be no interruptions, although she knew that Mrs. Fowler was apt to lurk behind the door.

Even with his eyes closed, he followed her movements behind him by the swish of her long skirt.

Leona took the brush in her hand, hesitated above his head and then, with resignation, began to brush his shoulder length straight hair that was greasy with pomade. The room was cold and her dress was still wet from the wash.

He turned to look at her. "You cold?"

"Yes, Massa. Just a little, sir."

"Well, this won't take long. You can warm up afterwards when you're through."

"Yes, sir," she said quietly, knowing that he'd purposely not made a fire. Her wet bodice clung to her shivering body and the nipples of her breasts stood erect.

"Now, I want you to cut it evenly. I don't like it too short, you know."

"Yes, sir," she leaned her body into him. She felt him lean his weight against her. Leona took his long thick hair and wrapped the ends around her fingers. She held the scissors in her hand and snipped the ends. She took another strand and did the same. She saw him watching her in the mirror. He saw her watching him. She forced herself not to think of how sharp the scissors were.

He visibly relaxed under her touch. "I operated on a patient today," he said with a note of satisfaction in his voice. "The chucklehead had an infection in his leg. I had to cut it out. I gave him something to ease his discomfort," he chuckled. "He didn't feel a thing. I tell you that new medicine worked like a charm. Too bad it's wasted on a stupid bastard who cut himself trying to fell a tree. The trick is not to use too much of the chloroform ...just a little once in awhile, gives one a euphoric feeling. Yes, and relaxing."

And makes you crazy. "Yes sir." Leona made no comment about the amount of blood that had smeared the sheets.

"I poured my tonic over the surgical wound. He should be fine in a few days. I told him to keep off that leg."

"Yes, sir," she said, shivering.

"Now, I want you to cut it evenly. I don't like it too short, you know." He reached up and touched her hand. His fingers caressed hers. She moved her hand away and loosened her grip on the scissors.

"Why I should pay a barber to do what you can do just as well is beyond me. A waste of money and time, I'd say."

Leona made no comment but concentrated on getting the ends straight.

"That's what happens when you go to one of these barbers. You sit and wait your turn and listen to the gossip. Oh, once in awhile it's good to get away, find out what's going on in the

15

county. But one hair cut can take hours. Waste of time and money, I'd say, especially when I have you."

Leona checked to see that the ends of her master's hair were even all the way across before she cut it even shorter. She was aware of his body odor mixed with the tonic he used earlier to clean the man's wound. Both seemed to smother her with their scent and she wrinkled her nostrils in protest. A floorboard creaked in another part of the house. Leona knew it was Mrs. Fowler sneaking around. Leona felt trapped.

She looked out and saw a shadow cross the window; it was a large black bird, a Raven, that landed on a branch. His sleek body arched toward her. He tapped on the glass with his beak, danced backward along the branch, then forward to tap the window again and dance back again. *A dance of freedom*, she thought. *He's mocking me.* She turned from the window and her glance landed on the scalpels and knives lying on the instrument table. She stole a look at the mirror and watched Dr. Fowler breathe easily in sleep. *It would be so easy.* Her hand hovered over the scalpel. But she wouldn't, she couldn't.

Ω

Leona came back to the present and snuggled close to her brother while he ate, but she still felt the touch of Dr. Fowler's clammy hands on her and she shivered.

"You cold?" George said, putting his arms around her. George wished he could see his sister's face. Her large, cat-like brown eyes glowed when she was happy and flashed when she was angry. She had smooth, mocha colored skin and full lips that pinched in a thin line when she was expressing disapproval. Her eyes danced with joy whenever he did anything to make her laugh.

As a young boy George remembered watching his sister braid

her thick, curly hair in two braids and wrapping them on top of her head. One of them would always come apart and unravel, making it an attractive target for pulling.

Though she was unaware of it, his sister was beautiful. George knew it was a matter of time before some white man would have his way with her—to rape her. More than likely it would be Fowler. George expressed his concern out loud.

"You wait till you get older. You'll see what I'm talkin' about. He take a good look at you in the light next to his wife and he gonna git him some, cause he ain't gettin' none from that bag a bones."

She raised her hand to hit him playfully, but his remark found it's target. Her hand landed hard on the side of his face.

"Hey, what you wanna do that for?" he rubbed his cheek.

"I don't like you talkin' that way. I don't like that kind of talk," her voice trembled.

"He touch you?"

She hesitated.

"He *did* touch you."

She lied. "No, no…not…not really. He don't touch me but…"

"But, what?"

Tears of shame ran down her cheek. "Sometimes, he…like come up behind me and…and…he…rub up against me, like he was bumpin' into me. Or he move in too close or…he…" she broke down and sobbed.

George put his arm around her and let her cry on his shoulder. "Don't worry. You go and you tell his wife 'bout it."

Leona shook her head. "No, she…she…don't do nothin.' Jest stay in her room all the time. I think she know what he be doin', but she don't wanna know; so she look the other way."

Mrs. Annie Fowler married the doctor but she detested his profession. To appease her, he turned one room of their rambling clapboard house into his office; equipped with a separate entrance and exit. That way, his patients would not disturb her. Mrs. Fowler hated to be around sick people. Yet, she was forever complaining about her own illnesses. She was so afraid that one of his patients might have some contagious disease, that she gave strict orders that nothing in the doctor's office could come in contact with anything in the household.

Mrs. Fowler also detested Leona, whom she pinched and hit whenever her husband wasn't around. No, Mrs. Fowler would do nothing to stop her husband from harassing her. She preferred, instead, to punish Leona.

"Well next time he try somethin', you just tell him you got yourself a brother who gonna come over and beat him."

That sent a shock of terror through her. "Don't talk like that, ya hear? Don't you even think it. You don't know how mean he kin be. All he gonna do is take it out on me. He told me he don't want me to see you. I had to sneak out tonight. He'll take it out on me. And you too—somehow."

And so her baby brother just rocked her in his arms as she sobbed softly. They had always been close. Leona was cautious, hesitant and slow to rile. George, on the other hand, was a risk-taker and joker, quick to smile and quick to anger. They had been sheltered by their Aunt Sara from the cruelties of slavery when they were young. Aunt Sara's mistress was kind-hearted and promised that one day all of them would be free. However, one day the mistress died suddenly. Unfortunately, Aunt Sara was unable to convince the heirs of the validity of that promise.

The one thing Aunt Sara managed to do was get the heirs to agree that they would not sell Leona and George too far apart from one another. They now lived several miles apart: George as a field hand on the Mercer plantation, and Leona as a house slave to a doctor.

The brother and sister held on to one another in silence, one feeling the heartbeat of the other; two hearts beating in rhythm.

"It time for me to go," Leona said, reluctantly pulling away. "I got to get back 'fore they wake up. Don't you go gettin' into trouble, ya hear? And don't you start talkin' 'bout runnin' or puttin' up a fuss."

"I won't Le-le. You just take care. And stay as far away from Fowler as you can. Hide if you got to."

"Oh yeah. What kinda house girl I'm gonna be if I keep hidin' from the folks I'm supposed to serve?"

"That why we can run, Le-le. We can run and everything gonna be all right."

"Stop. Stop talkin' like that," she pleaded. "I gotta go." She rose and handed him a bundle of clothes. "This here I saved for you. Should keep you warm," she said, handing him one of Fowler's old coats. He put it to his nose.

"Ugh, white man smell. Gotta brush this 'fore I turn into a white man," he said, laughing. She laughed with him, kissed him on his stubbly cheek, and got one more hug before she took off again.

As she skirted the Mercer plantation and headed toward the trail that took her back home to the Fowlers, Leona thought about what George said about Dr. Fowler. She remembered an argument she'd overheard between Fowler and his wife. Mrs. Fowler screamed and begged Dr. Fowler to come to her bed.

"I have patients!" he screamed back.

"It's not the patients you're interested in," she'd overheard Mrs. Fowler say. "You mind yourself. Or you'll have hell to pay," she threatened. "I know what you're up to and you won't get your way with her, not as long as I'm alive."

Leona dashed past their door in time to catch the last part of their argument before Fowler stormed out. He went back to his study where he slept most nights. Leona heard Mrs. Fowler crying.

გჳ

Leona picked her way through the heavy brush, stepping gingerly among the rocks and fallen trees. She saw her breath in the cold night air, which was about the only thing she could see. With the moon disappearing among the clouds, it was like walking through ink. Luckily, she had made these secret trips in the dark to see George before. She felt confident she could find her way back home, and to her room, before the Fowlers awoke.

There would be no time left to sleep. It would take her another twenty minutes to make it back. Then she would steal upstairs to her attic room to keep from disturbing the Fowlers. She would have to be up by five; start the fires, cook breakfast, sweep the floor in Dr. Fowler's office, and lay out the linen. No, she wouldn't get much sleep, but getting to see her brother had been worth the trip.

Leona stepped into a clearing and was ready to spring across to the other side when she heard a horse approaching. She couldn't tell which direction it was coming from, and decided to take a chance and run for it. The horse and rider seemed to come from out of nowhere. The horse overtook Leona as she ran through the frost-covered meadow with her skirts hiked up. She plunged into the underbrush, trying to keep her lead, but she stumbled and fell and her skirt became entangled on a prickly bush.

The rider hunched over and grabbed Leona by her coat collar. She toppled and fell again; but the rider kept his hold on her, dragging her across brambles as she flayed helplessly for a short distance until, finally, he dropped her. She lay winded on the frozen ground, her hands and face cut and bleeding. Her coat and dress both ripped, so that she felt the cruel cold against her naked shoulders.

Two booted feet stood before her.

"Where was you runnin' too?"

His voice seemed far away. She thought she would black out but blinked, hoping to clear her vision.

"Get up, gal!"

She couldn't move, her body wouldn't respond.

He bent over. "I said, get up!"

She struggled to get to her feet as he pulled her up by her braided hair. She staggered against him. He instinctively shoved her away.

"I asked you a question. Where was you runnin'?" His tone as frosty as the night air.

Her eyes focused, but it was too dark to see his face, just the outline of his body. She knew he was white and young. *Patroller*!

"You tell me where you was runnin'?"

"I…I wa…wa…sn't…run…run…" She was so terrified that she chocked on her words.

"You was headin' somewhere in the middle of the night. Now you answer me before I beat it outta you."

"Nowhere. Wasn't runnin' no where."

"Then what you doin' out here this time a night if you wasn't runnin'?"

She didn't know what to say. *If I tell him I went to see my brother, I'll get him in trouble too.*

"I went to…to…I…"

He laughed. "You cain't even lie right. You was runnin' all right. Well, we'll just take you in and let the sheriff deal with you."

"No....please, I...I was just goin' home. Dr. Fowler is my master...he just live over yonder," she pointed off in the distance.

"He know you out this late?"

Leona shook her head.

Maybe it was because he'd had no sleep, was cold and tired, or maybe his fear numbed his compassion, but Jesse Frye had had enough for one night and wasn't inclined to be lenient. He pushed her forward. "Okay, gal, you comin' with me. I got a rope. I'm tying your hands. Then we'll just march to the jail and let them figure out what to do with you."

The young patroller mounted his horse and set an exhausting pace covering the three miles to the jail while Leona stumbled beside him. By the time they got there, the sun was up. She was bruised and battered, her clothes torn and her wrists and feet bloody from the ropes and the walk. He untied her hands and pushed her roughly in the arms of a deputy.

"See you caught yo'self a pretty little nigger gal, Jesse," said the slack jawed deputy named Russell. He slapped Jesse on the back. He shoved Leona in a cell with one hand, and gnawed on a piece of chicken with the other. "'Bout time you caught somethin'," he said, almost chocking from laughter.

Young Jesse Frye nodded "Yeah, somethin' besides my death of cold," Jesse grinned and wiped the snot from his dripping nose. *Or Cholera.*

CHAPTER THREE

Outside Ripley, Ohio—near dawn

Captain Thaddeus Moxley scratched his beard that he was sure was crawling with lice as he listened slacked-eyed to the young Kentucky planter drone on about the difficulties of keeping slaves. Moxley was stuck near Ripley when the alarm sounded that several slaves had escaped from Kentucky. Until they were captured or the authorities gave him an all clear, his steamer, the *Annabelle,* was docked indefinitely and he was a captive audience to a snot-nosed boy who fancied himself a gentleman planter. He would have been half-way to Cincinnati by now with his cargo and that much closer to buying his steamer out-right.

Luckily for him, the young Ephraim Mercer had deep pockets as well as a loose mouth. Moxley looked around for the tavern owner, but did not see him. Only a handful of customers were here this time of morning, waylaid no doubt because of the hunt for fugitives. Some were asleep at the long wooden tables, while others were drinking. A family was huddled around the enormous fireplace that kept the tavern warm. They were a miserable lot—weary travelers going nowhere.

It could be worse, thought Moxley, we could be stuck in Ripley and I'd have to listen to this jabbermouth without a drink. In a town with more than fifteen hundred people, Ripley was as dry as a bone. Thank God, just outside of the city limits "coffee houses" flourished. Moxley tipped the whiskey to his lips and drank greedily while he feigned interest in what the young planter was saying.

"You see captain, it's not like the old days. Slaves nowadays think they can get away with anything. Plus they're liable to run away thanks to them confounded abolitionists. They're more organized than ever, especially since that Compromise went through. They are determined to steal a man's property; and then they wanna be self-righteous about it."

"Ya don't say." Moxley stifled a yawn. The planter's monotone was putting him to sleep. Still he had more drinking to do, especially since the young man was buying.

"I do say," the young planter went on. "You see, unlike me, smaller planters are fit to be tied. If the slaves run away, they have to hire bounty men to find them. If these slaves continue to be recalcitrant, doing things like sabotaging the machinery or stealing provisions then they must be dealt with immediately. Like apples, these slaves have to be gotten rid of before they infect the whole barrel. But the small farmer still has to pay an agent to take the bad one's off his hands. All of us are losing money. Small and large planters alike. I have a fairly good-sized operation, and even I am feeling the expense every time I must get rid of my unwanted property."

"Ya don't say." The captain cocked his hat to one side and scratched his full head of hair. He felt something crawl along his fingers and squashed the bug.

"Captain, care for another round?"

"What? Oh, yeah. Sure, Mr. Mercer, sir."

The Kentuckian snapped his fingers. When that didn't work, he yelled. "Hey, you over there."

The tavern owner came running barefoot to the table.

"Another round for me and the captain please," Mercer said flourishing his empty glass. "And make it quick sir."

The tavern owner scurried from the table to get their order.

"And now," Mercer continued, "...we have to contend with this confounded Raven."

"A bird?"

"Hardly. Raven is a slave rescuer, or at least that's what he calls himself. He sneaks into the area, steals our slaves and takes them across the Ohio. Then he taunts us by leaving a black feather and even brags about his exploits in the paper. Look at this." Mercer went into his pocket and took out a folded newspaper. The young man sighed and pointed to a passage. Then read:

> *Who is this trickster, this dark knight.*
> *This spirit guide, this demon bright.*
> *They whisper Raven on the wind.*

"With every successful exploit he publishes these...these...poems to mock us and make fools of the law-abiding Southern men whose property he steals." Mercer crumpled the paper and let it lay in a ball on the table.

The tavern owner returned to their table a few moments later with a bottle. Moxley took control of it and poured himself a large drink. He continued to endure the planter's endless complaints, scratching his lice infected head and beard as he listened.

"You are lucky sir," Mercer leaned over the table and gave the captain a glassy-eyed stare. "How I wish I could ply the waters on a steamer such as yours, having adventures, meeting all sorts of people. Instead I am confined to the farm I inherited as well as the blasted slaves that came with it," he slurred.

"Have yourself another, son. It cain't be all that bad." Moxley slid the bottle over to Mercer. The young planter sighed and poured a drink.

"How I envy you," he spat.

Moxley gave the boy a disdainful look. He knew that the planter would not last two days as captain of a steamer. Moxley had lived most of his life on the river, first as a young deck hand, and later as a pilot. He had been captain of a barge and had finally scraped up enough money to buy the *Annabelle.* He owed his creditors, however, and the only way he could keep a crew was by keeping them plied with whiskey and bribed with stolen cargo.

By the time the *Annabelle* left Ripley for Cincinnati, he was sure he would lose another one of his crewmembers. *What the hell.* His men were as dispensable as the machinery he constantly had to replace on the boiler. He would find some roustabout. Keeping a loyal crew was not one of Captain Moxley's strengths. He worked them long and hard. On the trip up the Mississippi River, he had lost one crewmember due to fire and another when they hit a shoal at night, throwing the hapless boy overboard. By the next landing, Moxley had replaced both.

"All of us are in the same boat, so to speak." The planter continued with his ramblings. "Debts. Taxes. They're constant. The only thing we can do is sell off something—slaves mostly, but never the land."

"Well, it seems to me that you boys need to sell your slaves as a group instead of individually like you is doin' now. That way you only have one agent to pay. Ship 'um down to New Orleans. Them folks down there always lookin' for slaves, especially nigger gals pretty enough to be fancy girls to fill them bawdy houses of theirs. Or strong field hands for the cane and cotton fields. They die off pretty regular doin' that work."

26

The planter was holding his drink as he stared blankly at the captain. "What?" was all he could manage to get out.

"*I said* why don't you sell 'um all at once and ship 'um down to New Orleans. That way you save on shippin' and agentin' fees. Hell, I know some folks in New Orleans, buy 'um off you sight unseen. That's how bad they need slaves."

"We'd not thought of that. Yes, yes. We could." Mercer eagerly downed his drink. "Would you be willing to take them?"

"Cargo is cargo to me, son. Don't matter whether it's a bale, hogshead or human. Tell me how many you got, and I'll negotiate a fair price. I'll take my share from the sale." Then he leaned over toward Mercer. "I'm takin' the risk, just so you know. Slaves on a ship is a tricky proposition. They like to jump overboard, don't you know. If ya still interested, just name the place and time. And a handshake will seal the deal. I'll act as your agent."

"Let's see, I'll have to go back and talk it over. But I'm sure the rest of the planters would agree. How will I get in touch with you?" Mercer asked, eagerly.

"The *Annabelle* is headed to Cincinnati where I got business," Moxley informed him. We'll lay up for awhile in Louisville and start the trip to New Orleans. We'll work the lower Mississippi, then come back this way if I get my quota of cargo."

"Good." Mercer could barely contain himself now. "Then I'll get word to you in Louisville. I'll tell you the place and date. I know it won't be until December or maybe January."

"Don't make it too late in the season," the captain cautioned. "The Ohio can ice up. Cain't guarantee we can get through if it does."

The young planter smiled broadly and held up his glass. "You've got it, Captain," he said, holding out his hand. The Captain pressed his palm into the planter's soft, cool flesh that felt like the underside of a dead fish.

And while wiping tables, the barefoot tavern owner lurked unnoticed within earshot of the two men.

ଔ

Near Ripley, Ohio—dawn

Reverend Trout took another sheet of heavy linen paper from his desk drawer and stared at it by the tallow candle light. He was hoping something would come to him before sunlight peaked through the window, but his mind wasn't focusing on the task. His troubles were pressing on him, drowning out any thoughts of blood-washed salvation. He had recently received a missive from a presiding elder urging him to break from the church's pro-slavery doctrine. Furthermore, he was to persuade his congregation to aid in anti-slavery activities. While Reverend Trout sympathized with the cause, he could not comply with the missive because it was against the law; and he was a man who lived by the rules.

He felt himself sinking deeper—mired in confusion, fear, and doubt. His faith in his fellow man and in his own actions seemed to belie God's love. He knew it was time to pray, for he was a troubled man.

Reverend Trout rose and walked toward the window, looked out on the gentle signs of the approaching dawn, and with some difficulty, pulled his nightshirt around him and lowered himself to the floor. He clasped his hands together.

"Dear God, you have delivered me through all the storms in my life," he said in a reverent whisper. "Deliver me now through this one. I am your humblest of servants who needs your help."

The Reverend John Trout shifted his ample weight and sighed. "When I see suffering I must do something about it...that extends to our darker hued brethren whose inferior breeding

28

and lack of intelligence prevents them from rising above their station. Because of my belief, I have done all I can, including supporting the Colonization Society's efforts to send them back to the jungles from whence they came. For their land beckons them to return, unshackled and free. They are not a God-fearing lot with their primitive ways. And so, they belong with their kind, leaving us this land."

Then he heard a rustle and the muffled sound of feet on his doorstep. The front door creaked open and someone entered. It was rare, but not uncommon for marauders to be afoot. The reverend's modest home was on the outskirts of town. There was the occasional assault on sleeping innocents.

His first thought was to hide, but the years of his wife's cooking and passive lifestyle left him overweight and too slow to rise without effort. From where he was kneeling he couldn't see who was sneaking into his parlor.

He heard the person walk stealthily across the floor and stand in his study doorway. He heard short-winded, uneven breathing. He turned his head and saw, by the flickering candle, a black woman who clutched old rags in her arms. The woman's clothes smelled of mud and hung heavy with dampness. The rags moved and a whimper issued from them. It was a baby.

" 'scuse me, sir. I see de light and …and …thought …I …my baby and me…we's powerfully tired sir. Can you help us? A little food?" Her voice trailed off as if talking was exhausting.

The Reverend John Trout rose stiffly and stood in front of the bedraggled woman. "Massa, I seen de light." she cowed, backing herself in a corner, clutching her child protectively. Reverend Trout glanced at the dancing flame, then at the window. He realized he had inadvertently signaled that his was a safe house.

"Of course, the light. You followed the light."

"Yes, sir. I come from over yonder, 'cross the river...Kentucky," she said softly, her eyes shifting toward the door, ready to escape.

Reverend Trout was torn. This woman needed help, yet she was a fugitive; an escaped slave. If he helped her, he would be committing a crime. He stood paralyzed.

"Massa a piece of bread? A drink of water? I'll be gone before the sun is full up," she begged. He looked toward the ragged bundle she carried and could not turn her away.

"I'll start a fire. Your baby must be cold. He gently escorted her to a chair then he stoked the fire to a roaring blaze. The slave woman spread her legs wide to make a lap cradle for her sleeping child. She turned her face toward him.

"Thank you, Massa."

"How did you get across?" he asked as he threw another log on.

"I got word to go to the road tonight and wait 'til I hear a bird call, so I wait in the bushes. That's what I done. I waited. Seem like forever. Then I hears this wagon comin' towards me. This white man, he's on top of the wagon. And this old black woman drivin' it. And when I come out, the man jumps down and takes my hand.

"I's scared to death," she said, holding out her hands to the flames and shaking her head. Her eyes fixed on the fire. "I cain't go back. And I was too afeared to go forward, sir." The slave woman stared into the roaring fire. Her baby moved in her lap. "Please sir, my baby done had no milk. I...I got to..." she looked down at her breast.

Flustered, the reverend averted his eyes, embarrassed by the fullness of the slave woman's dark breasts.

"Yes, yes, I quite understand. I…I'll get my wife," he stuttered. The Reverend Trout turned to go, but then turned back. "What happened when you got ashore?"

The slave woman stopped, her hand hovered over her open bodice. "Yes, sir. I made it along with another. But when they let us out, the woman, the one what steered the wagon and took us by boat, was gone. The white man what was wit her tol' us to move to the light what was up on a hill. The other slave, he was a man, he started to climb the hill, but I cain't. It was too much, not with me and my baby, and he, the other nigger, don't help me.

"I wasn't gonna make it fo' sun up. So I headed back down and wandered in the bushes. Seem like hours, then I see your light. I waited to see if it was safe. I see you at the window…lookin' out…like you was lookin' for somethin' and then I…I think maybe you would help and I come here." Her dark eyes, lighted by the flames, searched Reverend Trout's, looking for reassurance.

Reverend Trout nodded his understanding. The signal was a light in the window, if it was dark, or a dozen other signals that indicated a house was a safe haven for a fugitive. The fugitive slaves wandered through, stopping for a few hours or a few days at a safe house until they could move on to another.

"Do you know your next stop?"

The woman shook her head. "No, Massa. All's we was told was to go to the light on the hill," she said, rocking her child as the baby suckled. "I been out in these woods, wanderin' for a while. Couldn't rightly tell you where I was or where I am now," she said rocking and cooing at her child. The woman's eyes closed and she fought to keep them open. It was apparent to Reverend Trout that this runaway was too tired to go any farther.

While climbing the stairs to wake his wife Martha, Reverend Trout passed the picture of Jesus at the Rock of Gethsemane. He had passed the picture many times without a second notice, but this time Reverend Trout stopped and in the dim light from the early morning sun, he saw the face of Jesus, and realized in a flash of insight that this woman who found him had come in answer to his prayers.

Reverend John Trout who prided himself on never taking an action that would offend, or have an opinion that would incite, decided that very moment that it was his duty as a man of the cloth to help the fugitive slave woman seek sanctuary. He would break the country's law as well as violate the Plan of Separation, adopted by his fellow Southern Methodists. He would be like Moses leading her to freedom. He would conduct her to the next safe house himself.

CHAPTER FOUR

Ripley, Ohio—dawn

The pounding was incessant.

Valentine heard it through the fog of his nightmare—always the same—he was running and hiding. It was the pounding of the horses as they raced behind him, hunting him down. He heard them coming closer and was too afraid to look back. He ran on as the air seared his throat. His muscles ached. His legs felt like lead, but still he ran, anticipating shouts of triumph from the horsemen as they drew nearer. He had to find some place to hide. A cave...a barn...some place where they could not find him. This time, they would kill him. The pounding grew louder.

They were right behind him. They were so close he could feel the hot breath of the horse on his back. He screamed. "Please God, no!"

He jerked awake, panting for air and looking around his darkened room only to hear the pounding once more. At first he thought the noise was coming from above him... *Solomon drunk again*... only to realize that someone was at the shop door.

"I'm coming. I'm coming," Valentine shouted as his bare feet touched the cold wooden planks and he shivered. He struggled into his pants, retrieving them from the floor. He fumbled in the darkness to find the shirt he'd thrown over the chair. Valentine shuffled to the burlap curtain that separated his shop from his living quarters.

The pounding continued; it was a steady hammering that matched the ache in Valentine's head. He had had less than three hours sleep and had been looking forward to sleeping in this Sunday.

"Coming," he shouted to the person on the other side of the shop door as he rushed to the front. His shop windows were shuttered so that everything in the room was a uniform, undefined blackness. As he stepped into the shop, he had to feel his way through the darkness and stumbled, stubbing his toe on the cold wood stove.

"Damn!" The pain was so excruciating it took his breath away. He rested his hand on the back of the barber chair and sucked the wind back into his body.

The pounding wouldn't stop.

"Lord God, this better be good." Valentine limped toward the door and jerked it open. He stood there in the freezing morning cold, half dressed, staring into the face of a grizzled stranger who smiled at him drunkenly.

"May I help you?" Valentine said tersely, looking up at the drunk.

"Yeah, yeah. I come for a shave." The grizzled man said, weaving in the doorway. "I come to get cleaned up. Shave and hair cut. Lice," he said smiling through a beard glistening with saliva and matted with tobacco juice.

Valentine's head still pounded. It was in rhythm with the pain in his toe. He stared up at the giant intruder through the weak morning light that highlighted the stranger's profile.

"This is the Sabbath. We don't open until after church, in the afternoon." And he pointed to the hand painted sign over the door. The man's eyes followed Valentine's finger and squinted, trying to focus. He shifted his gaze back to Valentine and sagged against the entranceway, smiling.

"Cain't see. I come for a shave and hair cut. Goin' to 'nnatti …Cincinnati. I'm Cap…Captain Moxley of the *Annabelle*. They searchin' the river for some runaways. Won't let my steamer leave 'til later this mornin'. I got time."

"I don't open 'til noon on the Sabbath. Come back then." He tried to close the door but the man lodged his huge hand between the door and the opening; a hand that looked as if it had strangled chicken and human necks without making a distinction

"Pay you well. Hair cut and shave. More'n you'll make this whole day."

Valentine sighed and closed his eyes. He wasn't in the mood to argue. "Let me see your money."

The man reached into his pocket and pulled out a fistful of crumpled bills.

"All right come in and take a seat. It's going to be awhile before we start. I got to heat up the stove, boil water, and sharpen the razors. Just sit over there while I get things ready."

The man weaved toward the outline of a straight back chair in the corner. He flopped down and let out a heavy sigh, then belched.

"You got anything to drink?" he slurred.

"I can make some coffee when the stove's hot," Valentine replied, lighting several oil lamps in the shop to chase the glum.

"That'll do…I guess," the stranger said slouching low in the chair. His feet stuck out in front of him, and his head rested on the wall that was lined with newspaper to keep the wind from blowing through the cracks. Within seconds he nodded off.

Valentine Kass disappeared into the back room where he slept and took his time with his daily ablution. Last night's adventure had left him bone weary. Two rescues, three if he counted the baby, all safely deposited in Ohio.

Valentine had spent hours getting into costume and make-up at Solomon's insistence.

"Pretend you're one of Macbeth's witches," Solomon had quipped as he had corked Valentine's face to make it darker and pitted. Little did either of them know at the time that the cork would irritate Valentine's eyes so badly, that he would be nearly blinded.

They'd gotten Captain Julius and the boy Tom to take them across the river, arranged to have a funeral wagon and coffins waiting for them, then made the long drive to pick up the two runaways. One was a middle-aged man who feared he was being sold to pay off his master's debts. The other was a young woman with a baby who was willing to run to escape her master's affection until she saw that she had to hide in a coffin. Then her superstitious nature took over.

"I should have stayed in the theater," Valentine said to himself as he plucked the last of the caked make-up from his face and rubbed the axle grease from his hair. He brushed his thick hair, patting it in place with the tips of his fingers that were lightly scented with fragrant oil of Bergamot. He dressed with care, making sure his broad necktie was properly flounced and his apron neatly tied.

This fastidiousness extended to his living quarters. It was almost monastic, with the exception of the dress and wig he still had from last night. Valentine made a mental note to return them to Solomon's apartment.

Valentine was a stickler for appearance and cleanliness even though most of his customers were quite the opposite. After a busy day, his shop often smelled of unwashed bodies and unkempt teeth, and he would have to open both the front and back doors to air out the place. He also burned a mixture of rosemary and sage oils nightly to remove the stench of dirty hair and foul body odor.

Valentine leisurely crammed wood and paper into the stove and struck a match, setting the whole thing ablaze. Then he went outside into the cold, pumped water into a bucket, trudged back into the shop and set the bucket on the stove to boil.

ଔ

He glanced over at his first customer of the day who was still sleeping fitfully. Valentine stacked clean towels on one side of the counter, checked the boiling water in the bucket and then ladled some into the coffee pot where he spooned several heaping tablespoons of coffee to brew. He then opened the shutters, allowing the dawn to peek through with what morning light there was. Next, he lined up in a row his tortoise shell and bone straight razor set and sharpened them methodically against the razor strap, beating out a syncopated rhythm as he sharpened the points and heels of each one. Valentine owned one of the finest German straight razor sets around, and he kept their edges smooth and in excellent condition with periodic grinding.

Once done, Valentine was ready to begin, but he wanted to bask in the silence of his shop before he awakened his customer. He poured hot coffee in a tin cup and sat down in the padded barber chair he had imported from Philadelphia. He designed it and was pleased with the hand-carved, serpent armrests, rubbed shiny with use. The plush green velvet tufted seat and back allowed for customer comfort. And a mechanism at the iron base, which he had once seen on a dentist chair, allowed him to recline and swivel his customer. It was one of a kind, but it was worth it, he thought as he slid down in the seat and propped his legs up on the footrest.

The river town of Ripley was awakening. Through the window, Valentine could see early morning wagons and people on horseback. The Sabbath was holy for some, and just another workday for others. Ripley was always bustling with work: flatboats, barges, keelboats, and steamers carrying cargo and passengers to the Mississippi and back. Only Cincinnati was busier. *More people, more customers.* He looked over at the slumping drunk and sighed. The man would not appreciate his art; his were the clothes of a river rat.

The coffee served to revive Valentine and he stretched, yawned, and poured more coffee into another tin cup. He glanced at his razor selection and decided that a wide-edged one would be appropriate to trim the man's thick curly beard. Before he touched the man's hair, he would wash it with strong lye soap to delouse him. Valentine sipped the hot brew and set it down to test the razor's edge against his finger. Satisfied that it was sharp enough to begin, he walked over to his customer, coffee in one hand and razor in the other. When the man's eyes opened, he began talking to Valentine as if they were continuing a conversation.

"Take 'um to New Orleans, that's the deal." Saliva drooled down the man's beard. "Gotta pick up the slaves ..." the man mumbled and shifted his weight, righting himself.

Valentine inched closer. "Where?" He whispered. "Where will you pick...?"

The man's eyes jerked open wide and he jumped to his feet, knocking over the chair. He waved his arms in a defensive posture as he shouted, "Nigger what the hell you think you doin'?"

Valentine did not shrink from the man's aggressive outburst, but calmly held the coffee out again.

"Sir, you wanted a shave and a haircut. I am your barber. Valentine Kass is my name."

CHAPTER FIVE

Ripley, Ohio—Sunday morning

The light snow swirled and danced in front of Reverend Trout as he navigated the wagon in the flow of traffic that was moving through the center of town. Unconsciously, he scanned the other drivers, the pedestrians, and the shops, looking for danger. And although it was chilly with the wind whipping off the river, he was sweating in his topcoat. It took all of his willpower not to look back at his load and stare at the bundles of clothes, food, and blankets to see if Ruth and her baby were safely hidden.

Occasionally he saw a familiar face. He smiled and waved heartily at them, ignoring their invitations to pull over and converse.

Reverend Trout felt the sweat beads across his forehead and wiped them away with a handkerchief. He was hoping no one would wonder why he was sweating when the weather was cold. He was more frightened than he had ever been in his life. He knew that what he was doing was aiding and abetting a fugitive. In his heart, he justified his actions. Yet, in the cold light of day, with Kentucky being a slave state and just across the river, and bounty hunters swarming the Ohio borderland, he felt like a drowning man with no hope of rescue.

The minister turned his head and spotted the freeman barber...*What was his name?* He was a portrait of arrogance, particularly galling coming from a young colored. The barber was leaning against the shop door. Reverend Trout had heard stories and gossip about him. A man from the East, in his early twenties, who came to Ripley to start his own business, rumor had it. He had materialized in town a year before with a wagonload of supplies and a fist full of money. He'd bought the building on the corner of Second Street, using the first floor as his residence and renting out the top floor to his friend and traveling companion. The companion was a recluse whose mental soundness was in question, as he was prone to wander the streets at night talking to himself. But the barber…*What was his name?…*had assured those who asked, that Solomon Tucker was nothing more than a melancholic, looking for peace and quiet.

The two men had caused quite a stir upon their arrival since one was colored and the other white. Most of the talk around town centered around the barber's uncanny business sense. He under priced his competition, bragged about his cutting prowess, and had, before long, obtained a loyal following of men. His clientele consisted of planters and river men alike. His shop. "The Razor's Edge", became a natural gathering place to hear the latest news that floated up and down the river.

If the barber had ever expressed concerns about the plight of his own race of people who were enslaved, the Reverend Trout had not heard. As far as he knew the barber …*Something to do with heart…or Valentine…yes, that was his name…*was friendly, agreeable to most anyone, even obsequious when it came to his wealthy clientele. Yet, there was something else about him, an air that discouraged familiarity; that did not allow one to get too close.

☙

After his first unwelcome customer of the morning left, Valentine asked the orphan boy Tom to snoop around and find out what he could. He told Tom to try the outlying taverns first, since that was most likely where the customer had come from. Tom reported back that Captain Moxley of the *Annabelle* had been drinking through the night with a young Kentucky planter who wanted some slaves shipped to New Orleans. The tavern owner was a sympathizer who willingly worked with the abolitionists groups, funneling valuable information to help its conductors plan slave escapes. This time Tom said the owner knew no more than what he had overheard. He had no date, place or time.

Valentine took a break and walked down to the banks of the Ohio River. The overcast skies made the already uninviting waters of the Ohio appear dreary. Steamboats belched clouds of black, billowing smoke that seemed to add more gray to the skies. Rotting wood, rusting metal, dead animals and human waste littered the shoreline.

Boats loaded with precious cargo moved sluggishly along the Ohio's main artery of transportation. Valentine smoked a cheroot as he watched the procession of boats and mused at the ugliness of it all. He looked across at Kentucky and wondered how many more slaves were trying to escape; how many more needed his help?

Kentucky had become an escape corridor for slaves who came from as far away as Louisiana. They traveled through the state, hoping to reach their destination—Ohio— then farther north to freedom. Many of them came on their own: afraid, hungry, cold and hoping to encounter welcoming help along the way. Others had help from the network. This year the enforcement of the Fugitive Slave Law made political pawns of fugitive slaves for either side of the slavery question. Ohio's border, in turn, had become a haven for slave catchers and anti-slavery advocates who were ready to do battle in the streets. It was open season on fugitives.

Valentine still reflecting, turned his back to the river and walked to the doorway of his shop. He looked up briefly and caught the attention of Reverend John Trout as he drove by seated on a wagon. Valentine waved to him. In the instant their eyes met, Valentine felt something pass between him and the minister. *Strange that the reverend should be out of church this early.* Valentine squinted. Something about the reverend felt different.

Valentine was not able to study the matter any further, because a tall man, in dark, well-tailored clothes was approaching the shop. Valentine bowed and opened the door for this new customer. He glanced over his shoulder before entering and saw the reverend steer the wagon down the street toward the outskirts of town.

The new customer peered around the shop, scrutinizing it before he stepped over the threshold. He was holding his hand at a peculiar angle and didn't bother to remove his hat that sat, cocked to the side.

"They told me I could get a shave here," he said, massaging the swollen knuckles of his right hand. Valentine grinned broadly.

"Yes, you can, sir. What specifically would you like done?"

"Shave and a trim."

Valentine appraised his customer. *Ah, a gentleman.* The man's clothes and accent spoke of refinement. His frock coat had a notched velvet collar. His matching vest of patterned dark silk fitted properly against his thin frame.

"Looks like your chops are pretty neat as it is. Suppose I just give them a once over?"

The man nodded, not bothering to answer.

"You can hang up your coat and hat over there," Valentine pointed. "And take a seat." He watched as the customer took off his coat, brushed it down with his hands, carefully placed his cream-colored felt hat on the rack and straightened his broad tie in the mirror before sitting in the barber chair.

Valentine was pleased that he was getting someone who appreciated his skill.

"You're not from around here I take it?" Valentine asked as he pulled the full-length covering firmly around the man's neck.

"No, just in town for a day…or two. Have some business; then I'll be on my way."

Valentine selected a razor, one that had a slender blade. He sharpened it on the strap and ran his thumb along the edge to feel for jags.

"Well, if you're staying for the night, I'd suggest the Ripley Hotel or Rivertown Inn. Can't go wrong with either. Accommodations are clean."

"I've made arrangements at the Ripley, thank you." His customer said curtly, leaning his head back on the chair's head rest and closing his eyes.

"My name is Valentine Kass. I am the proprietor of this establishment. And you are…?" he said, holding out his hand.

The customer opened his deep-set eyes and squinted up at Valentine. He shifted his gaze away, ignoring Valentine's outstretched hand, hesitated for a moment, then replied. "Slade," and closed his eyes once more.

Valentine nodded, pretending he hadn't been dismissed, and stood in back of Slade to trim the man's dark curly hair.

"You've been traveling long, Slade?" Valentine asked casually.

"Uhhhhahhhhhh," Slade said.

"River?"

"No."

"Going far?"

"Far enough."

"Well, enjoy your stay here. This is a nice little town. Full of friendly people. Not like the bigger cities where everyone is too busy to take the time to say 'hello.'"

"Mmmnnnnn." Slade grunted and shifted his weight in the chair.

"If you'll just hold your head to the side a bit," Valentine cocked the man's head to the right to trim around his ears. "There, that's good. Now the other…"

The tinkle of the bell over the shop announced another customer. Valentine looked up from his work as Joseph Greene sprinted in from the cold. Joseph was the owner of the tailoring shop. He dropped in most afternoons for a shine, trim, or the latest gossip.

"Just have a seat, Joseph. Tom's in town. He's making a run and he will be back shortly to shine your shoes."

Joseph nodded, blew on his hands, and took off his hat. "How's he working out with that old river codger, Julius?" Joseph asked, placing his hat on the rack.

"Old Cap? Fine, I suspect I'll lose another boy to the lure of the river. Cap says Tom can pilot a pirogue, a flatboat, and a keelboat as well as any river rat."

Joseph stood a moment admiring the fine cut of Slade's coat. He straightened his own and sat in one of the straight back chairs, slicking down what remaining strands of hair he had on his head. He took out a handkerchief and wiped his spectacles that had fogged from the warmth of the shop.

"Gettin' colder outside. Snow'll stick soon. River'll freeze," Joseph said fitting his wire-rims over his ears and blinking behind the thick lenses.

"Yes, I expect you're right," Valentine replied, not looking up.

Joseph was a short man with an ample paunch who was particularly fond of tailcoats that only emphasized his portliness, but he felt it made him look prosperous. Valentine didn't have the heart to tell him that only old men wore them.

Joseph was always in perpetual motion. Either he was measuring, fitting, and waiting on customers, or supervising his apprentice while nagging the seamstresses. And just as he couldn't sit still, he couldn't stop talking either. He stood and walked to the mirror on the wall to admire his new tailcoat. "New material from New York." He turned around so that Valentine could see the cut of the coat.

"A little finefied for these parts. Don't you think?"

Joseph looked over his glasses at Valentine. "You should talk. I don't see you hauling cow manure in your get ups." He grinned good-naturedly at Valentine.

"Not me, Joseph. Thank God I never hauled manure or wore farmer's smocks."

"Those are handsome clothes you're wearin', sir." Joseph looked down at Slade, appraising him.

Slade nodded acknowledgement.

"Mr. Slade is just passing through on business," Valentine said, submitting to Joseph's curiosity.

"I see that kind of material and cut farther South. You a Southerner, sir?" Joseph asked.

"In a manner of speaking," Slade said without opening his eyes.

Joseph stared at the man for a long time, then broke off his gaze and turned pointedly to Valentine. "Speakin' of Southerners, I heard there was quite a commotion yesterday, over'n the Kentucky side. Seems these two slaves escaped from plantations over there; disappeared into thin air."

"Don't say," Valentine said, noncommittally.

"Do." Joseph confirmed. "Woman and man. Woman had a baby. Ain't nobody seen or heard from them since. They say they were kidnapped by that Raven. Or so that's the rumor.

"Stopped river traffic two miles east and west of here, lookin' for 'um. Disappeared. Just like that," he said, snapping his fingers, and then glancing down at his hand that showed roughness from handling cloth and sharp needles.

"You got some of that lotion concoction for your hands? Mine feel like dried sawdust."

"Look on the shelf, the green bottle to the right," Valentine said as he carefully snipped along his customer's ears.

"Yep," Joseph continued, moving the carefully lined bottles in Valentine's glass cabinet. "This it?" he held the bottle up.

Valentine looked over his shoulder. "Yeah, that's it. Just a little and work it into your hands."

Joseph shook a few drops in his hands and smelled them.

"Odd odor. Opens your nose. Bet this would be good for a cold, he inhaled deeply then put the cork back in, placed the bottle back on the shelf, and rubbed his hands vigorously.

"I tell my wife, she should get some from you, but she tells me that she's not going to use anything a barber concocts on her hands, thank you very much. Says she'll stick to her almond lotion. I keep askin' her why, since it don't do her no good. Her hands feel like they been plowin' the fields.

"'Course I don't tell her that, mind you. Women, they got peculiar notions about what is and isn't proper. It's okay for them to go to the apothecary and buy some fancy smellin' lotion that don't do no good, but it ain't okay to come into a barber shop and buy somethin' that works, even though it smells up everything around it. "

"I'm not sure she objects to stopping by a barber's, Joseph." Valentine said pointedly, knowing that what Mrs. Greene really objected to was Valentine's race.

Joseph wandered back to the front of the shop and looked out the window at the street traffic. "Busy day. Had a coupla farmers come in. Wanted to know if my gals could cut that cheap cloth they make them slaves wear. I told them I didn't. They'll have to find someone else. I told them to try up at the nig...colored settlement, maybe them folks can help 'um."

Slade, who had been languidly listening with his eyes closed while Valentine shaved him, now opened them and turned toward Joseph unexpectedly, catching Valentine off guard. "You say there's a nigger settlement not too far from here?"

"Sir, you'll have to sit still if I'm going to trim those chops of yours." But Slade brushed Valentine's razor aside.

"What about this nigger settlement?" Slade insisted.

Joseph realized that Slade was talking to him and turned, "Oh, well I told those farmers there's some gals up there who can help them if they bought the cloth. The women there could cut the patterns and sew them themselves. But like I said, I don't do that kind of work. Not worth it to me."

"The settlement, where is it?" Slade persisted.

"It's north of town. They call it Africa Hill. A hundred free people live there more or less. Been there since God knows when, am I right, Val?" Joseph said, glancing from Slade to Valentine.

Valentine spoke up. "Yes, I heard that some owners a long time ago manumitted them when Ohio was just a territory. Their former owner bought them the land and their descendants have been on it ever since. Would you mind leaning back so that I can trim the other side?" Valentine asked Slade.

"You know them better than I, Val. They'd probably do it, wouldn't they?"

"I'm sure they can use the extra money. They do my laundry."

"Nice people. Keep to themselves. Don't cause any problems. Come into town to do a few errands. Most farm though. Sell the vegetables in the market—that kind of thing. Wouldn't you say, Val?" Joseph blinked behind his glasses.

"Nice people." Valentine chimed in.

"How long will this take?" Slade said, annoyed.

"Not long, if I can just get to that other side." Valentine smiled indulgently at Slade.

Slade impatiently plopped his head down once more while Valentine walked to the other side of the chair and began working.

They heard a scraping sound overhead and all eyes turned toward the ceiling.

Joseph glanced knowingly at Valentine. "Solomon again?"

Valentine nodded. "He had a bad night, last night. He must be stirring."

Joseph shook his head. "They tell me he was out by the stables the other night, reciting poetry to the horses."

"He does that sometimes."

"Are you sure he's harmless?" Joseph asked. "We frown on public drunkenness around here. Drove the liquor saloons out, not that that makes much of a difference since people just get drunk outside of town. But at least the town has an upstanding reputation. Our temperance society, of which I am one of three hundred members, is proud of our progress."

"Yes, Joseph, I know. Solomon is nothing more than a man who's lost hope," Valentine said, sadly. "His mother, you know."

Joseph pondered this last remark and then changed the subject. "When did you say your boy'll be back?" Joseph reached into his waistcoat and pulled out his watch.

"I sent him out a half hour ago when we had a break. He should be back any time now. Why don't you have a seat?"

But Joseph, used to being on his feet for hours at a time, just paced in front of the window and commented on who was out and about in Ripley.

"I see old man Rankin and his sons come down from that hill. Guess they're here to buy supplies. Stay up on top of that hill like they're guarding the gates to heaven. I guess that's what you have to expect, being as contrary as they are," he said, lowering his voice.

"You know I heard he vowed he'd never be taken from his land. You know there's a price on his head across the way. The man's a radical. His sons are too. You mark my words, he's gonna see a lot more trouble and all the preachin' and proselytizing in the world ain't gonna do him one bit of good when the authorities come down on him and a few others in this town for aiding runaways. Nope, not one bit of good." Joseph picked up steam.

"Now if he wanted to help, instead of flaunting the law, he should do like the good Reverend Trout. He's takin' a bunch of supplies up to the colored settlement. Asked me for a donation just now. I gave him a coupla yards of cloth. Not much I can do with it. Poorly dyed. Can't get my money back. Bought it on the cheap, you see. Even asked if he could buy a yard of heavy muslin, the kind you can make into a blanket for a baby. Well, I gave him what I had and told him that if he'd only given me a few days notice, I woulda been able to round up more." Joseph pondered.

"I was surprised. I told him I thought he collected around Christmas, but he told me that he heard the settlement was in need of more supplies. Although I don't see what a yard of cloth for a baby could possibly be of any use, but..." he shrugged.

Valentine felt Slade's muscles stiffen. He saw Slade's hand grip the serpent-armrest, but when Slade spoke it was off-handed and even.

"This minister believes in helping the cussed niggers?" Slade asked.

Joseph blinked behind his glasses and seemed to be framing his reply carefully. "Well, sir I'm not saying the minister is a darky sympathizer, by any means. I think he cares about the plight of needy people. Certainly, nothing near our Reverend Rankin and some of the others in these parts who count themselves strongly abolitionist. No sir, our Reverend Trout is a…uh…moderate, I do believe on the Negro question. Southern Methodist is what he calls himself." Joseph again looked at his watch.

"I guess I best be movin' on. Tell your boy he owes me a shoe shine," he said as he retrieved his coat. "Can't wait here all day. No telling what happens when I'm away from the shop. Be back for a trim.

"Oh, and when your grinder comes, send him my way. Shears and scissors need a good edge." He turned to Slade. "Hope your stay is a pleasant one…uh…Mr. Slade. If you're in the need for a suit of clothes or new coat or trousers, please remember Greene Tailors," he said, as he tipped his hat and closed the door behind him.

The barbershop seemed unusually quiet after Joseph Greene left. The only sound was the crackle of wood in the stove. Valentine's hands deftly wielded the razor across Slade's chin and dabbed the last of the soap off Slade's face with a clean towel.

"Would you care for a scent?" Valentine said, stepping back to appraise his work.

"No, thank you." Slade stretched his right hand, then curled it slowly and winced. "It bothers me in the cold sometimes, especially if I've been out for a long time."

"I see. You work outside?"

"Mostly."

Valentine walked to his cupboard and removed a glass bottle.

"I use it myself occasionally, and you saw how Mr. Greene, our tailor boasted about its soothing qualities. It's an oil with special herbs to help relieve the pain. Five cents is all I charge," he said unstopping the cork and holding it under Slade's nose.

Slade took a sniff and wrinkled his nose. "What's in this?"

"Oh, a mixture of herbs. A bit of this and that, and the special ingredient is from the Eucalyptus tree. A British sailor who'd been to Australia introduced me to this wonderful plant in Philadelphia. He carried the leaves with him wherever he went and swore that they were good for fever, breathing problems, and pain. What I found them to be most helpful for is as an ointment for skin and joint aches. Try some. Rub it gently on your hand and feel the relief."

Jackson Slade took the bottle and rubbed some on his hand. "It smells."

"Not unpleasant I hope."

Slade flexed his hand. "Five cents, you say?"

"Yes, sir. Five cents for the oil, ten for the shave and five for the trim. That comes to twenty cents."

"I shouldn't think that would break me," he said, pulling change from his pocket and handing it to Valentine. "You've done a good job."

Before Slade could get his coat, little Tom came running into the shop. A rope tied the black boy's cut-off pants; his coat sleeves were rolled up and his wheel cap was pitched to the side. Tom was one of the dozen orphans who earned their living running errands and working the river.

"Sorry I'm late Mr. Valentine, but old Cap'n Julius wanted me to help him," he said, breathlessly.

Slade had his coat and hat on and brushed by the boy as he opened the door to leave.

The boy looked up at Slade. "Shine, sir?" he grinned expectantly.

Slade gave him barely a nod and walked out.

"Thank you, sir and come again," Valentine called out. Then he turned to the boy and gave him a knowing look.

"He's a catcher?" Tom asked, watching the man leave. Valentine peered intently at the boy.

"It seems so. Make sure Cap'n knows that there's another one in town. Tell him we'll be going fishing tonight."

CB

CHAPTER SIX

"*Solomon*, get up!" Valentine yelled as he raced up the stairs and threw open the door to Solomon Tucker's inner sanctum.

"I was turning over for another nap. Sorry about the noise I made earlier. I had a bad dream and damn, if I didn't roll off the bed." Solomon fumbled to light the oil lamp as Valentine came nearer. "Have a seat. I'll be with you in a minute," he said, throwing his legs over the side and sitting up.

Valentine's feet hit several empty wine bottles as he moved across the floor to open the shutters pulled across the window.

"Don't, I can't stand the daylight, not right now. You know I work best after dark," Solomon said in the cultured English accent he had affected in Philadelphia during his theatre days.

Valentine stopped and turned angrily on Solomon. "When we brought the slaves across, did you escort them to the next station?"

"Uh? You mean Rankin's?" Solomon hesitated. "Yes, well, no. I showed them the path. I told them to take it." He yawned and stretched. "Then I went to my favorite drinking hole just outside of town. Actually, I bought a case of wine back, if you're interested."

"For Christ sake, how many times have I told you to follow through?" Valentine threw open the window. The sunlight stabbed at Solomon's eyes and he squinted blindly while holding his pounding head.

"Close the windows, for God's sake," he yelled.

"Serves you right for drinking to all hours. Now get up. We've got work to do."

Curly blond hair fell across Solomon's brow. His blue eyes, fogged from lack of sleep and too much drink, focused lazily. "Why?"

"Because we have another slave catcher in our midst and I think he's looking for the woman with the baby. The *same* woman *you* were supposed to take to safety."

"Valentine, I told both of them to go to Rankin's on the hill. She couldn't have missed it. The old man keeps a light shining every night."

"You should have taken them," Valentine said sharply.

"And be found out? Our agreement with the underground is that we rescue them and bring them safely over. They guide them. We did our job. Let them do theirs."

"Well apparently they didn't or there was a mix up. For some reason I think she stumbled onto Reverend Trout. He's trying to take her to the Negro settlement now."

"The funny little reverend isn't the sort to extend himself. Who told you it was him?"

"Joseph Greene," Valentine said, pulling out a chair from the ornate desk Solomon used for writing, and sat down. Papers were strewn across the desk. Ink bottles lay open; dry ink crusted the openings.

"Whatever you may think of Joseph," Valentine continued, "...he is a wealth of information, and had it not been for his prying, I would not have gotten wind of our slave tracker. His name is Slade. Joseph happened to comment on Slade's dress. 'Dresses like a Southerner', or words to that effect. Then I remembered something that someone mentioned to me about a peculiar slave catcher in this part of the country who'd come up from the Carolinas—a tall man with sharp features and dark hooded eyes. Slade fits that description. The fingers of his right hand are curled, like a claw. And now he smells of my lotion. You shouldn't have a hard time finding him."

"Let me rest, will you." Solomon said disinterested.

"Solomon," Valentine said, impatiently. "The man comes from the South." He ticked off the points on his fingers. "He appears just after we've made a raid and he's here on business for a day or two. He looks like a fox, perpetually hunting prey. You should have seen the way he looked when Greene mentioned giving the reverend some cloth for a baby. I thought he was going to jump out of the chair." Valentine studied a wine glass.

"I think he is on to poor Reverend Trout's trail. From what I can surmise, Trout is on his way to Africa Hill, carrying a wagon load of supplies to them."

"For God sakes, why? They certainly have everything they need."

"That's just it. I would have heard if they needed anything. No, I think the reverend is carrying supplies as a ruse in order to get that mother and child to the settlement. I saw him this morning when his wagon passed and when he waved to me, he looked... well, he looked anxious, now that I think about it. He would have taken Creek Road, that's the easiest way even though it's the longest. And he certainly wouldn't know the route our people would normally take," Valentine concluded.

Solomon thought about this for a minute. "And you think this tracker, Slade, is on to Reverend Trout?"

"Most assuredly. Slade asked Joseph about the settlement. My guess is he's going to waylay him before dark."

"And what is the Raven going to do about it?" Solomon said as he stood and stretched. "We'd be foolish to try and pull something in daylight. And they have a head start."

"No, but Slade will be dealing with two people, and that's cumbersome. More than likely he'll need to arrange for a wagon and driver to meet him. I want you to be that driver," Valentine said with finality.

"Then I suppose I'll need a disguise."

"Well, hurry. I want to make sure that you're the one he chooses. Chances are he'll be looking for a man down on the wharves."

"Don't worry," Solomon said, walking to the heavy armoire. He threw open its large walnut doors. Inside were racks of costumes: wigs, hats, and an array of false moustaches and beards. He picked through and found an eye patch.

"Val, you still have that herb, the one that makes everything yellow?"

"Tumeric?"

"That's the one. I'm going to need some."

C&#x8;

When Solomon left, Valentine began straightening Solomon's desk. Valentine stoppered the inkbottles, stacked the papers in a neat pile, and lined up Solomon's pens. He looked around the room. Solomon had brought with him his four-poster hand carved bed, the desk, several chairs, an ornate rug, several matching tables, and the heavy armoire that took up one wall of the room. The beauty of the fine European furniture was obscured beneath layers of clothing, bottles, and discarded papers. Valentine opened a bottle of wine he found underneath the desk and leafed through Solomon's papers while he waited for his friend to return. There were pages of verse, lyrics to songs, and random scribbling. He picked out one sheet of verse and read it:

The Raven swoops down late at night;
Avenging angel in the fight,
To save the slave who bares the scars,
Of cruel oppression and freedom barred.

Torn from mother, father and country dear,
The son of Afric' wanders here,
On land that nurtures only pain,
And keeps him bonded and in chains.

His heart cries out for freedom's light:
"Can no man set these wrongs to right?"
The Raven can, he hears the plea,
And cries. "Oh, slave, you shall be free.

Across the river t'ward a land,
Where you are counted as a man,
We'll go by ones, and twos, and threes,
To live in peace and liberty."

Valentine wondered what abolitionist newspapers Solomon would choose for that one. Solomon had written a dozen or more poems, always signing them "The Raven" 'to fuel the curiosity of the people', he had said. And he was right. Rumors and gossip sprung up about the Raven because of his exploits.

Some speculated that this phantom operated in the deepest cypress swamps in the South. Others thought he conducted fugitives across Lake Erie to Canada. Some said he was most definitely white, for how else could he slip through the snares and traps laid for him so easily? Some said it was a man; others thought it was a woman dressed as a man. If they only knew, the Raven was the cooperative imaginings of a confused, angry fugitive slave, and his eighteen-year old actor friend.

୦୫

Solomon had been working as a light comedian with his mother's Philadelphia stock company in a series of hackneyed melodramas and tedious English imports; but, what he most enjoyed was being on center stage, upstaging the more experienced actors. Solomon had just finished a performance when both he and Valentine had been invited to the lavish home of an "arts patron" and abolitionist. The "patron," who enjoyed the company of handsome men and women of all races and persuasions, was from an old, established Philadelphia family.

Valentine and Solomon had been left to entertain themselves in the man's library, sampling his fine wines while the rest of the invited guests were scattered throughout the mansion. They were unaware that their host had passed out in another room from too much opium. The two men were in the throes of a heated discussion about the abolitionist movement, and the slow, arduous process involved in petitioning to free slaves.

"Well," Solomon said. "don't just whine about it. Do something! Some of you abolitionists can talk up a bloody storm, but when it comes to action, you're nowhere to be found. Arm yourself with bowie knife and rifle and gut the wretched slavers," Solomon gestured dramatically.

"Easy for you to say—you're white," Valentine countered. "Besides, our stand is to appeal to the nation's conscience. We will defend with Bible not with guns."

"Tell that to poor Mr. Lovejoy and those who've followed him to the grave. Bible and rhetoric did not deflect the bullets from Mr. Lovejoy's heart," Solomon taunted. "Besides, if I were colored and free, I'd be willing to fight for what I believed in, not complain endlessly about the plight of my fellow man while sipping champagne," he had challenged.

Valentine fell silent. He knew there was truth in Solomon's comments. Words and moral deeds were no longer enough to change the minds of slave owners and slavery advocates. The time was fast approaching when more drastic action was necessary. After months of discussion and arguments, they invented the quintessential hero—the Raven.

And now, the Raven was charged with having helped every fugitive from Maryland to Missouri. With the steadily increasing numbers of runaways, the price on the Raven's head had tripled. Five thousand dollars was a tempting sum, and there were plenty willing to kill for less.

Solomon thought it a lark to drive the law and the pro-slavers crazy with Raven exploits, but that made the job even more dangerous. His taunting verse heightened the danger, not only for themselves, but also for other abolitionists who risked their lives as well to guide slaves to freedom.

For a year, they had skillfully maneuvered within the system. To their credit, they had succeeded with over twenty rescues, and escaped with fifty fugitives. Though they were more than a bit reckless, they were also effective; leaving only a black feather to mock their pursuers, and a poem to herald their exploits.

One year. How much longer before our time runs out? Valentine wondered, sipping wine as he browsed through Solomon's voluminous writings.

ભ

Jonathan Jackson Slade held his cream-colored felt hat against the steady wind that blew across the Ohio River. He sidestepped several bales of hay that had fallen from a stack, and walked around men loading barrels onto a wagon. He took his time looking for just the right man for the job he needed done.

Slade was unsure whether the minister was responsible for the woman's escape. But he wanted both of them. The minister and the fugitive slave woman would make glorious trophies—a sign of his tracking prowess-- when he took them to Kentucky. *And who knows, maybe our minister is the Raven. It wouldn't be the first time that a man of the cloth felt it his duty to flaunt the law.*

Slade recalled Charles Torrey, a former minister, who died in a Maryland penitentiary of tuberculosis several years back. Torrey had been sentenced to six years of hard labor for helping fugitives escape. Both black and white abolitionists had made him a martyr and worshipped at his grave. Slade did not want that to happen to his little minister.

No, I'll leave his wagon. By the time they guess he's not been murdered by marauders, I'll be in Kentucky, collecting my reward and telling my story to the papers. The southern newspapers were always eager to print any story of fugitive slave captures to discourage anti-slavery advocates and runaways.

Slade needed a driver who would keep his mouth shut and was willing to take on a job with no questions asked. And then William Gladstone, a seedy young man with yellowed teeth, and an eye patch, approached him.

"William Gladstone at your service," Gladstone bowed low. "And what can I do for ya?" Gladstone's one good blue eye stared into space, giving Gladstone a vacant look. "Saw you was lookin' particular for someone, thought that someone might be me," Gladstone winked his good eye.

"Do you hire out?" Slade called to him.

"Depends," he said, casually glancing at Slade as he turned around and walked away.

"On what?" Slade replied, following him.

"On the price and the time. Right now, I got me a job to do.

What you want done?" He said, lifting a cask on his shoulder and carrying it toward the gangplank of a steamer.

"I want to rent your wagon—and you—for the night. I've got a special cargo that needs to be picked up and delivered back here."

Gladstone set his load down and placed his hand in the middle of his back to straighten up. He let out a groan as his good eye stared off into space.

"Well, it depends on where you want it picked up and when you want it delivered and what it is," Gladstone said, walking splay-footed back up the sloping wharf for another load. Slade became impatient.

"Look, you said you could help. I want you to drive out and meet me on the road going toward Africa Hill."

Gladstone looked at him incredulously, mouth open, showing stained teeth as he balanced another cask on his shoulder. As he walked, his feet slid in the trampled mud of the wharf to the unloading area.

"That road ain't safe in the daytime, much less at night," he shouted back at Slade who was leaning on his wagon. Gladstone waddled down the slope, dumped his cask near the gangplank, and then returned.

"I'll make it worth your while," Slade said, flashing several bills in front of Gladstone's face as he returned. Gladstone tilted his head so that his good eye lighted on the money. He licked his full, flaccid lips, unable to feign indifference. Slade waved the bills under Gladstone's nose.

"This is for saying you'll do it. There's more when you pick up the cargo and bring us safely back here."

"Us?" Gladstone reached for the bills, but Slade withdrew them.

"I need a man who can keep his mouth shut and mind his own

business."

"That's me," Gladstone said, as he longingly eyed the money in Slade's hand. "I keep me mouth shut and come through on the job. Ask anybody around here."

Slade slipped several bills into Gladstone's hand.

"That won't be necessary. You'll meet me on that road after dark. There'll be a couple of passengers. Then we'll come back here, and my cargo and I will board a boat," he said, jerking his head toward Kentucky.

Gladstone tilted his head toward Slade and lowered his voice. "I ain't fond of the law on me back. And I don't want no trouble so, I'll kindly take a goodly portion now," he held out his grimy fingers.

Slade grudgingly gave him several more bills. "You'll get the rest of this when you meet me."

Gladstone shrugged. "Fine by me," He said pocketing the money.

Slade smiled. "Good, I'm glad we understand each other," and started to walk away.

"Hey, what happens if you ain't there?" Gladstone called out.

"I'll be there. Just make sure you're there. When you see me, signal with your lantern like this," said Slade, as he moved his arm vertically. "I'll signal back like this," he moved his hand back and forth. "And bring a rope."

"Yeah yeah, a rope," Gladstone nodded and winked with his one good eye.

CS

Valentine was standing in front of Solomon's armoire mirror, trying on a woman's long haired wig when he heard Solomon bound up the steps. Solomon threw open the door only to burst out laughing.

"My God, love. Who are you suppose to be?"

"A harlot, I thought," Valentine said, mimicking the brazen stance of the streetwalker. "For this exploit, I thought perhaps a woman of dubious reputation with her male procurer might serve us until we're able to get beyond the patrollers."

Solomon's eyebrows arched. "Only if the procurer were blind. Take that thing off and try this on," he said, rummaging in the armoire and grabbing a brown wig with ear puffs the size of wheat rolls.

Valentine wrinkled his nose and looked skeptical.

"We're not marrying you off. Beauty is not a virtue here."

"What kept you so long?" Valentine asked, throwing the longhaired wig on the bed and slipping on the ear puff wig. Solomon stood watching critically as Valentine tugged and pulled to adjust the wig to his head.

"You wanted me to find Slade and get him to hire me. I did." He pulled out the money and waved it in front of Valentine.

"You could smell him a mile away. Plus he is just as you described; a predatory character with keen features and the sharp eyes of a bird of prey. Our slave catcher wanted a driver and wagon, as you thought he would. Meet William Gladstone," Solomon bowed.

"Good. So we meet him?"

"He said he'll have two passengers. He'll be coming back by wagon and transferring them to ours," Solomon said, watching Valentine wiggle into the cheap red muslin dress.

Valentine tugged at the dress. "You sure this is the right size?"

"Of course it is, you've just gained weight. Be thankful you don't have to wear a corset."

Valentine was still struggling with the dress. "I can hardly breathe," Valentine pulled the bodice up and slipped an arm into the sleeve. "The damn thing fits like a second skin," he said, trying to fasten the hooks on the side.

"You don't have to look presentable, just throw on a wrap."

Valentine grabbed the skirt of the dress and hiked it up. "Where are your pistols?"

"In the desk," Solomon called over his shoulder.

Valentine opened the drawer and took out two pearl handled pistols that he slipped in his pants he wore underneath the dress. He hoped they wouldn't have to use them.

"Now, all we have to do is wait until dark."

CHAPTER SEVEN

Creek Road—near dusk

With each mile they rode, the minister's spirits grew as dismal as the landscape. Reverend Trout had anticipated that they would reach the colored settlement shortly before sunset to drop the woman and baby off safely. Then he would rest and water the horses, and make it back home later that night. What he had not anticipated was his old wagon being unable to hold up on the rutted road. Two hours outside of town the wagon hit a hole, made a high-pitched grinding sound before wobbling for a few feet. Then the front wheel fell off.

"Woman, are you all right?" he asked, steadying the horses as they nervously danced and strained against the reins. He eased himself down and watched as Ruth made her way cautiously over the spilled cargo, hugging her screaming child against her. She and Reverend Trout both surveyed the damage.

"I'ma put ma baby down and we do it together."

Whether it was from manly pride or fear of discovery, Reverend Trout assured her that everything would be fine.

"No, you take the baby into the woods and hide. Try and quiet her. I'll do this by myself. Don't worry. We'll get there," he said.

She looked at him, skeptically, but he reassured her that he could do it alone. Ruth obediently carried the child deeper into the woods and hid as Reverend Trout took off his coat, hat, and jacket and rolled up his sleeves.

Since he was not a physical man, the repairs took longer than he anticipated. At one point, as he put his back to the wagon and lifted it in order to secure the wheel, he prayed that someone would come along to help. Then he realized that the only people most likely to be traveling this lonely road to an isolated colored settlement would be ne'er do wells. Instead, he prayed only for the strength to fix the wagon wheel without breaking his back in the process.

Once done, he reloaded the wagon, hitched up the horses and called Ruth back. As they proceeded on their journey, their funereal mood matched the approaching gloom of dusk. His wife had fixed biscuits and bacon for them, but he was just too tired and anxious to eat. The baby fretted and the mother, beside herself with fear, tried to quiet her child.

Waves of nausea now swept over Reverend Trout. While he often liked to remind himself that 'struggle breeds character,' fear was chipping away at his resolve. He kept telling himself he was doing God's work, but his muscles ached and he felt light headed. The most frightening of all was that he was resentful for having been "chosen" for this task.

Over the squeak of the repaired wheel, he thought he heard a sound behind him. He stopped the wagon to listen, but heard only the sounds of wild animals and birds. The shadows were getting longer and gnarled tree branches seemed to loom out at him. He had the feeling he was being watched. It was as though some hidden presence was lurking just beyond his vision.

ଓଃ

Creek Road

Slade spotted where Trout's wagon wheel had come off. He followed well behind the wobbly trail until he felt it was time to make his move to overtake the "no-gooders." He laughed aloud at the term he got from his mother. His laughter startled a bird that disappeared deeper into the dense growth.

The no-gooders moniker was his ma's description of poor immigrants who swelled their New York Irish ghetto where he grew up.

"They'll never amount to nothin' my Johnny. Nothin'. Good for nobody and no one, that's what I say. They take no pride in their family name. You, Johnny, are a Slade. Don't forget that…never forget you come from good stock. I ain't raisin' you to be a no-gooder. You'll be a somebody, some day," she would tell him in her heavy Irish brogue.

It didn't matter to her that they, too, were as poor as the rest of the unwashed immigrant masses. To her, they were different. She was different. She had ambition and drive. Her raw single-mindedness and pride were her legacy to her son.

His mother would brush off his hand-me-down clothes and send him to church on Sunday mornings. His father, in the meantime lay snoring on the floor, too drunk even to take off his clothes and crawl into bed. Young Johnny Slade was not to come back until the late afternoon. His mother had made that plain.

"Stay in church, Johnny. Let the good priests teach you somethin' about the ways of the world. Let them teach you how to be a gentleman."

She always felt that clothes made the man and she made sure he looked his best. She would send him off for most of the day so that he wouldn't have to see her fight with his pa—or make love to him—whichever method would keep the peace in the family. What she didn't know was that her Johnny rarely went to church; and was *never* there all day. He believed in God, but he put his faith in survival. He would prowl the rowdy tenement streets of the Five Points area of New York, looking for excitement and adventure. He always found both. There were as many taverns in Five Points as there were churches—and he knew every one of them.

When he saw some drunken dockworker looking the other way, Johnny would sneak a sip from his drink. Later, he would pickpocket that same drunk who would be sprawled out on a table. Young Johnny often spotted money, or a lost trinket as he crawled along the sawdust floors of the taverns. On a good day, he might find a wallet. He saved the coins that his ma gave him to put in the church basket, and he hustled for money during his visits to the taverns in Five Points. That was how he earned his money. That was his life—until things changed.

One Sunday when his ma sent him out to church, young Johnny came back later that afternoon and found his mother lying in a pool of blood. His father had finally beaten her to death in a drunken rage and left her on their tenement floor. This time she had not managed to control his pa's anger. The elder Slade was nowhere in sight.

Whatever compassion Johnny may have had for another human being, dried up and crusted that day, like the blood that oozed from his mother's wounds. His conscience became shriveled and hardened, corrupted with the realization that the only person who had ever loved him now lay dead on the cold plank floor.

Johnny—his mother's pride and joy—went to the loose board in the floor and pulled up his money. He searched through a chest of drawers and gathered his clothing: two good pants; a vest; and, a frock coat made of fine wool that his mother had cut down from a gentleman's jacket. He then turned and walked out of the one room apartment. The priest would later bury his mother in a pauper's grave. Jonathan Jackson Slade was twelve years old.

Since that time he had lived on his own. He took various jobs that involved labor, from dockworker to factory worker, but he quickly tired of them and moved on. He traveled down through New York and the Eastern Seaboard until he reached the southern states. There he found his calling. Rich people: merchants, doctors, lawyers and planters all seemed to lose things like their stickpins, their money—their slaves.

He became a slave catcher since he was good at finding things. Slaves. They were the worst of the no-gooders: poor, helpless, and less than human. They had nothing. Not even their names were their own.

He learned how to read along the way, and he would look for advertisements for runaway slaves. Then he would approach the owners with a proposition to find their runaways for a price they were willing to pay. He usually found the fugitive slave and brought the property back alive, even if the property was not in the best condition.

One time he struck a deal with the owner of a North Carolina plantation to find a runaway. He tracked the man for months and found him shacked up with his wife, who had been sold to a Tennessee farmer. He and his captive traveled back through blizzard and freezing temperatures. They made it back by early spring. The slave had gotten frostbite on his fingers. Slade presented his captive to the North Carolina farmer, but the farmer refused to pay.

"That there boy is damaged," the farmer said. Slade leveled his gaze at the farmer, pulled out his pistol, and shot the slave in the head.

"That's damaged."

The farmer did not attempt to prosecute Slade, and the incident taught Slade a lesson—always get a retainer.

Jonathan Jackson Slade was well dressed and well spoken. He also was good at what he did. Unlike the no-gooders, his name meant something. His mother would have been proud.

ೞ

Creek Road

Reverend Trout whispered with urgency, "Woman, there's someone coming. Hush the child."

"Gid up," he said, flicking the reins. The horses strained against their load, but only managed a trot while the wagon bucked and bounced along. He heard the rider coming up fast.

The baby still protested, whimpering weakly in the back. The reverend began to sing loud and off key:

> *Oh, worship the King All glorious above;*
> *Oh, gratefully sing His power and His love,*
> *Our Shield and Defender,*
> *The Ancient of Days,*
> *Pavilioned in splendor*
> *And girded with praise!*
>
> *Oh, tell of His might,*
> *Oh, sing of His grace,*
> *Whose robe is the light,*
> *Whose canopy space!*
> *His chariots of wrath*
> *The deep thunder-clouds form,*
> *And dark is His path*
> *On the wings of the storm.*

"Stop the wagon, sir." Slade shouted above the singing. The reverend turned and made out the rider as a darker outline against the deepening background of the woods.

"Sir, I cannot. And if you mean to rob me, then I must tell you that you are robbing from the poor. I am a man of the cloth on a mission of mercy," he shouted to the stranger. Reverend Trout fixed his gaze on the cream-colored felt hat that sat jauntily askew on the man's head; the man's face was in shadow. The reverend detected a pungent odor from the stranger that he was unable to identify.

Slade leaned toward the reverend and smiled. "Would you not talk to a friend who may be lost, sir?" he said, affably.

"Then I can only tell you that this road leads only one way and that is to a colored settlement up ahead. That is where I am going. You would be wise to turn back and retrace your steps." The reverend slowed the wagon.

"May I ask your business?" Slade grabbed the reins and halted the horse.

Reverend Trout clawed unsuccessful at the reins.

"I wouldn't do that," Slade said, menacingly.

"Who are you, and what right have you to stop me? I have told you that I am on a mission of charity and you are interfering with the work of God, sir."

"Am I, little minister? Or am I interfering with an Underground conductor who is breaking the law?" Slade's tone was menacing.

"How dare you accuse me of criminal activity." Although the reverend couldn't see his expression, he felt the man was mocking him.

"I have reason to believe that you are harboring a fugitive slave for the purpose of helping her escape. "

"Nonsense," Reverend Trout said, hoping the fear in his voice would not betray him. "I have no reason to do any such thing. Unhand my reins and let me be on my way," he said, once again trying to grab the reins back from Slade.

Slade deftly grabbed his arm in a vise-like grip. "You will let me see what you have in the wagon, or I will be forced to harm you."

Both men turned when they heard Ruth's voice.

"Please sir, don't hurt him," she pleaded as she struggled to free herself from underneath the cargo. Even in the near dark, Reverend Trout saw the fear on her face. She held her baby to her and cautiously sat up.

Slade loosened his grip on the reverend. "Now, both of you will come with me."

"Sir, she is on Ohio soil," Reverend Trout protested. "You have no right to take her back. By rights she is free."

Slade pulled a gun from his pocket. "By rights she is a fugitive and you are a kidnapper."

Reverend Trout tried to speak, but nothing came out. Slade waved the gun in the reverend's face. "You sir, are under arrest as a person who knowingly and willingly aids, abets and assists a fugitive to escape, or harbors and conceals a fugitive," he said, reciting from memory. "I thank you to turn this wagon around and follow me back to town where both of you will cross the river with me into Kentucky. Your punishment can be decided in a court of law or by me right here in this desolate place."

The reverend panicked and whipped the reins frantically. The horses reared and bolted, careening the wagon across the uneven, rugged road until the front wheel wobbled drunkenly. The wagon bucked high into the air before crashing, spilling Reverend Trout on the ground, leaving him stunned. It then rocked precariously and threatened to turn over. Several sacks of supplies had protected Ruth and the baby from injury and she gingerly picked her way across them and on to the ground while Slade looked on. With a hollering baby in her arms, Ruth knelt down to see what she could do for Reverend Trout.

"He bleedin'. We got to get help," she implored Slade. "I think his side's hurt too."

Slade made no move to dismount. "Give me the child," was Slade's only response.

Ruth stood motionless.

"Give me the child and tend to that stupid bastard," he repeated, angrily.

Ruth still stood frozen.

Slade aimed his pistol at the child. "I'm sure your master won't mind. He can always make another one. It's up to you. Give me the child," Slade insisted.

Ruth looked at the injured minister and then at Slade. Silently, she held her child up to Slade who transferred the pistol. And grabbed the baby with his free hand.

"Now, get him on his feet," he demanded. "The damn fool ruined the wagon. Both of you unhitch those horses. We have a long ride back."

CHAPTER EIGHT

Creek Road

"*That* was close," Valentine said, undoing the shawl from his head. "Did you have to squeeze me so hard?"

"The patroller was looking straight at me. I had to do something. God knows, if he had shown the light on you, I'd be arrested for having poor taste in women. "

"Next time, you play the harlot then," Valentine answered peevishly.

"Love, a black man and a white woman would be cause for scrutiny. We would be arrested, no questions asked," Solomon reasoned as he fidgeted with his eye patch.

"Well, then next time I'll play your servant and you play the damsel."

"That's a good idea. How's this?" Solomon pitched his voice high, "Sir, my man is taking me home. You don't expect a lady to travel unescorted. Franklin here is very reliable. He'll see to it that I get there safely."

"Mmmmm, not bad. Let's do that one. You fit better in women's clothing than I do," Valentine said pointedly.

"That's because I've had more practice. I must have played dozens of different female roles on stage when we were growing up. Can I take this eye patch off now? I can barely see the road."

"No! You've got to stay in character, Valentine warned. "William Gladstone you are; or as your friends would call you, One-eyed Willy."

They had crossed paths with three patrolmen but only one stopped them to take a closer look. Valentine was careful by leaning his head on Solomon's shoulder and wrapping the shawl to cover his face. Solomon had then affected an air of indignation and embarrassment at being caught with a colored woman of dubious reputation. He even offered the man a swig of wine from a bottle and asked the officer not to mention their sighting. The officer tipped his hat and went on his way.

"Let's stop here. And hand me that wine." Valentine tightened the shawl around his shoulders before taking a swig of wine. "Couldn't you have brought something stronger to fight the cold?"

"Oh," Solomon mimicked Valentine's moralizing baritone, "...and risk getting drunk in a town known for its self-righteous temperance members?"

"You're wearing a top coat. I've got only this wool wrap and thin dress," Valentine reminded Solomon, taking another swig. "Damn it's cold. The river will start to freeze."

This caused both men to fall into a brooding silence, since they knew it simply meant that more slaves would try to walk to freedom across the ice floes. Valentine and Solomon had seen the frozen remains of fugitives who didn't make it when they washed up on the Ohio shore during the spring thaw. It was a grotesque sight, especially the children. Valentine broke the somber mood.

"I forgot to tell you. A riverboat captain was in this morning in a drunken stupor He alluded to the fact that he would be carrying slaves south. I had young Tom do some investigating, and it seems that a number of Kentucky slave holders may be persuaded to sell their slaves, and have them all shipped to New Orleans. I'm not sure of all the details, but I've got Tom and some others trying to get more information."

"Maybe Grinder can snoop around, too." Solomon replied noncommittally.

"Yes," Valentine agreed, "... I'll get word to him. It shouldn't be hard to get that information. We might be able to round up some of the men."

"Sounds interesting." Solomon said. "Now, listen to this poem," he said, changing the subject. He cleared his throat and began to recite in his stage voice that carried on the autumn wind:

> *He crosses rivers, woods and streams,*
> *Eluding traps and snares with ease;*
> *For no one yet has seen his face*
> *Nor knows his name or hiding place.*
>
> *To village, city, hamlet, town*
> *He steals the slave in bondage bound;*
> *Then sneaks away in dead of night,*
> *To plan again at day's first light.*
>
> *And like the bird whose name he bares,*
> *Is trickster, player, prophet, heir,*
> *Of legend, omen, death, despair;*
> *Cross his path and then beware.*
>
> *For he is not of mortal man.*
> *A specter, phantom roams this land.*
> *A righteous sword he doth command*
> *To smote the foe of freedom's stand.*

"Well? What do you think?" he said, turning expectantly toward Valentine.

"I'm not sure," Valentine said, thoughtfully. "You forgot to mention Raven."

Solomon dismissed the comment with a wave of his hand. "I'm not through yet. Besides, I'll just sign the damn thing "Raven." They should get it. The abolitionist papers have been diligent in printing my poems. I only wish the local papers would do the same. It seems to me a waste of my time—preaching to the converted," Solomon shrugged. "Then too, the locals might not print it at all, in which case it would be a shame to waste the effort." Then Solomon brightened. "So, I shall send it to both," he decided, enthusiastically.

"Your taunting poetry only makes our job harder; makes everyone's job harder," Valentine said, patiently.

"Yes, but it's so much fun," Solomon chuckled. "Listen, I've got a shorter one, just in case they don't quite get the poetic nuances...or the name."

> *Raven flying overhead,*
> *Searching for the slave who's fled,*
> *Leading him to safety's shores*
> *Where he'll be a slave no more.*

"Even little children can sing that. Clever, eh?" Solomon grinned.

"One of these days your cleverness is going to have us rotting in jail or swinging by a rope. Wake me when you hear them," Valentine said, burrowing down in his wrap.

☙

Valentine again recalled the times in Philadelphia when Solomon constantly questioned Valentine's role as an abolitionist. Young Solomon, rambunctious and rebellious, laughed, and challenged him to do something more decisive about slavery than just talk. At one point, he even maliciously teased Valentine about being up to the task.

This brought Valentine to his feet, and he angrily hovered over Solomon, ready to challenge him to a fight. "What right have you to tell me what I should do? You're nothing but a snot-nosed, pampered child. And you sit here in your finery, never having done a hard day's work, and call me a coward!"

"Good show, love. Best performance I've seen in ages. And you said I was overly dramatic. You should never have left the theater for a barber's apprentice; but again there was no call for a blackamoor actor. The audiences much preferred your roles as adorable pickaninny. Unfortunately, you grew out of those roles," Solomon joked, before he continued on a more serious note.

"I did not, nor will I ever call you a coward, for I know too well your killer instinct once your ire has been aroused. I only urge you to become a person of action and decisiveness. It just seems to me that ever since you've been involved with those abolitionists, all you do is preach and petition. What has it gotten you, eh? Two broken ribs, a bruised ego in street fights, and a lot of money thrown around," Solomon chided.

"You've gone too far," Valentine fumed.

Solomon winked. "No; not far enough, in my estimation."

ଔ

As Valentine dozed off to the motion of the wagon, a thought crossed his mind. Here he was disguised as a colored prostitute to waylay a slave catcher. Both he and Solomon had become so deeply involved in the dramatics of the Raven that maybe this life and death struggle for freedom had turned into a game for both of them; a game that one day could result in their deaths.

Slade had given the baby back to its mother who had fashioned a sling from a blanket to strap to her back while she rode. Slade had bound both their wrists. Reverend Trout was barely able sit upright on his horse because of the injuries to his ribs. It was a torturous journey.

Slade hoped that Gladstone would have the good sense to meet up with him and not wait for them at the crossroads as planned.

The ointment the colored barber had given him had worn off, and now he felt a dull throb in his right hand. Plus, his arm ached from holding the lantern. He shifted his weight on his horse and hooked the lantern to the saddle horn. To take his mind off the journey, Slade focused on a more pleasant vision.

He saw himself taking the two prisoners back to Kentucky, and informing the authorities about how he had single-handedly captured another fugitive, and possibly, the notorious Raven. He would personally write the story himself, in case the locals proved inept. Publicity was always useful in his line of work.

There is nothing like being able to show the results of your work to a new client. A testimonial letter from the constable wouldn't be bad either. He saw himself accepting his reward from the grateful plantation owner. Then he congratulated himself on having had the foresight to travel to this part of the country.

The Kentucky and Maryland borders, as well as the towns along the Mississippi, definitely needed his services. Fugitives escaped from those regions more than from any place else. If they lived farther south, they stowed away on boats with help from the colored crew. There were a number of ways they were able to elude capture, once in Ohio.

They were helped along the way by freemen who worked as porters, farmers, businessmen. Do-gooder religious folks also felt it their calling to aid fugitives. *We make it so simple for them.*

If a slave in the lower south was smart or lucky, he reached Canada in two or three days, depending on his mode of transportation. *Luckily for me most don't have the good sense to know that.*

Most of the runaways he had talked to knew only to run north, like it was some magical place. They didn't know how to find a boat going upriver, or a train. They tried to make it on foot, some of them traveling for months to reach this part of the country, only to be captured and returned to their owner.

Slade looked back and shone the light on his two captives. They squinted in the glare. The fugitive woman looked numb with fear. The light caught the reverend silently praying. Like a frightened animal he turned his face away from the light. Slade could see he was trembling. "Bet you never thought you'd be put in jail for "God's work", huh, minister?" Slade yelled at him. "You still think that helping fugitives is your calling?" he taunted.

"God showed me the way, sir. Yes, I still believe in doing God's work." But Reverend Trout's voice wavered. He slumped forward on his horse.

"Keep up the prayin' minister. You'll need all the help you can get." Slade turned around, shining the light back on the path. *When will that stupid bastard meet us?*

ശ

Solomon nudged Valentine. "Wake up, I think I see a light."
Valentine sat up in the wagon. "Where?"
"Through those trees. They're coming around the bend."
Valentine stared in the darkness and saw the flicker. He took a deep breath and willed his stomach to settle down.
"I see it," he said, climbing into the back of the wagon.
Solomon signaled with his lantern.

"He's getting closer. Jump."

"I can't get the damn dress unfastened." Valentine said, frantically. "I'm stuck. I've got to tear it off."

"Christ, don't do that. You know how much that cost me?"

"I thought you said you got this off a prostitute?" Valentine shot back, still tugging at the hooks.

"Yeah, that's what I meant. Hide in the back. I can see their outline. He's not in the wagon. They're riding horseback."

"Steady the wagon. You want me to break my neck?" Valentine called back.

"He sees me. He's signaling. Get off before he gets closer," Solomon cried out.

Solomon heard Valentine trying desperately to scramble down from the back of the wagon. He heard a thud and saw, out of the corner of his uncovered eye, Valentine taking cover in the darkness along the side of the road.

"Damn, I hate this eye patch." He flipped it up to get his bearings and flipped it back down again before Slade came closer.

Solomon sang out to those approaching, "Yes sir, here I am, just like ya told me to be."

Slade rode up, the lantern held high in his hand. By lamp light Solomon could see Slade's haggard face. His eyes were sunken even deeper in their sockets. He looked like walking death.

"About time. Set your lamp down and help these people in the wagon," he shouted.

Solomon scrambled down from the wagon. "Yes, sir. Right away sir."

Ruth nearly collapsed in his arms. He untied the baby and placed it into her shackled hands. As he gave her the child, he whispered in her ear. "Don't worry, love. You're going to be all right."

82

The woman raised her eyes to his, but said nothing.

Next, he helped Reverend Trout from his horse. The reverend had a large knot on the side of his head and a wound caked with dried blood. He could feel the reverend's body tense.

"Unhand me, sir. I've done nothing wrong." He tried to wrench himself from Solomon's grasp, but Solomon wrapped his arms around the portly minister and squeezed. The minister yelled from the pain.

"Don't struggle, you're hurt. Just play along and don't be a fool," Solomon whispered through clenched teeth. The minister was about to reply when Solomon shoved him roughly forward. "Get in there, you," he raised his voice, "And don't cause no trouble." He turned around to Slade. "Well, that's it. All nice and cozy. What now, sir?" He stopped short when he saw by lantern light that Slade had drawn a gun on him.

"Now my friend, you'll step aside and allow me to drive the wagon."

"But sir, I...I can't do that. This is my wagon team. I'm the driver. I..." Before he could utter another sound, Slade aimed the weapon at Solomon's head. Solomon took a step backwards while his one eye scanned frantically for Valentine.

With Solomon in his sights, Slade dismounted and tied his horse to the back of the wagon. He set his lantern along side the other and hauled himself on the seat. Solomon desperately tried to forestall him.

"But...but sir, ya can't drive the wagon and watch them, too. Let me drive while you watch."

"I have no need of your services anymore."

Solomon was taking several steps forward hampered by his limited vision from the eye patch, so he didn't see when Slade aimed his gun and shot, barely missing his feet.

"I said, I don't need your services. Step back or else I'll not miss the next time."

While Slade laboriously turned the wagon around on the path, Solomon looked frantically for Valentine. He heard another gunshot that echoed in the darkness. He hit the ground. When he looked up, he saw Slade blindly return the fire, aiming to his right through the trees.

A whirl of motion and another shot caught Slade off guard. Solomon rose and saw Slade aiming his gun. Solomon rolled and covered his head. He heard the clanging of fallen lanterns, but didn't see Valentine until he grabbed Slade and threw him to the ground.

Slade still had the gun in his hand as they wrestled in a swirling mass of muslin, legs and flailing arms. Valentine straddled Slade, smothered him with the skirt and beat him with his fists until he lay unconscious. Valentine rose, breathing heavily as he staggered forward, his red dress ripped at the shoulders.

"You know, you could have helped," he said, between gulps of air.

"Hell, I didn't know what you were planning. All I could see was a gun pointed at my face. Could you have cut it any closer?" Solomon snapped.

"I was trying to wait until I could get good aim. What's wrong with your pistols, anyway?

"There's nothing wrong with my pistols. Something's wrong with your aim. Good Christ in heaven, a child can shoot better than that." He saw that Valentine was holding his shoulder. "You all right?"

"Yes. Just bruised and a little worse for the wear," he said. "Nothing serious." He took off his wig, shook it free of dirt. "Let's get him tied up before he comes to."

"Did he get a good look at your face?" Solomon asked.

"If he did, what could he say? A colored woman in a red dress jumped him? Not the kind of thing you want to spread around if you're a slave catcher, I would imagine. What about you?"

"All he saw was One-eyed Willy, a teamster with a dubious reputation."

They dragged Slade to a tree, and tied him securely to it with a rope from the wagon.

"He'll be okay for the night. Someone is bound to find him," Solomon said, jamming Slade's hat down and sticking a black feather in it. "Our signature."

They walked back to the wagon.

"That was rather dangerous, shooting blindly in the dark. You could have hurt someone, namely me."

Valentine ignored Solomon and turned his attention to the passengers. "Are you all right?" He said holding the lantern to see the captives.

The reverend, who had been laying in the corner of the wagon, now looked up and saw Valentine with his red dress sans wig in disarray. The reverend blinked then stuttered. " I...I know....I know you sir...you are...aren't you the barber?"

Valentine said nothing.

"Minister, I'll take you back to Ripley," Solomon said, helping him down from the wagon. Are you all right?" But Reverend Trout was riveted to the sight of Valentine.

"Yes, yes, I...I think we're all fine; the woman and I." He turned his attention to Solomon. "Thank you for rescuing us. We were on our way to Africa Hill when that man caught up with us."

"Yes, we know minister, and we'll get her there safely, but you will come with me and return to town," Solomon said sternly. "Can you ride? It's still a good long ways."

"Yes, sir. I think I can," he said mounting a horse. "But sir, I am confused. How did you know? I didn't tell anybody?"

"It doesn't matter, sir. Just keep this to yourself."

Solomon saluted Valentine as he and the minister took off on horseback toward Ripley. Valentine boarded the back of the wagon and crouched down toward Ruth who was huddled with her baby in the corner.

"How are you?" he asked gently while he untied her.

"We alive, guess that's God's plan," she wanly smiled.

Valentine patted her shoulder. "Well, we need to make it to the settlement before daybreak. They'll give you food and water. Then send you on your way. It'll be too dangerous to stay. The Quakers will take you the rest of the way."

Ruth nodded her understanding. Valentine proceeded to crawl over her onto the wagon seat, but she kept staring at him.

He turned back toward her. "What is it?"

She shook her head. "I…I don't know. Seem like I seen you before, too."

"Then forget you've ever seen me, you hear?"

ಆ

CHAPTER NINE

The two men carefully followed the road back to Ripley in the dark aided only by the feeble light of the lantern. Their silence was interrupted periodically by the sounds from nocturnal animals. Solomon looked over at the reverend who was slumped and listing to one side of his horse. He realized the minister was having a difficult time.

"I can build a fire and we can camp for a few hours, if it won't be too cold for you," Solomon volunteered.

Reverend Trout smiled feebly. "I'll take my chances with the cold. I'm not as young as I used to be and the excitement tonight has me exhausted. My heart is still pounding and my side aches."

They rode in silence until Solomon found a spot near a stream. He helped the reverend secure his horse and sat him down while he foraged for dry wood.

"How do you feel?" Solomon asked, glancing at the reverend's pale face through the crackling flames of the fire.

"I'll be all right, I suppose," he said wearily. "Nothing broken except my pride."

"I'll stay awake and tend to the fire, you get some sleep. We're only a few hours away from Ripley. We can be there early in the morning."

Reverend Trout curled himself into a ball and within minutes was snoring. Solomon passed the time making up rhymes in his head, reciting poetry and monologues from plays. As the sun rose, Solomon sat languidly against a tree, smoking and looking out over the serene landscape when he caught the reverend looking at him.

"Is there something you'd like to say, minister?"

"I, well, I think I know you…or know of you. That's all." The minister dipped his hand in the water and splashed it on his face.

"Yes?" Solomon asked, impatiently.

"It's just that from what I've heard…a…a melancholic who never ventures out in daylight. Somewhat of a mystery in town, you see." And leaning over, he whispered confidentially. "You are the Raven, aren't you?"

Solomon tilted his head and smiled pleasantly at the reverend. "Sir, I think if I were you, I'd try and forget the entire incident. It is not beyond the power of the southern establishment to make an example of you still. All Slade has to do is convince the authorities in Kentucky to investigate this matter. And if they find that you are a party to absconding with another man's property, they can extradite you on a charge of kidnapping. And if convicted, sentence you to many years of hard labor. Judging by your ample physique, I doubt seriously if you'd last six months," Solomon said, blowing smoke rings in the morning air.

"So, Reverend Trout, my advice to you is that you never say another word about what you've seen or what you've done." Solomon tossed a pebble into the stream and watched it ripple out in concentric circles. "You see reverend we're either in this together, or not at all. And like my rock there, your talk could send unpleasant vibrations rippling throughout the Ohio Valley."

The reverend, whose face dripped with water, blinked at Solomon's bluntness. "Yes, sir. I absolutely understand what you mean. And I will take steps to never put you or anyone else in jeopardy." He wiped the water off his face and without guile or hesitation pronounced. "I asked for a test of my faith, and I got it. The slave Ruth was my opportunity to test my faith. And I failed.

Had you not come along—well," he bowed his head in shame. "I sympathize with the slaves and their desolate lives, but I do not want to die for them nor do I want my family to suffer. So, today sir, I make you a promise that you will never hear of this from my lips."

Solomon regarded the minister somberly. "Sir, some men are brave because they know what they can do. And some men are brave because they know what they cannot do."

When Reverend Trout finally reached home, he took Martha into his arms and kissed her desperately. He did not tell her about the complications. He only said that he had accomplished his goal. When she pressed him about the bruises on his face and body, all he said was that he was not hurt badly and the slave Ruth and her child were in good hands.

൦ঌ

The Africa Hill community was known for aiding fugitives and yet, it was becoming more dangerous to do so. The Fugitive Slave Act of 1850 made it unsafe for fugitives as well as free blacks. Members of the community feared being waylaid and kidnapped back into slavery. The community elders even talked about moving on. Some of the members had already moved to Canada. Those who remained were armed and would not hesitate to use their weapons to prevent a slave catcher from invading their community.

This was the free black community where Valentine took Ruth and her baby. While Valentine rested, the community fed Ruth to fortify her for the next leg of her journey. They coddled the baby in warm blankets, fed and rocked it to sleep. The community arranged to take Ruth and her baby farther north to a Quaker community. There, the Quakers would arrange for free papers and passage on a coach to Sandusky. The money for the coach ticket was from the Quaker's own coffers.

In two or three days, if Ruth arrived safely in Sandusky, she would join a handful of fugitives who would board a boat and cross Lake Erie to Canada where there were several colored communities. This is how the network operated. Each community knew its responsibility and purpose. And if you asked the people who participated in the Underground if they were law-abiding citizens, they would all nod in the affirmative. Then they would add that they were also doing God's work, and God's law always took precedent over man's.

☃

As for Slade, some farmers found him the next afternoon when they heard him yelling. The curious farmers untied him and questioned him about what had happened, but Slade only said that he had been waylaid and his valuable property stolen. The farmers offered to take him to the authorities, but he refused. Instead, he searched the Ripley wharf for William Gladstone, but no one seemed to know the man with the one blue eye.

Reluctantly, Slade gave up and boarded a ferry to cross over into Kentucky. He then waited an appropriate interval of time before he delivered the bad news to the planter who hired him.

"I regret sir, that as your agent, I must tell you this disturbing news because I know how much you wanted her back," he said, standing before the man, hat in hand, feigning as much humility as he could possibly muster.

"Her lead was too long. Helped I'm sure by numerous people who would deprive you of your rightful property. I tried, sir, but her trail was too cold. And I am only one man," he said humbly.

They were in the planter's library, one that was fashioned after an English country manor. Slade's gaze drifted out the window and over the frost-kissed lawn littered with fall leaves. His employer owned several hundred acres of prime farmland in the middle of Kentucky, a fashionable home in Louisville, and two or three warehouses. Slade hoped that in addition to his retainer, he might be compensated for the time and effort he'd put into the chase. Instead, the planter, who had said nothing during Slade's rehearsed narration, slid a newspaper across his walnut and mahogany inlaid desk, and with a ringed index finger pointed to a piece in a local Kentucky paper:

A man in black came to Ripley town,
Was looking for a slave and found,
His task a daunting one, you see,
The Raven was his enemy.

This man in black, he hunted men,
Their crime, he said, 'their dark hued skin',
That made them slave and so, you see,
He would not, could not, let them be,

But Raven caught him one dark night,
And there ensued an awful fight,
For Raven won and took the slave,
And spared the catcher an early grave,

For Raven wanted nothing more,
Than to keep the slave on freedom's shore,
He tied the hunter to a tree,
And left him there for all to see.

Now, this man in black whose name is Slade,
Is finding work a bit delayed,
For catcher he is no damn good,

Ann Eskridge

His prey he loses in the woods.
The Raven

Slade left the plantation without compensation, but took the newspaper with him. As he rode, he clutched the paper in his right hand, now crippled with pain. Each reading fueled his anger. As he headed west, he passed a village where he spotted a flock of noisy black birds. Whether they were Crows, Magpies or Ravens, he did not know. And he did not care. As he watched them circling overhead, he drew his gun, firing off six shots in rapid succession, killing one of them. The bird fell earthward. It flapped haplessly for a moment and then became still.

Slade dismounted and walked over to the lifeless creature. With the heel of his boot, he crushed its head. He then vowed to do the same to the man, or men, who had heaped humiliation on him and tarnished his good name.

CHAPTER TEN

Maysville, Kentucky

The morning after her capture, Leona huddled in a corner of her cramped cell. Her coat and dress had been torn and the dank cold coming from the stone walls made her shiver. All she had against the cold was her shawl wrapped around her shoulders. The deputies had given her only threadbare, lice-infested blankets. She had not been given any food; only a tin cup of lukewarm water to drink. She smelled of grime, and felt lost in hopelessness and fear.

The cell door then opened, and Dr. Nathaniel Fowler stood in the doorway, smirking. The heavy wooden door closed with a thud. He looked around the cell, then rested his eyes on her. He held in his hands a plate wrapped in a cloth. He uncovered the plate and took out a chicken leg that he waved in the air before he threw it on the dirt floor.

"Eat it. It's the only decent meal you'll get here unless you decide that you have regretted your actions."

Leona looked at the meat. All she had to do was take it. Hungry though she was, something in her—something she couldn't explain—wouldn't let her reach out those few inches. The toe of his boot nudged the chicken leg toward her.

"Eat it. I know you're hungry. You're probably cold as well. I'm surprised you haven't caught your death in here." He squatted on his haunches and stared at her. His eyes were roiling pools of darkness. She smelled the medicine on his clothes.

"Oh, Leona, what am I to do with you? I want an explanation. I need an explanation. Why would you defy me so?"

She averted his eyes, looking instead at the meat, while trying to ignore her growling stomach. "I wanted to see my brother, Massa. That's all."

His head shot up like a snake poised to strike. "And you would go against my orders?" he shouted. "I, who have fed and clothed and trusted you for these many years? You would dare to defy me? I said there were kidnappers afoot; evil men who would do you harm if they caught you. You are lucky you were caught by the good deputies, but even they can do you harm."

"I just wanted to see my brother," was all she could say.

Dr. Fowler rose. "You will stay in this cell until you apologize. Only then will I allow you out. Only then will you return. You have done me an injustice and I will not tolerate it. Do you hear?" he shouted. She did not answer. He screamed: "Do you hear?"

"Yes, Massa, I hear," she responded meekly.

He bent over and touched her face.

She shrank from his touch.

"Oh, Leona why...why do you inflict me with such feelings."

"Do you not know the power you have over me? You cannot stay here. I can not protect you here. Those men, they will try to despoil you. They will do terrible things to you. Can't you see that I'm the only one who can protect you? Say the words. Say them and we can go home."

She closed her eyes while tears ran down her face.

"Leona, what do you say?"

She couldn't stop sobbing and trembling.

He pushed her away. "I could have them beat you. Lash you in full view. Those are my rights. I am your master. I could have them starve you. I could have you stripped naked and paraded around the town. You will apologize to me," he thundered. "I know of a master who left his slave in jail to rot for over a year. Is that what you want?"

Still she was silent.

He crushed the chicken leg with his boot and then he turned and opened the cell door, glancing back before he closed it behind him.

When she heard his footsteps retreat, she grabbed the chicken leg, brushed it off, and ate greedily. She couldn't articulate why she refused to apologize. So she sat in jail. Each morning at sunrise, she made a line on the dirt floor to mark the new day. She could count up to ten.

The fourth night she was drifting off to sleep to the raucous noise of the deputies drinking in the next room. They roared in drunken abandon as they joked with one another about the job of taking slaves to Gibbon's Farm near Minerva, and whether some of them would be hired for that. "Mercer gonna hire Jesse. He done captured hisself a runaway," one of them said.

"Yeah, and she pretty too. Pretty for the likes of Jesse here," they laughed.

"Some say Mercer gonna get rid of his cook gal. Now that one's a looker. Bet she gonna be one of them fancy gals in New Orleans."

"He ain't got no more use for her. Not when he's to marry," one deputy said.

"More'n likely, Harry, Mercer got to get rid of the wench 'for he take his bride. But if I was him, I'd keep that gal around, just in case." The deputies hooted and howled with laughter.

"Yeah Jack, I bet you would like a taste, 'fore the goods are sold. You wanna find out what's so special 'bout Mercer's gal. Wanna see what she got?"

"Don't need to wait to get no dark meat. We got us, dark meat right here."

Moments later, Leona heard a sound at her cell door. Through the fog of sleep she looked up and saw a face lighted from behind by the lanterns on the walls and framed by the iron bars set in the door. She heard the heavy wooden door scrape open and before she was fully awake, two men rushed into her cell and grabbed her.

They played with her like a rag doll, tossing her from one to the other. She lashed out at them, clawed and spit, but the two toppled her to the ground and one felt underneath her clothing. She struggled against the man who held her hands while the other one pulled up her dress.

"Better leave her be," a third voice commanded them, sounding much older than his years.

"Who the hell, you tellin' us whatta do, Jesse?" The man holding her head said.

"Yeah, we do as we please," said the second, as he tightened his grip on her hips.

She struggled for air as the first man forced her head back toward him.

"Kiss… gimmeakiss, nigger gal." His mouth covered hers in saliva and stink.

"Harry, Jack, I wouldn't be the one to answer to Dr. Fowler. I hear he said she weren't to be touched. And he give strict orders to that effect. You saw him. He don't look like a man you'd wanna cross," Jesse said from the doorway.

"Yeah, well he ain't here."

"No, he ain't. But when he takes her back my guess is she gonna tell him for sure just what you done to his property, Jack. You know what'll happen if'n he finds out who spoilt her. You seen him half crazed. You ask me, he a straw short of a haystack, but he the only doctor 'round for miles. You want him to dress your wounds, knowing what he know about what you done? One slip of his knife and you less of a man."

Leona felt hands slip away from her private parts. The man named Harry who grabbed her head, let her go and she was able to breathe.

"Come on, boys save it for the march. Let it be. She ain't worth gettin' cut up by a crazy doctor. Besides, if that Fowler don't come and get her in a fortnight, we got a right to sell her," Jesse reminded them.

Harry and Jack grumbled, but preceded Jesse out of the cell. As he left, Jesse glanced back at her. The light from the wall lantern illuminated his young face. She saw his lips twitch, as if to say something, then changed his mind. He yanked the cell door closed behind him.

Leona wondered how many marks made a fortnight.

CHAPTER ELEVEN

Ripley, Ohio

Valentine turned the chair so Joseph could appraise himself in the gilt mirror.

"Just trim the sides and leave some on the top," Joseph Greene said as he leaned his head back and let out a contented sigh, then sank down in the velvet barber seat and closed he eyes.

"Joseph, I don't want to be the one to tell you this, but some is all I can take off," Valentine teased.

Joseph cocked his head to one side and ran his fingers through his thinning hair.

"I used to have a thick head of hair until I started my business and got married. The hair started falling like snow in a blizzard. Next thing you know, I'll be as bald as an eagle. It's the constant demands on my time, Val. Mrs. Greene wants me to do this. My customers want me to do that. My employees don't want to do anything. I'm surprised you're not going bald yourself what with the shop and your Solomon. How is he, by the way?" He swung back around.

"Solomon is doing well. He's working on a few more poems and he told me he was starting a play, but he won't let me see it until he's finished." Valentine brushed the thin blond strands on Joseph's head; hair that he trimmed—hair that, no matter what concoctions he mixed, would never grow back. Nonetheless, Joseph insisted on trying anything, hoping for a miracle.

"Did you hear the news?" Joseph said, sitting straight up.

Valentine gently nudged Joseph back down in the chair only to have him bob back up with excitement.

"No, I have to tell you this before I forget," Joseph said, blinking frantically through his thick glasses.

"As if you would forget anything."

"Well, Mrs. Trout came into the store an hour ago and asked to see some bolts of cloth. She needed to make a traveling outfit for herself. So, I ask her, casual like, if she is planning to take a trip. And she says that she and her husband, the good reverend, have decided that their fortunes lie on the frontier.

"She tells me, mind you, I didn't do any prompting, that Reverend Trout had a vision of their whole family moving to the new state of California where all those 49'ers are. Well, isn't that unheard of? He don't even wait for a new minister. Just ups and leaves," Joseph said, peering candidly through his glasses at Valentine.

"Take off your spectacles, Joseph so I won't spill anything on them."

"Well, you don't seem at all surprised," said Joseph as he removed his wire rims and put them in his waistcoat pocket.

"To tell you the truth, I'd heard something about that only a few days before."

"You did no such thing," Joseph said in a bit of a huff. Joseph prided himself on being the first to hear any gossip and rumor that floated around town.

Valentine sighed. "Joseph, the reverend came to me and asked me to recommend a set of tools he'd need on a trip. It was then that he told me what he was planning," Valentine lied.

It was true that Reverend John Trout had come to Valentine. It was not, however, to ask the barber what tools to take with him on a long trip through the frontier. Instead, the reverend had furtively met with both Valentine and Solomon in Solomon's quarters to thank them once again for rescuing him. It was then he told them of his plans to leave Ripley.

"I don't doubt sir, that I would be in the same predicament as Mr. John Van Zandt," he said.

John Van Zandt had been charged with aiding and abetting nine fugitive slaves when he agreed to conceal them in his wagon. When caught, Van Zandt was indicted and convicted. He appealed to the United States Supreme Court, who upheld the findings of the lower court. Van Zandt had to pay twelve hundred dollars for his humanitarian action.

"I do not have that kind of money, nor can I afford to languish in prison and so, gentlemen, I am in your debt and that debt will be repaid by my silence," he assured them solemnly.

"You didn't tell me?" Joseph blurted.

"Didn't tell you what?" Valentine came back to the present.

"About the reverend," Joseph pressed Valentine.

"Oh, I didn't tell anyone. He said he wanted to keep it private until he was able to announce it to his congregation. I would suggest that you do the same. It's only fair to the reverend."

The duly chastised Joseph leaned back in the chair. Valentine reached into his cabinet and pulled out a clear bottle.

"Let me try something. I made up a new herb concoction. I know that certain herbs stimulate growth. Let's see if this helps. I had the apothecary mix it to my specifications."

Joseph was one of Valentine's best customers. He came in every few days to get a shave, and every other week for a cut. Joseph didn't need either, at least not as regularly as he seemed to think. Valentine suspected that he came in just to pass the time. Valentine was hesitant to offend or lose his best customer by telling him that he could make fewer appointments and still be well-groomed. It was Joseph's business how he chose to spend his money.

Valentine poured a few drops of oil in his hands and began to massage Joseph's head. He could feel Joseph's muscles relax. Joseph let out another sigh of satisfaction.

"I don't know what your magic is, Val, but I swear coming into your shop takes years off of me."

"Well, you deserve a respite from the day's labors. You work extremely hard," Valentine acknowledged, as he rubbed the ointment into his customer's temples.

"You have no idea. Why, I was trying to tell Mrs. Greene the other day that I really wasn't up to hosting an elaborate party for her niece, but she insisted. Said she'd read in one of her ladies magazines that they're about to make Thanksgiving a national holiday; some kind of movement along those lines, and we should be part of it. She would give a Thanksgiving party as the perfect opportunity to introduce the girl to Ripley. It won't stop there, mind you. She's thinking of planning a round of festivities. And I was so looking forward to having some peace."

"Oh, your niece is staying with you? How long?"

Joseph grunted. "God knows. It's her brother's daughter. Seventeen or eighteen I think. Decided she wanted to come up from Tennessee to visit. My guess is that Harriet's brother wants to marry Delphine off, and sent her up here to find some unsuspecting, near-sighted fellow."

"That bad?" Valentine teased, rubbing the back of Joseph's neck.

"No, not really. She's a pleasant enough girl... just... just... a little... uh... plain, I suppose you'd say."

"Certainly, there are eligible men in Tennessee?"

"Yes, but I think the competition is a bit too much for the girl. Sent her up here to a bustling river town so she has a fighting chance. Maybe she'll fare better. And now I'm in charge of rounding up suitable men for our soirees. Is my work never done?"

"I'm sure you'll find someone."

"Yes, I suppose so," he sighed again, winding down, but immediately revved up with more news. "And then there's the matter of the help. All these fancy parties and one of our gals just up and leaves. I don't know if you know her. A gal we hired, let's see, about two months ago to help our cook in the kitchen. May. Yes. That's her name. One day she was working out fine; the next day she was gone. Just like that…" he snapped his fingers. Joseph rambled about the ungrateful help while Valentine continued to massage his head.

Valentine did know May, but that wasn't information he was likely to share with Joseph. She had run away and passed herself off as a free person. When she got wind that her master was looking for her, she appealed to the abolitionist underground. He supposed the Grinder, through his contacts, had arranged a wagon to take her on a zigzagging trip up the middle of the state from Brown to Highland County and from there up to Sandusky and across Lake Erie to Canada.

"…and say, do you think that your friend, Solomon, would be interested in coming?" Joseph sat up erect.

"What?" The question took Valentine by surprise.

By now, Joseph's eyes shone with inspiration.

"Yes, won't you just ask him? It would really get me off the hook, you see. I mean, he is an intellectual and all; would be something different. I've invited some couples and a few of our church people. Then there's that school teacher, can't remember his name, not been here long enough. And the merchant over by Red Oak. Of course he's rather old…and then there's…" Joseph continued telling Valentine who he'd invited to the Thanksgiving dinner for Delphine.

Valentine interrupted. "What would Mrs. Greene say? I mean, after all, Solomon can be a bit…uh, contrary at times."

"I'll just say that he's had a bad stroke of luck and that maybe we'll be helping him out by inviting him. He's a good lookin' fella and those times I've had occasion to converse with him, he seemed… well, he seemed in his right mind."

"I really don't know if he's…"

"Oh come on Val, do this for me. Frankly, I'd be looking forward to it myself. A little flavor, you see. Something different, you see…an artist."

"Lay back, Joseph. Let me start cutting. I'll ask Solomon for you. It might do him good to get out in polite company."

"Do that," he said, as he laid his head back in the plush barber chair, closing his eyes. In a few moments, Joseph was snoring contentedly. While Joseph dozed, Valentine thought, about how, in Philadelphia, he would have at least been invited.

In Philadelphia, Valentine was not a social pariah because of the color of his skin. He had been active in the influential center of the black abolitionist's movement. As a result, he was privileged to be in a circle of influential black and white men who believed in their moral obligation to free slaves.

The Reverend Richard Allen was the early guiding force for the black abolitionists. A former slave himself, Allen taught himself to read and write, and eventually purchased his own freedom. His true gift was ministry, which led him, along with Absalom Jones, to establish the African Methodist Episcopal Church later on. Allen and Jones became the nexus of the black abolitionist's movement that included James Forten, a free black man.

These were among those first black men of stature who

argued their right to be in this country as free people. They held this view in opposition to The African Colonization Society. This society, led by whites, wanted to send all freed slaves back to Africa, even though the majority of these slaves were now born and raised in America.

The free black men who opposed the Colonization Society were eventually joined by like-minded white men, and together they supported other alternatives including colored settlements in Canada. They sold subscriptions to abolitionist papers, and held town meetings to rally support for slave emancipation. Valentine admired these black abolitionists. In his mind, they stood as examples of what a black man, given the opportunity, could be in life. Some were wealthy, articulate, and influential— everything Valentine wanted to be.

In Philadelphia, those whites who believed in the cause often hosted lectures, meetings, and charity bazaars. Valentine was a frequent guest in their homes as they were people who claimed to fight zealously for the rights and equality of all men. He was, as Solomon once said. "an abolitionist gadfly", flitting around to various homes of the prominent elite.

Valentine should not have felt hurt when Joseph didn't invite him to dinner; but it did hurt. He considered Joseph a steady customer, even a friend; one who seemed to pay no attention to color, or so Valentine thought. Valentine combed Joseph's thinning hair and with scissors, snipped more than he should.

CZ

CHAPTER TWELVE

Ripley, Ohio—Joseph Greene's home

Solomon leaned casually on the pianoforte that graced the Greene's front parlor and scanned the room. A fire crackled in the fireplace, the smoke lending the room a woodsy scent. The parlor walls of the Greene's Georgian-style home were painted peach, and along the molding was a hand-stenciled border of green ivy; a décor meant to impress people from rural Ohio villages since browns and blues were more the norm. But Mrs. Greene had read several months before that contrasting colors lent culture to the home. Shortly after that, the parlor was repainted peach and green over Mr. Greene's objections that it was costly and gaudy.

Twenty people sat facing Solomon in delicate chairs that had needlepoint-decorated seats, and were arranged in two rows. The women wore their finest Sunday dresses. The men sat stiffly and uncomfortably, after having filled themselves at Joseph Greene's ample table.

A curl fell from Solomon's frontal wave as he leaned his head forward with an air of intimacy. Dressed in a dark tailored suit with bold scarlet vest and matching silk tie, he was somewhat out of place in a room of somberly dressed men. The men were at a loss in their impression of this flamboyant man. The women felt no such ambiguity, and they beamed with delight.

Solomon's delicate mouth curled into a seductive smile. His blue eyes shone wistfully as he gazed in the direction of Delphine who blushed in response:

> *When you and I are old this earth*
> *Will lose for us its tone of mirth;*
> *The flowers fair, the skies of blue*
> *Will but reflect a somber hue.*
> *We pass but once along life's way,*
> *The sweets we fail to sip today*
> *Perhaps tomorrow will be sour;*
> *Drink deep then of each golden hour.*

He stopped and sagged as if the mere recitation of the poem had sapped his strength. The affect was that of a man who felt deeply the ebb and flow of life, and who at times, drowned in its eddies. That image was not lost on his audience. This was particularly true of the young, impressionable and plain Delphine who seemed overwhelmed by the fact that Solomon had dedicated the poem to her.

Delphine's long curls bobbed up and down as she almost bounced out of her chair. Her eyes shone brightly. She smiled, showing crooked teeth in a horse-like face.

"Oh, please Mr. Tucker, have you anymore? We'd loved to hear something else," she snorted.

It was obvious to Solomon that he had captured the attention of the young woman. The poem he had just recited hinted at the promise of years to come. It was a bit too sentimental, written some years back when he was in love with a young woman of questionable reputation with whom he'd had a brief but torrid encounter.

Solomon had never played before a more enthusiastic crowd. He affected a cavalier stance, at once commanding, but with an air of humility.

"Please, you flatter me most kindly," he said, raising his hand to hush the applause.

"But you must recite more, Mr. Tucker. You must," Delphine urged.

"Perhaps one more then, something…something that is most exciting," he lowered his voice. "But somewhat dangerous. Would you like to hear it?" he teased.

"Oh, yes. Yes," Delphine cried.

"All right then. A poem I heard recited among an unsavory lot." Solomon took a breath. He scanned his audience and waited until he had their full attention. Solomon closed his eyes, took a deep breath and began:

> *The Raven swoops down late at night,*
> *Avenging angel in the fight,*
> *To save the slave who bares the scars,*
> *Of cruel oppression and freedom barred.*

He heard murmurs and gasps in the crowd. He opened his eyes and saw that the men were frowning and the women were whispering behind gloved hands. He stopped, bewildered at the reaction.

"Uh, I can't remember the rest, to tell you the truth. But I heard another. Something shorter, more lively," He coughed and cleared his throat then started again:

> *Raven flying overhead,*
> *Searching for the slave who's fled,*
> *Leading him to safety's shores,*

Where he'll be a slave no more.

Solomon waited for applause, but only silence greeted him. He was confused and slightly taken aback by the silence. The amiable Joseph Greene came to his rescue.

"Mr. Tucker, nicely done," he clapped a bit too loudly. "Taken from the writings of those abolitionists who see the Raven as a hero most certainly. A commentary on these controversial times, you see?" he said, turning to the audience while putting a hand around Solomon's shoulder and blinking excitedly behind his spectacles. "A man who has picked up the tenor and tone and mimics the abolitionist spirit. Very well done, sir." Joseph stood before the audience. "And now, I would invite Mrs. Thorton to come up and grace us with a popular Ethiopian musical number," Joseph Greene said, as he urged the audience to clap.

Solomon took his seat next to Delphine who leaned toward him and whispered, "That was so brave of you to recite an abolitionist poem. Bravo, Mr. Tucker. I don't suppose you'd teach it to me one day," she said, her nostrils flaring with excitement.

The audience's cool reception to his abolitionist recitation did not register with Solomon. It never occurred to him that although Joseph Greene visited Valentine's shop, Greene did not necessarily consider Valentine an equal. In his naiveté, Solomon assumed that his audience was composed of people who might be sympathetic to abolishing slavery. Instead, these men were merchants who relied on Southerners for trade. Ripley's foundries, tanneries, mills and stores were reliant on southern patronage. Their pork packing industry supplied pork products to slave owners from Kentucky to New Orleans since owners believed that pork was more economical and contained more protein than beef. The Ohio women, in turn, relied on their men to provide them with a comfortable lifestyle from that trade.

There were fervent abolitionist groups in the northern part of Ohio, but there was strong pro-slavery sentiment in the southern part. The political geography escaped him because Solomon was too self-absorbed to be bothered with politics. He leaned his body closer to the young Delphine and whispered,

"Shall I teach you the poem when we are alone?" She whinnied and shyly covered her mouth to hide her crooked teeth.

Over the course of the evening's Thanksgiving festivities, he'd learned that Delphine was a rather well-to-do young woman whose father doted on her. Solomon was more than happy to flirt with her as they listened to Mrs. Thorton's rendition of *Oh, Susanna,* a popular tune that was sweeping the country. People were singing it in parlors and beer halls alike. Mrs. Thorton's rendition was loud, lively and off-key, but no one seemed to mind. They clapped in cadence to the music, and once through she waited until the applause died before she began a second number. It was a Mozart aria about Turkish lovers that was so poorly executed, Mozart himself might not have recognized it as his composition.

ᎧᏃ

While Solomon charmed his young hostess, Valentine sat behind his shop in the biting cold and watched as Grinder sharpened his barber instruments. Grinder was named after his profession and it was the only name he was called. The small, stooped man with knurled hands and wiry beard that flowed to his chest was German by birth and an abolitionist at heart.

Valentine knew very little about the Grinder who had plied his trade in Philadelphia before working both sides of the Ohio River and down along the Mississippi. Grinder traveled wherever he could get work, which included taverns, barber, tailor shops, and plantations. He sometimes traded his skill for rides up and down the river. Finally, Grinder was Valentine's link to the other abolitionist groups.

Grinder knew the identity of every abolitionist between Cincinnati and New York. He also knew the routes and stations and, more importantly, the names of major conductors and stationmasters in Ohio, Indiana, Illinois, and some parts of Pennsylvania. This information he carried in his head. As far as Valentine knew, the Grinder, Captain Julius and young Tom were the only people who knew that Solomon and Valentine operated as the Raven.

Grinder pronounced his "w's" like "v's" and his "th's" like "d's" even after spending years in the United States. His thick German accent and the grating sound of metal on stone often made it difficult for Valentine to understand everything Grinder was saying.

The two men were discussing the latest abolitionist idea of selling non-slave made goods in stores. The free labor movement was an attempt to strangle the South, economically. The problem was that goods made from non-slave labor were rare—and costly.

"But Levi in Cincinnati runs his store. He got goods enough to make money," Grinder argued.

"That's just one store, Grinder," Valentine contested.

"*Ja, aber* one store more dan *nichts*," Grinder replied, smiling.

"What?" Valentine shouted over the noise.

"I said, one store more dan nothin'."

"Ever the optimist," Valentine snorted. "You heard that a group of Kentucky planters are selling slaves?"

"*Ja,*" the Grinder said, keeping his eye on the wheel. "Men *und* some women, de troublemakers mostly."

Valentine nodded. "I have that same information." He watched as the old man took each tool and wiped them off with his sleeve.

Grinder's feet pumped the ancient whetstone wheel until it spun furiously. He lightly laid the tool edge against the wheel and with one eye closed, watched the stone sharpen the razor. The Grinder coughed and hacked again. He wiped the spittle from his mouth and selected another dull razor.

"*Ja*, dey say dis de largest group. I hear tell dey gonna march dem to one location."

"I never heard when and where," Valentine said as he imagined the rag-tag black men and women being herded in the cold, dressed inadequately with their feet in rags. He could still hear the cries of the children who were left behind, screaming for their parents. He recalled the memory vividly since he had been one of those children himself. He closed his eyes to block the sight.

The Grinder coughed and spit. "All done in secret. Each planter got to make his own arrangements to get his slaves to de gathering."

"It's going to be a hard walk for them," Valentine pondered aloud as he ran a thumb along a razor's sharpened edge.

The Grinder nodded. "*Ja, aber* dis way dey don't have the likelihood of kidnappers gettin' the whole bunch until de end. 'specially, not *mit* de Raven loose," the Grinder, looked at Valentine, pointedly. "Dey fear the Raven more dan dey fear losing some to the cold."

"Do you know when?" Valentine asked.

"Naw, but dink you find this planter named Mercer, you be able to find out the date."

"That means going to Kentucky."

Grinder nodded.

The wind picked up. Valentine said nothing, but pulled his coat tighter around him. "How long would it take you to get a group of men together?"

"Dat ain't the problem. Gettin' men I can trust together, *Ja?*" he coughed, gagged, then spit. "Maybe four or five men."

Valentine closed his eyes and thought. Four or five men, but there was no telling how many armed guards. *Could it be done?*

The Grinder blew on his exposed fingers and picked another razor from Valentine's set. "Where's the boy?"

"He's at a…uh… function called a Thanksgiving party with some of the other town's people," he said, then hesitated because the thought that Solomon was invited and he wasn't, still smarted. "A party for a young woman. The niece of the tailor."

"Ah, the fat *kleiner Schneider*," he smiled. "Always lose his help, *Ja?*" Grinder winked. "Well, both of you keep still for the time bein'. Hear tell dere's a few people done decided to trap a *Großer schwarzer Vogel*—a big black bird."

"We'll do that," Valentine said.

The Grinder nodded. "*Ja*, I read in de paper. De bounty hunter, he go toward Louisville, tail between his legs."

"I don't think he'll be coming back."

The Grinder gave Valentine a wry look. "Man like dat don't take kindly to bein' laughed at. Man like dat, got hisself a bone to pick," he said, as he lowered another razor to the whetstone while his feet madly pedaled the wheel.

CB

Valentine was in the back of the shop, lying on his bed when Solomon pulled back the curtain with a flourish and stepped in to the darkened room and danced around.

"I brought something for you," he said, waving a mincemeat pie under Valentine's nose.

Valentine shoved it away and turned his back on Solomon.

112

Solomon arched one eyebrow. "Well, you aren't in a very good mood. I'd think that the smell of mincemeat pie would have you drooling like a lap dog.

"I'm tired, Solomon."

"I see." But Solomon didn't leave, instead he lighted the lamp on the heavy oak table that served as Valentine's desk and dining table. He flopped in a chair, one leg draped over the arm to devour the mincemeat pie himself.

Unlike Solomon's well-appointed room, Valentine's was utilitarian: the table, several chairs, and a pine rope bed were the only furnishings. His room reflected his personality.

"I think the plain, yet frisky Delphine liked me," he said, between bites. "I've promised to see her one afternoon this week... a casual visit. A polite call to see how the lady is faring." He leaned close to Valentine who still hadn't stirred.

"Did you know the lady in question is rich? I mean...very rich. I understand her father owns a number of businesses and a plantation. Wouldn't that be ironic? Me, a slave owner?" He thought that this might get a rise out of Valentine, but his friend lay inert.

"Of course, we'll live in the North—on her money—while I teach her the finer things in life." He paused, finally exasperated. "Valentine, for God sake, say something."

Valentine rolled over on the bed, his face appeared ashen in the light.

"My God, Val, what's wrong? You look like you've taken ill. Are you ill?"

"The Grinder was here today. He confirmed the information about the forced march."

"And what do you want to do?"

"I want to try. It's what I've been working for," he said, looking candidly at Solomon. "My nightmares will end if I'm able to do something ...anything...to save those people."

Solomon looked at the earnest, pained expression on Valentine's face and realized that the psychological wound slavery had left might never heal no matter how many slaves Valentine set free. He knew the story all too well. Just like the two of them had invented the Raven, Valentine had reinvented himself.

ଓ

Valentine's birth name was Sam. Sam's mother was the cook on a Virginia tobacco plantation. The owner, Sam's birth father, came on hard times. In order to save his farm, he sold Sam's mother to pay taxes. The last time eight-year old Sam saw her, he was coming from the tobacco field and caught a glimpse of her red head wrap in the distance. He ran after the wagon for miles, but was unable to catch up to it. The overseer dragged him back to the plantation, but the next day young Sam was gone. He had run off and gotten lost. Sam stayed hidden for a week, eating berries and whatever plants he could find, but eventually the owner found him and chained him to a young slave girl while they both worked in the fields so that he could not run away.

Sam overheard that his mother had been sold to another Virginia planter farther south, near Richmond. That was over a hundred miles from where he was, but Sam vowed to find her. He found his chance to escape six months later.

One day he complained that his stomach was cramping and he told the overseer that he might have caught something. To make his story convincing, Sam had eaten the leaves of the Blessed Thistle plant that grew wild on the plantation. He had seen his mother use it with pregnant women to increase their milk, but too much of it caused vomiting. The overseer, fearing that whatever Sam had would spread to the slave girl, and then to the rest of the slaves, unchained Sam from the girl. Then he told Sam to go back to the cabins.

Instead, Sam headed straight for the provisions he had hidden. Then he fled in the general direction of Richmond. The patrollers caught him three weeks later and only five miles away from Richmond. They threw him in jail to wait for his owner to come get him and bring him back home.

As punishment, young Sam received spare rations, brutal floggings, and was isolated from the other slaves in the back room of the overseer's cabin where he slept chained on the floor. He did not try to escape again for another year. This next escape was purely unplanned.

The overseer was taking a gang of slaves to hire-out on a construction project. The wagon carrying them lost a wheel and several men were injured. Sam slipped away while the overseer was taking care of the injured. He hid in the woods by day, forded streams, climbed trees and slept in them at night.

By the fifth day of his escape the youngster was exhausted, starving, and suffering from exposure. He stumbled into a camp of itinerant actors, traveling the Eastern Seaboard circuit. One of the women who was sleeping, was awakened by a moan. She got up, walked outside of her wagon, and saw the boy lying in a heap in the bushes.

Over everyone's objections, Arabella insisted they hide young Sam. The other actors knew he was a runaway, but Arabella persuaded them to say nothing. She disguised the ten-year-old boy in girl's clothing to pass him off as her maid. She renamed young Sam, Valentine because she said he was her little sweetheart. She gave him the last name of Kass, which was the name of her lover at the time. By the time the players had finished the circuit and returned to Philadelphia, Sam had become Valentine and the companion to Arabella's six year old son, Solomon.

ಐ

"We need to go to Kentucky." Valentine said softly, rousing from his stupor.

"What?" Solomon was startled at Valentine's sudden statement.

Valentine sighed. "I'm going to Kentucky," he said, swinging his legs off the bed.

"You know that can be dangerous," Solomon replied wiping crumbs from his mouth.

"Not if I carry a set of my papers on me and not," he said, looking directly at Solomon, "...if you go with me to make sure I don't get mistaken as a runaway." he said. "So where's the mincemeat pie?"

Solomon held up the empty dish. "I told you it was good," he smiled, sheepishly.

CHAPTER THIRTEEN

Kentucky countryside

Geographically, there was little difference between the southern most tip of Ohio and the northern most tip of Kentucky, where the river kissed the shores. The ragged banks sloped upward then gently leveled off. Town buildings faced one another across the expanse of river.

The trees lay bare from the early frost. Weather on both sides was the same, but in Valentine's mind, every time he set foot in Kentucky it meant plunging into the gaping mouth of hell. One misstep and he would be tumbling into his own nightmare. If someone challenged his freeman status, he could be sent back into slavery. So, he tried to make his trips South infrequent. But in some cases, like now, he needed information, and then he would shove his fears aside and force himself to make calls on his familiar southern customers and their neighbors.

He peddled his barbering skills from farm to farm offering services to the master and help. He and Solomon traveled in an ever-widening circle, fanning out from the town center and scouring the countryside for information. Solomon stayed near town while Valentine called on clients. They were never more than a half-day's ride apart, just in case Valentine needed Solomon to vouch for his status.

Valentine's method for garnering information was simple; he carefully poked and prodded his customers with questions as skillfully as he kneaded their scalps. He knew exactly what he was looking for: a master who could not meet his taxes and had to sell property; or one who was looking to get rid of a female slave deemed by a wife as "inappropriate;" or one who needed to get rid of a lazy slave or a defiant troublemaker. An inconvenient or aggressive slave who showed little respect for his master's authority might also prompt the need to sell. Valentine knew the cues. It was an irritation in the master's voice, or a downturn of the mouth, or stiffened muscles. By the time Valentine was through plying his trade, he would have the information he needed. Mercer's plantation, where the young, drunken planter had sealed an agreement with the captain of the *Annabelle* was one of his first stops.

The Federal-style home of Ephraim Mercer was box-like with windows evenly spaced on either side of the main entry, one supported by high, white columns. Large Magnolia trees, whose gnarled limbs sheltered the entrance, also shaded the front from heat in the summer. Black walnut trees dotted the expanse of manicured lawn, and stately Chestnut oaks acted as a canopy to the well-worn road leading up to the mansion—welcoming the visitor.

Valentine stood at the back door, the one used by slaves and peddlers. It faced the chicken coops, hog pens, stables, and barn. The smell hung like a sickening cloud in the still air; and it was insufferable when the wind was blowing. Valentine raised his hand to knock, when a statuesque mocha colored woman who bore her height like a queen, came to the door. Her hand was on her hip as she leaned against the door frame. A saucy smile hinted through her pouting lips. Her hair was tied elaborately in a white cloth that gave her even more height and she wore a dress befitting the mistress of the house instead of a slave. She looked Valentine over, as he clutched his bag of instruments.

"What you want, you?" she snapped.

118

"I've come to see Massa Ephraim Mercer. I'm a barber. I thought he might need my services," he said thrusting a calling card in her hand.

She took the card and barely glanced at it, but flipped it back at him. "He ain't here. Now git," she said shifting her weight onto her other hip.

"Do you know when he'll be back?" he persisted.

"He don't tell me nothin' and I ain't ax."

"Perhaps I can wait."

"He don't like no strangers comin' round."

"Then maybe I can attend to his slaves?"

She let out a throaty laugh. "What he want to give his slaves a hair cut and shave?"

Valentine explained patiently that many slaves, because of their ignorance, were unable to groom themselves carefully, and thus, carried diseases of the head that could infect the entire household. These diseases, in some cases, disabled the slave and made him unable to work. Valentine had seen it dozens of times.

"If not treated, the slaves, including women, are left with bald patches from scratching. Their hair begins to fall out in clumps. In some cases diseases are so bad that the hair never grows back and the woman is left to wear forever the head wrap to disguise her baldness," he said, pointedly looking at hers.

She eyed him suspiciously, and then closed the door in his face. Valentine waited. Fifteen minutes went by before she opened the door again.

"Git 'round back in that shed," she pointed. "I'll send them to you. Your money'll be on the steps when you through." She then slammed the door again.

The Mercer plantation grew hemp and tobacco. It was large compared to others in Kentucky. Ephraim Mercer made money from tobacco but he also raised livestock and hired-out his help to work on other farms.

Valentine set up in a shed used to store tools and equipment. He built a small fire to keep warm and to heat water. He was just setting out his instruments when a young, gangly slave who called himself Thor, came in and sat down on a stool. He gave Valentine a wide gap-tooth grin of embarrassment then took off his hat displaying a thick, matted head of hair that looked and smelled like the boy had been wallowing in the slop he fed the hogs. While Valentine prepared, Thor began a diatribe against a fellow slave whom Valentine knew well because the slave operated in secret for the Underground.

"I tells master that Jubba don't know what he doin' and I can do the hire-out work. But no. He keep tellin' me let Jubba do it. Jubba all the time get to go to town and work on the river, while I got to stay put. Man ain't got the sense God gib him. Dumb as a fence post.

"Done broke a wagon. Massa got to pay for a new one and he mad 'cause he say Jubba done cost him too much money. But he ain't thinkin' 'bout punishin' Jubba. Oh, no. Jubba do the work a two men, he say. So what he do? He beat me 'cause I the one say Jubba done it on purpose. But he *had* to. You cain't tear up no wagon like that lessen you take an ax to the axle. Hell, I could see that. Massa say I lie, and to mind my own business.

"Ouch! what you doin' back up there, nigger...I mean, Valentine?" He turned his tar black face towards Valentine.

"I'm puttin' some turpentine and kerosene on your head to clean it from this lard you been puttin' on it to slick it down.

The skinny young slave rubbed his sore head. "Why you wanna go and do that?"

"Cause it stinks. I'm surprised you can't smell it."

The young male, who was no more than fifteen, grinned. "I be workin' 'round them hogs. I thought it was them I be smellin'."

"Yeah, well after I clean your head good, I'm going to cut it short. You keep it short. You wanna put somethin' on your head to make it smooth down, try just a little axle grease."

"You gonna make me pretty for the gals?" Thor laughed.

"I don't know about all that, but at least they'll be able to get near you without swatting flies," Valentine retorted as he rubbed a cloth along the slaves matted head.

"Yeah, this one slave, name George, he got his self a sister. She is a good lookin' woman. Don't get to see her none in the daytime. She come at night now. George don't think we knows, but we do.

"From what I seen of her, MMMmmmmm, sure would like to get close to her. Yes, sir. Wouldn't mind that at all," he grinned. "But when you talk to George, you don't let on, you hear? He kinda funny like that. I 'member one time somebody done said somethin' 'bout his sister, he done 'bout tore the skin from that boy's bones."

"Don't worry, I won't tell George what you said." Valentine rubbed the man's scalp. "Your master has a nice little farm here, he told me he's interested in buying up some land and expanding. I wonder where he'll get the money."

Thor squirmed under Valentine's hand. "Don't know about that. He ain't got the workers, you ask me. Ain't got no money neither. And he workin' us to death on this piece a land he do got."

"You don't say," Valentine said while he tried to get at Thor's roots to clean his scalp. Thor got comfortable, kicked off his battered shoes and wiggled his toes while Valentine rubbed his scalp.

"Do say. Hell, the only way he gonna get money is to sell some of us. And for my money, it'll be that cook he got. You met her? She 'bout the most shiftless, evilest gal I seen…and she cain't cook. But you cain't tell that to Massa Mercer, oh no. Cain't say nothin' to him 'bout her."

"He must like her cooking," Valentine said, noncommittally

"Hummph," Thor laughed. "More like he liken somethin' else. But then I hear tell he got his self someone else. A young white gal what be the daughter of a big planter in the next county. He be ridin' over there eber week seem like, tryin' to get her to marry him. Thataway, he get her money and in line for her land, 'cause she the onliest chile. You get what I'm sayin'?"

Valentine didn't comment. Marrying the daughter of a wealthy planter was one way of doing that. He recalled the striking, angry colored woman who answered the door and knew she must be the cook Thor was talking about. An unhappy female slave, especially one who couldn't cook, wouldn't be welcomed by a new mistress.

"You think Master Mercer will marry?"

"He be takin' her little presents and such. 'spect she'll say 'yeah'. Ain't that many good prospects 'round here."

Valentine continued to rub the cleaning mixture in Thor's head, massaging his scalp while the young slave hummed.

"He'd have to get rid of her, if he married."

Thor stopped humming. "Yeah, he'd sell her."

"You wouldn't know when?"

"Who me?"

Valentine changed the subject. "What's that you're humming?" he asked as his fingers dug deep in the wadded hair.

"That there a song we hear somebody else sing on a plantation and he say he hear it from someone what come from Tennessee. It be that *Oh, Susanna* song, but we got our own words."

"Oh, you mean the one that starts, 'Well, I come from Alabama with my banjo on my knee'…that one?"

The young slave nodded his head. "Yes sir, that the one, but we got different words," he smiled sheepishly. "This what we sing…but you gotta promise you ain't heard it from me." The young slave began in a soft low baritone and tapped his bare foot on the earth floor to keep the rhythm:

A black bird come into my life and landed on a tree
He whisper sweet things in my ear and tell me I should flee.
Oh, little black bird, why don't you set me free
'cause I'm leavin' Alabamy and the life of slavery.

I follow him into the night and listen for his cry
This black bird guide me to the light and on his wings I fly.
Oh, little black bird why don't you set me free
'cause I'm leavin' Alabamy and the life of slavery.

It rained all night the day I left could hardly see the trail,
But blackbird he done said go North, and on a boat I sail,
Oh little black bird why don't you set me free
'cause I'm leavin' Alabamy and the life of slavery.

The dogs was out; they hunt me down if I can't keep ahead
But black bird he done trick them dogs and let them think I'm dead.
Oh, little black bird why don't you set me free
'cause I'm leaving Alabamy and the life of slavery.

When I first step on 'ol freedom's shore, no more I was a slave
'cause black bird is the Raven and I sing his name in praise
Oh, little black bird you went and set me free
'cause I done left Alabamy and the life of slavery.

Thor grinned. "What you think?"

"I think you shouldn't be caught singin' that song, not around here."

"Yeah, I suppose you right. Don't do no good to let folks know what you really thinkin'."

"You thinking about runnin'?"

Thor looked at him and looked toward the door, then down at his bare feet. "Was thinkin' me and some others, but we ain't sure how to go. Ain't none of us been off this plantation, ever. He only hire out big dumb folks like Jubba who ain't got sense enough to run."

Valentine felt sores on the man's head as a result of insect infestations. "Look, I'm gonna have to shave your hair off and let these sores heal."

"So, that what be itchin' so?"

Valentine took his sturdiest pair of scissors and clipped off patches of hair. Then Valentine shaved his head, being careful to shave around the young boy's sores.

"How it feel to be free, sir?" Thor asked quietly. "You a freeman, ain't you?

Valentine didn't answer right away. He finished shaving him and rubbed his bald head clean. He stooped down to look him directly in the eye.

"Free is something that you earn and that you respect and no man can take that away."

Thor listened and nodded. "Well, sir. I guess I wanna be a free man, just like you. I just don't know how ta go 'bout doin' that."

Valentine looked at the door and lowered his voice even further. "One day when you decide that you want it bad enough, you start hiding food in a place nobody can find. You don't tell anyone and you don't let them see you. You need food and extra clothing. Maysville is northeast of here. When you get to Maysville, you can go see this boat captain. His name is Julius.

Julius Stout. Julius will take you across. You should be careful. Maysville and Ripley are both guarded by slave catchers. Anybody you talk to could inform on you..."

Both stared knowingly at each other. Then the boy stood up.

"Thank ya sir for the hair cut," he said, feeling his baldhead. The boy walked away when Valentine called him back.

"Part of being free is earning that freedom."

ca

CHAPTER FOURTEEN

Near Maysville, Kentucky

"**So**, you told him about Julius?" Solomon griped.

Valentine nodded as he hunched over the fire and rubbed his icy hands.

"Yes, I told him about Julius," Valentine snapped back.

"Without Julius knowing?" Solomon asked.

Valentine had been listening to Solomon whine for two hours and was tired, cold, hungry and most of all, fed up with Solomon constantly questioning him.

"Look, it was the chance I took. Julius knows we wouldn't put him in danger. This boy Thor sounded sincere. That's why I told him and now would you just shut up about it," he said, snatching several twigs and throwing them on the fire.

"I'm only asking because we may have to use Julius. If he's off ferrying some fugitive across to Ohio, what happens if we need him?" Solomon continued.

"What's the likelihood of that? For God sake, don't you have anything else to do besides pester me? I've shaved and cut so many diseased heads I'm not sure I don't have things crawling all over me," Valentine shivered.

Valentine and Solomon both sat around the roaring fire in a deserted cabin once used by a family who had long since left for better lodgings. Their horses shared a space with them because of the pelting icy rain. Between the cold, cramped quarters and the smell of horse manure, neither man was keen on being there.

One of the annoyances of traveling was not being able to secure lodging, particularly if you were colored. Valentine knew almost every deserted house, lean-to, barn, and stable in Mason and Bracken counties. He planned his trips so that he wouldn't be more than a day's ride from one of his shelters. When there was no shelter available, he slept outside.

It was also annoying to listen to Solomon complain incessantly about their living situation. Solomon, who could room anywhere he chose, chose to room with Valentine while they were on southern soil. That didn't mean Solomon had to like it, and he made sure that Valentine knew what a sacrifice he was making.

"Look at where we are. Sharing our beds with two horses and God knows what other creatures that want to come in from the cold. It's a wonder we don't get the flux the way we've been living for the past several days," Solomon complained. "And for what? Nobody's said a damn thing about a forced march. And believe me I've been in every saloon, tavern, inn, mercantile, warehouse, and plantation within thirty miles of here. Not one word," he spat out.

"When have you known Grinder to be wrong?"

"I'm not saying he's wrong. I'm saying if there was going to be such a march, someone would have said something by now. You haven't heard anything and neither have I. Maybe they just called it off. Too risky. I don't know," he shrugged.

"There's a march," Valentine said flatly. "We just haven't gotten the right information."

They sunk into a maudlin silence. The fire crackled and snapped, sending sparks dancing upward. Gloomy shadows quivered on the naked walls of the cabin. Valentine and Solomon listened to the fire and the stomping of the horse's hoofs against the floor. Both men were exhausted and more than a little frustrated.

"I heard a song today..." and Valentine sang what he remembered of the song the slave Thor taught him. Solomon laughed and asked him to sing it again until he'd memorized it.

"Wish I had composed that," Solomon said, poking the fire with a long stick. He watched the sparks fly upward. The mood had been broken and both were lighthearted again.

"You know, I did hear something curious, though. It seems the local authorities are holding a young slave woman. Her master refuses to take her back—something about her disobeying his orders. The sheriff told the man—I think he's a doctor—that she can't stay there indefinitely. Still, he refuses to take her back unless she apologizes, and so far she hasn't."

"Good for her."

"Well, it seems that her master told her not to see her brother. And she went and did it anyway," Solomon continued. "Cheeky thing to do, I'd say. So, anyway, she's rotting in jail and the sheriff has threatened to sell her if her master doesn't take her soon. Says that it's not his business to house slaves," Solomon poked at the fire, reflectively. "So, unless her master changes his mind or she apologizes, she's to be sold."

Solomon waited for Valentine to comment. When he didn't rise to the bait, Solomon continued. "Well I thought, you know, if her master doesn't want her and the jail can't keep her, then maybe..." he said wryly. "Maybe the Raven could intervene?"

Valentine caught the implication.

"That's a little dangerous, don't you think? The Grinder warned us not to pull anything."

Solomon dropped the stick and turned toward Valentine, "I want to do this myself." Solomon begged.

"We've always worked together. That's always been our plan. It's too dangerous alone," Valentine argued.

"Well, only if I get caught," Solomon said as the reflection of the flames danced across his face. "But I don't intend to get caught."

"No," Valentine said emphatically.

Solomon sat morosely then let out a sigh. He turned to Valentine. "By the way, do you have any of that stinky lotion with you? My hands are giving me problems."

Valentine rummaged through his bag and found the bottle of lotion containing Eucalyptus oil. Solomon sniffed it and screwed up his face. He mumbled. "If it's good enough for a slave catcher, I suppose it's good enough for me." He took the bottle and shook some of the oil in his hand, then sniffed again. "God, they will remember this smell," he said, wrinkling his nose.

"You say something? Valentine mumbled half-sleep.

"Just talking to myself. Say, do you remember the time when...." Solomon began a long story about a play he had been in. Valentine, barely listening, fell asleep snoring softly.

As Valentine slept, Solomon made a mental note of all the items he would need: blackened cork for sideburns, light colored hat, dye or a black wig for hair. He had to make arrangements with Captain Julius to take him and the slave across. Most important, he had to find some way of getting rid of Valentine.

ᘓ

Maysville, Kentucky—December

Leona heard the familiar voices of the deputies who tried to rape her and a third strange one. All boomed with laughter in the other room. She heard the scrape of boots shuffling on the floor and more laughter and talking as the voices came nearer. Then a face peered through the barred opening. The key clanged in the lock and she shrank in a corner of her cell silently praying.

"Okay, nigger gal, get on your feet," said the deputy named Harry. His voice was slurred and he swayed as he stood.

She was paralyzed with fear. The door opened wider and three men stood in the entrance with the light from the hall throwing shadows on the cell walls.

"I says get up and move," Jack yelled. "This here is an agent been assigned to take you. You been sold gal, to a new master some place in..." and then he turned to look at the man beside him.

The dark man was dressed in black and wore a light colored hat pulled down over his face so that his eyes barely showed. He stood there with his hands in his pockets, reeking of some odor.

"...Virginia."

Jack and Harry didn't wait for her to move; in two steps the two deputies grabbed her.

"You heard the man, come on."

She was jerked forward and held in such a tight grip that she winced with pain.

"Thank you boys. Appreciate the kindness," the stranger drawled.

"No problem, Mr. Slade. Thank you for the liquor and the coins. A might nice payment for havin' to feed her for the last several weeks. That Dr. Fowler, a tight-wad if ever there was one. Thinks he can just leave his slave for us to take care of." Harry belched.

"Always try to be accommodating, Harry," the agent said as he stepped forward to chain her wrists.

Jack pushed her toward the man called Slade who grabbed hold of her and led her out of the building as she struggled against him.

The sun was now setting. Leona shivered against the wind that was blowing cold rain in her face.

"You sure you don't need some help?" Harry shouted, then turned to Jack and snickered, "Or maybe she tryin' to get away from his stink."

"I think I can handle her," the man named Slade yelled back. "Come on gal, we got a long ride ahead of us." He shoved her toward a wagon loaded with bags and she slipped on the icy ground, catching herself before she fell forward. The agent lifted her onto the wagon seat, then went around the other side, stepped up, grabbed the reins, and urged the horses forward. He waved a jaunty salute at the two deputies and took off at a leisurely pace through the rain.

Leona glanced sideways at her new captor and was surprised to find him smiling and humming a tune. She glanced back at the jail that was now a dot in the distance. The man called Slade then whipped the horses; the wagon picked up speed.

"Get in the back and change clothes," he ordered. His voice had changed. It was no longer low and gruff, but soothing with a slight English accent. They were racing now out of town. The icy rain was lashing at her body. She didn't understand what he meant.

"Jump in the back. There's a set of men's clothes, hurry and change," he repeated.

"But I...the chains... I..."

His whole posture seemed to change. "For God sakes girl, you're not chained. I didn't lock the damn things. Jump in the back, we don't have much time. When those boys finally get around to actually *reading* those papers—provided they can read—and finding that feather, they'll be coming for us."

She didn't know if this was a trick, but she obeyed the stranger and crawled unsteadily to the back of the moving wagon.

"Stuff your old clothes in one of those bags and throw them over," he yelled back.

Overcoming her natural modesty, Leona peeled off the wet clothes. It was getting late and she struggled to get into the men's clothes, fumbling with the snaps and hooks in the waning light while the speeding wagon jostled her back and forth.

Leona didn't have time to think before the wagon veered left into a narrow cut through some trees. It bounced over the road, barely missing low hanging branches. She gripped the bags for support. It was all she could do to prevent from being flung over the side.

The road narrowed from there and the driver pulled up suddenly. They saw a signal light and in response. Her captor signaled back then jumped down from the wagon.

"Come on, love," he said, grabbing her arm and pulling her off the back of the wagon. "Run toward that light, over there," he said, pointing to the signal light in the distance.

"But...I don't...why?" she said, straining to see his face in the dark.

"I'm rescuing you."

She was confused. She didn't take in the words. "But I'm...I'm...my master...Dr. Fowler, did he send you?"

He laughed then. "No, love. The Raven did. Now move before we're all caught," he said, shoving her forward.

Leona ran, tripped over the pants as they slid down, grabbed them and pulled them up, and ran forward again toward the light as she tried to keep up with her captor. As she got closer, she saw a man on horseback holding the reins of a rider-less horse. He had a bandana over the lower portion of his face; his eyes shown through the slit between his hat and the bandana. The man got off his horse and handed the reins to the man called Slade.

"These are fresh horses."

"Can you ride?" her captor asked.

"I… I never… I…"

But he threw the reins at her before she finished. "Get on. Guide him with your knees. Hold the reins tight. We have some hard riding to do, love."

The man called Slade turned to the masked man and shouted last minute instructions over the stinging rain:

"Jubba, take the wagon, double back, and dump the sacks. I don't know how long it'll take them to figure out they've been had. He then turned to her. "Let's go." He jumped on his horse while the other man ran toward the wagon.

Somehow she managed to climb onto the horse. Once on, she held the reins in a death grip while pressing her knees into the horse's flank. The horse sprinted, almost yanking her out of the saddle. Leona was too scared to scream as the horse galloped at breakneck speed, following her captor's lead horse.

She didn't have time to question what was happening. She was too busy trying to stay on. They were riding fast, aided by the light from the lantern. She could feel the horse's muscles ripple beneath her with each long stride.

Her legs gripped the horse until they cramped. One hand clenched the reins, and the other, the man's flat brimmed hat on her head. She had no idea where she was going or why this man kidnapped her, but still she followed. They plunged through dense brush and over uneven terrain while rain pelted their faces.

The man in front of her slowed then pulled up short. Both she and her horse were panting wildly. Her captor held out his hand and touched her shoulder.

"This is the most dangerous," he whispered. "Down there. There's a flatboat waiting for us. But there are patrollers. I'll signal with my light. When I get a signal back, it means we're free to move toward the boat. Watch your step, the slope is slippery."

Below, she saw a small fire that glowed out of the seemly endless darkness. She heard water lapping the shore. *This must be the Ohio.*

The man held the lantern high, waving it back and forth three times. She looked sideways at him, but could only see him dimly as the light fell off beyond his face. He was a white man; that much was certain. *But what does he want with me?*

They waited for the return signal. Her horse's flanks trembled with anticipation. She shivered from the cold rain. From below, she heard strains of music and someone singing. She saw no movement as they waited for the signal. Minutes passed while the music and singing continued. Then it stopped. A few minutes later a lantern was lighted.

"There, now it's safe to go."

Every impulse told her to scream and run away, but it was too late. Their horses descended the slope toward the waiting boat. Once they got near, a dark-skinned boy and an old white man grabbed the horses and helped her climb down. The boy took her hand and pulled her onto the flatboat. Then he shoved her into a cabin and locked her inside.

In the locked room she heard bits of the men's conversation over the lapping waves and pelting rain

"What... you... long?" she heard her captor ask. She heard low rumbled laughter, but couldn't make out every word.

On top, Solomon rubbed the make up from his face. Captain Julius handed him a jug of whiskey and he took it gratefully. "God, it's damn cold, what took you so long? I thought my ass was going to freeze on that horse."

Captain Julius took the jug back and took a gulp, wiping his mouth.

"We was entertaining a patroller, the boy and me. Serenading him with song. We was so bad, the patroller just left without a word. I guess ya say he was not thrilled with our music," he laughed again. "He said the sound comin' from slaughtered sheep was better than what we was singin'."

Leona pressed her ear to the cabin door and heard her captor say. "I'll get off on the other side you take her to..." but the boat started to move and his words were drowned out by the lapping water.

Taking me to where?

There was nothing graceful about the boat's movement through the water. She was knocked from one side to the other in the tiny cabin.

The boat rocked and favored one side, smashing her against a wall. She slumped down on the floor and stayed there as the boat steadied. Then she lay on the floor for some time feeling the boat flow with the current. She heard feet shuffling on deck. *someone is getting off. Will I be getting off?* She strained to catch snatches of their conversation.

"...make it across..."

"... find something..."

"...she'll get off...Cincinnati.."

"...coffin shop..."

"I'll see you on the return..."

Solomon gave last minute instructions to Captain Julius. The old man gulped from his bottle and gasped as the liquor burned going down. "What about...you know?" He jerked his head toward the cabin.

"Tom knows where to take her once she gets off in Cincinnati. He knows to take her to Levi Coffin's shop. Just don't let her out until you've rounded the bend. There aren't as many patrollers there." He gave a jaunty salute. "See you on your return Julius. Tom, thanks."

She sensed the boat hugging the shoreline. It was pitch dark in the cabin and smelled of men's sweat and stale whiskey. The rocking of the boat was making her sick. There was more shuffling while the boat listed to one side as someone disembarked. Minutes passed as the boat moved choppily through the water. She hugged the floor.

Someone knocked on the door. "You okay in there miss?" The boy, of no more than ten, held a light in front of him. "You can come out now," he said, peeking in.

But she couldn't move. The boy held out his hand. "It's okay. It's safe now."

She took the young boy's hand and he pulled her to her feet then guided her on deck while she swayed unsteadily. The rain whipped her face and she clung to the outside walls of the cabin.

"Oh, you get used to it after a time," the boy said, grinning.

The captain glanced at her and smiled. "Hey, girly. You made it. Just another day and you'll be home free."

The words came tumbling from her; cart wheeling over each other. "Whereareyou taking me? Whatareyou...doing? Whyareyoukidnapping..me?"

"Shhhhhh, don't ya know they's slave catchers around?" He lowered his voice. "Don't worry. We huggin' the Ohio shore now. You already almost there. Once we get to Cincinnati, my boy here'll take you to a place where you can wait for them to spirit ya out of town." He glanced down at Tom who smiled, proudly.

"I knows where to take you ma'am. You don't have to worry about nothin'," Tom said, reassuringly.

She looked from the boy to the captain who was slugging whiskey from an old jug and gasping with each swallow.

"I don't wanna go. I cain't leave my brother," she yelled against the wind.

"It too late now, girly. You done made your bed. Once they find out you escaped, there's gonna be all hell breakin' loose."

She shook her head. "You cain't sell me. You have to take me back."

"Hush up, 'fore someone hears you. If you don't shut up we'll put you back in the cabin. We ain't sellin' you. We rescuin' you. That's the honest to God's truth. That is. Don't you know you been rescued by the Raven, girly? You famous now…and you got a price on your head for sure."

Leona remembered how Dr. Fowler talked about the hateful abolitionists who tricked slaves into running away. She screamed. "No, you won't eat me!" Without thinking, without even understanding what she was doing, she ran to the side and jumped in the icy water. The water swallowed her and she gasped for air as she sank. Her feet hit the bottom and she pushed her way back up. When she broke surface, she swallowed water, panicked, and flailed her arms in a desperate attempt to stay afloat.

Above her she could hear the boy and the old man yelling at her to come back, but she propelled herself forward, half-swimming, half-walking, flailing her arms wildly to keep from drowning. The pants she wore ballooned out and kept her buoyant as she struggled toward shore.

As she crawled up toward the rocky hill, she saw the boat had moved farther down river and the light from their lantern was disappearing into the blackness. Only then did she realize what had happened. She had just escaped being captured by the Raven and skinned alive by his abolitionist friends.

 భ

CHAPTER FIFTEEN

Higgensport, Ohio

Leona's hands slipped on an iced over rock and she belly slid down the embankment. What saved her from spilling back in the water were her pants that snagged on a jagged edge. She hung suspended, clawing frantically at the slippery rocks while edging the toe of her shoe in a crevice. When she secured her footing, she heaved herself up again.

She lunged for another outcrop and was able to make her way up, one foothold at a time until she felt flat ground. With all her strength, she pushed one more time until she flopped on the surface, breathing laboriously. She rolled over on her back. Leona saw the sky with its millions of stars twinkling back at her.

"Thank you," she whispered, and closed her eyes.

She was so weary that she wanted to fall asleep, except she knew she would freeze to death if she didn't find shelter.

Her men's wool clothes clung stiffly against her body like a frigid shroud. The water dripped down her face and froze in its tracks. She scraped the ice forming off her cheeks and shivered so violently that she thought she was having a seizure.

I got to get up... she told herself *... I got to move.* Leona rose stiffly and oriented herself to the lights shining in the distance. The lights were probably bonfires or houses. *Can I walk the distance and find shelter?*

Every step she took made her more aware that she might not make it. Freezing rain left every thing covered in a thin layer of ice that crunched underneath her feet. The sound reassured her since now her feet were numb. Her arms hugged her body to keep the heat from escaping. The faster she walked, the more intense the cold, but if she stopped, she knew she would die.

To keep her mind off her imminent death, she hummed a nonsensical tune through chattering teeth. If she stopped humming, her fears would engulf her. Her humming and the cracking ice were the only sounds that serenaded her on this winter night.

Leona tore through deep underbrush until she stumbled onto a dirt path that followed the bend of the river. Minute by minute, one foot in front of the other, Leona felt her way along the path until it lead to a dead-end and a clearing. She peered through the darkness at what she believed was a solid form. It was a shack. And then she saw the thin curl of smoke rising from a chimney. Leona gathered her last reserves of energy and hurried toward the house, and—by now delirious—hammered on its walls.

"Please, please let me in," she barely controlled her shaking voice as she moved around the shack, pounding on its outer walls, looking for the door. "Please, I'll die out here if you don't let me in," she cried desperately. She stopped to listen to any sound from inside. When she heard none, she beat harder, and clawed at the wooden slats with her ragged nails. She heard a door open to her right and moved toward the noise. A weak light shown through a crack.

ɔ৪

Ripley, Ohio—December— several days later

Solomon was slumped in the chair, his feet up on the desk, as he waited while Valentine vented about Solomon's foolhardy rescue attempt. He tried desperately to allow his mind to float, visualizing scenes of tranquility and peace. It was a trick he'd learned as an actor before going on stage. Arabella, his mother, had taught him this: "Allow yourself to float free, to sail in the clouds, detach yourself from your earthly cares and troubles, float, breathe deeply, surrender to the feeling of serenity. Close your eyes, my dear, and float," she had said. Solomon slumped farther down in the chair, closed his eyes and breathed.

"Are you listening to me?" Valentine shouted.

Solomon's eyes popped open. "To every word. Every word you've said." Surrendering was impossible. Solomon stared at nothing in front of him, his muscles were tense, and his head ached.

"So, please tell me how this could have happened?" Valentine had stopped his pacing and stood in the window of Solomon's room looking out on the near deserted street. He still had his barber's apron on and smelled of a woodsy fragrance. Valentine's hands were clasped behind him, his back rigid.

Valentine had arrived early that morning, having picked up supplies in a nearby town. He was badly in need of sleep, but no sooner had he laid down when the first customer came calling. He spent the rest of the day working. It was only after closing did he come up to Solomon's room to learn about the botched slave rescue. Solomon sighed and again repeated what he had heard.

"Julius and Tom said the girl jumped somewhere around Higgensport, maybe down farther, they couldn't tell. She was having a fit, or so they said. She screamed at them, saying something about she wasn't going to be eaten, and then she

140

jumped. They couldn't get to her. It was too dangerous between the current and slave catchers and all. They didn't know if she made it to shore or not. They had no way of knowing. Would you care for some wine?" Solomon asked, pulling a half-empty bottle from his desk drawer.

"No I would not," Valentine replied tersely.

Solomon pulled the cork out with his teeth and spit it in his hand. "Well, I am if I'm going to sit here while you rant at me." He found a dirty glass, wiped it off on his shirt, then decided to forego the crystal and drink straight from the bottle. He took a long swig and wiped his dripping mouth. *God, I hate it when he gets in these moods.*

"So, let me get this straight. You spent your time and energy, not to mention the money you paid old Cap and the boy, to rescue a slave who didn't want to be rescued. She thought you were going to eat her. So, she committed suicide by jumping?"

"We don't know if she committed suicide," Solomon added, taking another swig.

"What would you call jumping into a river in the dark in near-freezing water?" Valentine shot back over his shoulder

Solomon shrugged. "It's been three or four days. If she were dead, her body would float by now. Someone would have seen something."

Valentine walked toward Solomon and hovered over him. "Unless she's frozen at the bottom of the river. But damn it, that's not the point. The point is, we've just wasted our time, and I might add jeopardized our lives, for nothing."

Solomon had had enough, he turned on Valentine. "Excuse me, let me correct you. *I* wasted my time, jeopardized *my* life, and *my* money, not you. I'm not the one you should be angry at. These things happen. Some slaves don't understand freedom.

"I remember Grinder telling us the story about how this conductor had rescued two young girls who took off with their owner's dresses and jewels. They almost drowned from wearing so many layers of their owner's clothing. They thought freedom was a license to steal. Grinder said the conductor finally told them if they didn't remove the clothing, he'd leave them behind. He wasn't getting caught and imprisoned over the likes of them. Not everyone is worthy of their freedom, Valentine."

"Who are you to tell me what a slave deserves?" Valentine shot back. "What right have you to sit here with your fine clothes, your wine, and your arrogance and give me a lecture on slavery?"

"I..."

"You think this is all a game orchestrated for your amusement? We're here to do a job. One I might add, that could cost us our lives."

Solomon sprang from his chair and confronted Valentine; both men stood toe to toe. "Don't you dare lecture me about the poor slave. Don't tell me the pain and agony a slave goes through. Don't stand here and give me some sanctimonious blather about the noble cause of freedom. Remember who helped you gain your freedom? *My mother*. Had it not been for her, you'd be a fumbling ignorant, toiling in some tobacco field. It was *my mother* who risked her life for you." Angry tears streamed down his face.

"Your mother wanted a companion for her spoiled brat of a son; and, she got one cheap." Valentine shot back.

Solomon had never been much of a fighter. In fact, Valentine usually came to the rescue whenever Solomon got into trouble at some tavern or brothel. But this time Solomon blindly swung on Valentine and knocked him backwards into the armoire where he fell, sprawled on the floor.

"My money is paying for this building. My money is being spent on the expeditions, and my money has financed your shop.

"You want to rescue these poor souls; you can do so without me. This Raven is fleeing the nest. I have better things to do with my life than listen to your tirades." Solomon turned his back on Valentine, and walked over to the desk, snatched a bottle of wine, and his jacket.

"I'll find another place to live in the morning and send for my things shortly thereafter. I've had enough of you and your superior moral standards. I've had enough of living like a backwoods oaf. I've had enough of the Raven," he pronounced, and walked out of the apartment.

The silence was deafening.

Valentine got up and made his way down to his apartment where he sat in his Spartan room to mull over their argument. *He will come to his senses. He always does.*

⋈

Outside of Maysville, Kentucky

Dr. Nathaniel Fowler seemed to be a man descending into madness. His pupils looked like they were swimming in the dark circles that shadowed his eyes. He was disheveled, his hair unkempt. He was sporting a splotchy beard.

"I want her back," Fowler said, as he paced his office floor. He turned abruptly to face Slade. "I want her unharmed and I want her here," he punched the air with his finger, aiming it at Slade. Fowler paced again, like a caged animal. Each time he passed, Slade caught the stench from his body, but he gave no indication that either the smell or anything else about the doctor offended him. If he played his cards right, Dr. Nathaniel Fowler would be his employer soon. *It's all about gaining his trust,* Slade mused, rubbing his aching right hand.

There had been no time for introductions. Fowler had perfunctorily ushered him in. Now Slade stood patiently in front of Fowler's desk while the doctor continued his tirade as he fumbled with instruments on a side table.

"Those stupid bastards let her escape, and I made sure that higher authorities knew about their laxness. Most of these deputies and patrollers are just ignorant boys who only like the hunt, but have no strategy. I need someone who knows his business," he said whirling around, a scalpel in his hand. He approached Slade, blade gleaming.

"You say you've done this before?"

"Yes sir. " Slade watched furtively as Fowler wielded the knife inches from his mid-section. *The man is out of his mind.*

He was a man obsessed or possessed; Slade didn't know which word was better. Fowler's hands shook as he wielded the scalpel, punching the air with it to make a point. Slade knew better than to give any indication that he sensed something amiss. He scanned the room so as not to stare. His eyes lighted on an open cabinet. The bottles inside were scattered, several with their stoppers off and on lying on its side and spilling its liquid contents on the shelves below. It formed a pool that trickled on the floor.

Fowler sighed, brushed his long stringy hair from his eyes and laid the scalpel on the desk, patting it reassuringly. He turned his attention back to Slade.

"You have references? Anyone who can vouch for your success as an agent?"

Slade didn't want Fowler checking on his last assignment. He hesitated, cleared his throat, and said in a level voice. "The men who I've dealt with would hardly admit to a slave having escaped from under their nose."

This statement took Fowler by surprise. "I see. And so you think that your former employers, these men, somehow were careless?"

Slade saw Fowler's right eye give an involuntary nervous tick. He tensed and rushed to correct himself. "No sir. What I mean to say is that a slave will escape if he's given half a chance. They don't know what's best for them. Slaves are like wild horses; a wild horse doesn't know what's best for him, either. The animal doesn't know that he can be fed, sheltered, and taken care of if he will just submit and do his owner's bidding," he said in a soothing voice, as if to calm this wild horse before him.

"The wild horse will always try to escape. It's in his nature. Only when he is tamed and brought to his senses does he know what's best for him. That is my experience with runaways. I catch them, and teach them what's best."

"And how do you go about doing this?" Fowler asked, his face inches from Slade.

Fowler's tick fascinated Slade. He had to consciously pull his eyes away from the man and look beyond him in order not to stare. In doing so he noticed several bloody rags on the tables.

"Well sir after I find the slave...uh...there is a period of time when I must bring him in. In my own way, I...uh...persuade the slave to give up his foolish notion of ever escaping. I try to...uh, to show him the futility of his ways," he said.

"Ah, yes, that's good. That's very good." Fowler walked around his desk and plopped down. He gestured to Slade to have a seat. "So, how do you propose to return my property to me?"

Slade cleared his throat. "Well sir, I read in your advertisement that she had help escaping. You mention," and Slade pulled out the advertisement from his topcoat pocket,

"...that the Raven was involved?" He pushed the paper toward Fowler who glanced at it and nodded.

"They found a poem among the false documents and a black feather that was dropped outside of the jail. Both were marks of the Raven. The stupid bastards didn't bother to read through the papers. My guess is they couldn't read anyway. They just took this man at face value as an agent. They described him as a foul smelling man who called himself Slade."

Slade flinched inwardly. *The bastard is ruining my name.*

"Ah, did they say what this man looked like?" Slade asked, trying to control his anger.

"Something about him wearing a hat, and dark clothes," Fowler looked at Slade. "Nothing in detail. They were both drunk at the time." Fowler's hands nervously reached for the scalpel and fingered it. "They did not realize their mistake until a day later when I came to see her in the jail to ask again that she apologize for her betrayal. You see it was a betrayal..."

Slade watched him attentively as he rambled on, then out of the corner of his eye he saw a movement near the door.

"... I had done nothing to her. Nothing. I gave her everything. I treated her well. All I asked was that she not visit her brother. That's all I asked and the nigger bitch went behind my back and did it anyway. Of course, it was betrayal of the worst kind..."

Slade heard a board creak. He thought he saw a figure retreat into the darkened hallway, but pulled his concentration back to Fowler.

"...and so I told her that she could rot until such time as she was ready to apologize for treating me so shabbily..." His hand closed tightly over the scalpel until blood seeped from his fist. Fowler didn't seem to notice he'd wounded himself.

"So you see, sir, all she had to do was recant and submit, but instead she escapes." Fowler looked at his hand and saw the blood. "I went to her again, to give her a second chance," he said, as he loosened his grip on the scalpel, inhaled deeply then took a handkerchief from his pocket and wrapped it around the injury. He continued to talk as if nothing had happened. "When I found out about the escape, I went to the brother's owner, and I warned him to keep an eye on that nigger."

"And who would that be?"

"George, that's his name."

"No, sir. I meant the master. What is the master's name?"

"His name is Mercer; he has a plantation several miles from here. She may try to see him, I told Mercer. She could be hiding in the woods to wait until an opportunity presents itself."

"And what did he say?"

"He said that the boy, George, was being watched. Apparently he's rebellious. I wanted to question the boy, beat it out of him, if necessary, but Mercer wouldn't allow it. Said the boy was his property and he would take care of the situation."

"Your instincts were good. Having the boy under your control might guarantee that she would return," Slade lauded him.

"Yes, yes, that's right. That's what she would do, the conniving bitch," Fowler shouted as he unconsciously picked at the handkerchief around his hand.

"In my estimation," Slade said, "She would hide for as long as it took and then come for her brother."

"You know, I think you're right. You are very astute, sir. Very astute."

"If I were to become your agent, I would take advantage of her fondness for her brother; use him as bait. Lure her to him and then," he held his open hand out and closed it to illustrate his point, "...trap her as one would trap a rabbit."

"You know the mind of these people. They are tricksters, connivers, and schemers. They would do us all in, if they had the opportunity. They would..." Fowler rambled.

"The brother has to be kidnapped and held in a place where the trap can be set," Slade persisted.

"I understand perfectly," Fowler nodded. "And when we get the brother, we will get her. And we teach both of them a lesson."

"Yes sir. That is the plan." Slade watched as Fowler grew more excited. The man's eye throbbed uncontrollably.

"We can kidnap him and hold him here," Fowler looked around wildly. "I have a cellar, you know. We can hold him down in my cellar."

"We sir?"

"Of course, I want to be involved. I want to see her expression when she sees that I have power over her. I want to smell her fear," he sniffed the air.

This was not what Slade wanted at all.

"Yes, sir. But as I said, you must retain me as your agent. I will need money for expenses."

"Of course." Fowler opened his desk drawer and withdrew a pouch. He counted out the money with trembling hands. "Will this do?" Fowler thrust the money toward Slade. It was more than enough. Slade smiled inwardly and reached out to take the money with his right hand. A pain shot up his arm and he winced.

"You're injured?"

Slade painfully took the money. "In the cold it becomes stiff and aches.

"Oh, you must let me look at it."

"I'm fine, sir. Slade smiled. "It only bothers me occasionally. Nothing serious. I have some oil I rub on it."

Fowler sniffed the air. "Is that what I smell? God awful," he said, fanning the air. "You must let me treat you," Fowler said.

"Thank you sir. I appreciate it. But it's nothing." *You won't get near me, you ignorant butcher.* "Now tell me sir, is there something that she wore that we can use in order to bait the brother? Something that he would recognize as hers so that we can lure him away?"

Fowler thought for a moment. He scowled. "There might be something in her room. I'll see."

"Good sir, now if you'll excuse me I've had a long journey and would like to rest before tomorrow."

"Tomorrow? Why not right now?"

"Tomorrow we kidnap the brother and bring him back here and then I'll begin the hunt."

"Yes, you're right." Fowler stood and held out his hand. "Out of all the men I've talked with on this, you seem to be the one who knows what he's doing. The others were ruffians and rough neck keel haulers who couldn't find their asses," Fowler said.

Slade shook Fowler's soiled, bandaged hand and withdrew quickly. Then he turned to leave, but before he could open the door, Fowler called to him.

"Sir, one more thing. It's so silly of me. In all the excitement, I forgot to ask your name."

Slade never hesitated. "Jackson, sir. Jonathan Jackson, sir."

"Well, Mr. Jackson, we are partners in this."

"Yes sir. That we are," Slade said quickly closing the office door behind him.

Jonathan Jackson Slade rode away knowing he'd made a pact with the devil.

CHAPTER SIXTEEN

Higginsport, Ohio—just on the outskirts—same day

Leona took a deep breath and stepped onto the main road. Head down, she started to walk without knowing where she had been or exactly where she was going.

When she found the house in the clearing the night she escaped, she passed out. She awakened wrapped in layers of blankets, hearing the sounds of children shrieking and laughing. She was sweating and turned her head to see why. A woman had built up the fire and was sitting on a stool, pouring droplets of water over hot rocks.

Steam sizzled from the rocks and filled the small shack with warm mist. Leona breathed in the warm hazy air. She stared at the woman who dripped sweat. Her hair was braided down her back. Leona realized that she had been taken in by an Indian woman. The Indian ladled more water on the rocks and turned toward Leona. "You live," she said flatly.

It took several days for Leona to recover from the cold, during which time the woman said almost nothing to her except to order her to drink more of the foul smelling tea. When she had gotten better, the Indian woman thrust her out the door and pointed. "Runaway cause trouble. You leave and go to your people."

Now here she was on a road, lost. The sun's blinding light shimmered on the ice creating miniature rainbows that glinted off tree and bush. A thin layer of snow sprinkled the ground. The countryside looked like a crystal dreamscape. Leona didn't think she would be able to survive the cold even though the clothes she had been given kept her warm.

She walked the main road always on the watch for anyone who could identify her as a fugitive. When she did see someone, she hid in the brush until they passed. She did this throughout the afternoon, running and hiding. Toward dusk, she came to a fork in the road; one branch was heavily traveled. She saw several people walking ahead of her. She decided to take the other least traveled, but she hadn't gotten more than a few feet when she heard a shout behind her.

"Hey, you gal. Over here."

There was no place to run. She was exposed. She stood still, afraid to turn.

"Hey you..."

Her heart slammed in her chest. She couldn't catch her breath. She turned around, head down. She saw a white man standing up on his wagon, waving his arms. "Come here. Come over here," he yelled excitedly.

She had to obey him. Her legs wobbled underneath her as she approached. When she got to the wagon, she did not make eye contact. Arms wrapped protectively around her body, she stood in front of the man obediently waiting for the pronouncement that would send her back to jail: runaway.

"You from the Negro settlement?" he asked, eagerly.

She dared to look up and saw a well-dressed, middle-aged man whose cheeks were ruddy and whose spectacles were as thick as glass jars. She averted her eyes.

"Gal, did you hear me? Are you from Africa Hill?"

"Ahhh....yes....yes mas...sir." Leona replied cautiously.

"Well, I thought so." The man gingerly stepped down from the wagon and approached her. "I've got a proposition for you. I...well, no actually my wife needs...you'll have to stay with us. No running off back to your people. I don't care if you have a husband or children, you have to stay in our house. Sleep with the other servant we have. And every few weeks we'll allow you to go back to your family..."

Leona had no idea what he was talking about. She dared to glance up again at the man who was waving his arms excitedly. "...needs extra help. You know, kitchen things. Helping the other gal we have. Cook, clean, that sort of thing and I was wondering..."

"Yes sir?"

"Where are your papers?"

"Papers, sir?"

"Yes, gal papers. Do you have your papers on you?"

Leona shook her head.

"Damn, Well, I shouldn't do this," he said, leaning toward her confidentially, blinking behind his spectacles. "You know the law, I'm to look at your papers and then make arrangements ...that sort of thing, but I just don't have time and my wife is on me to get more help before we start with the holiday festivities. So, if you want to work...you'll have a warm bed, all you can eat...I just can't pay you much. But I'm sure it's more than you normally get.

"Now, don't say anything to my wife. She's very proper about these things. We'll just say that you were working in someone else's household, I don't know, we'll think of something on the drive back. Well, hop in. You can sit in the back with the supplies," he said, shoving her toward the back of the wagon.

Still confused, but not resisting, Leona crawled up over the supplies.

"Now, don't go taking advantage of me. The last cook gal we had took off. I hope you're more grateful." He jogged back to the front of the wagon and hauled his bulk onto the seat. He turned around.

"Your name?"

Leona opened her mouth and closed it. *My name?* "Mary, sir."

"Mary, Mary what?"

"Mary...George, sir."

"Mary George. You're Mary George from Africa Hill. Mine's Mr. Joseph Greene. I'm a tailor. I can't believe my luck," he said, flicking the reins.

Me too.

The wagon slowly made its way to Ripley.

⋄

Too tired to unload the supplies for his shop, Joseph Greene went straight home and unhitched the horses. He took Leona to the back into the kitchen.

"Your room is upstairs with the other servant," he said, whispering and pointing to the backstairs that led to the second floor of the house. "Now you run along. Nothing to do now anyway, too late. But in the morning I expect that you'll be up bright and early.

"I'll introduce you to my wife at breakfast. Make sure you're clean. There are some clothes the other girl left behind. They should fit you. Do everything that Essie tells you, and you'll do just fine," he said, patting her on the head, then leaving. Half way out the room he turned back. "Oh, and one more thing. If my wife asks for your papers...you do have papers, don't you?"

Leona nodded.

"Good, well if my wife asks you for them, just tell her that I've seen them and they're official. When you have a chance to go home, bring them back with you."

"Yes, sir."

And then he left.

Leona stood in the huge orderly kitchen and covered her mouth to stifle her tears.

ଔ

Kentucky—Mercer Plantation

While Fowler hid among the trees, Slade rode alone toward the cluster of slaves who mended a fence. He dismounted and walked toward a young slave who looked to be the same age as the boy, George.

The young slave's skinny frame was knotted with muscle. His head was drenched in sweat, even though it was a cold day. His nimble fingers hammered the nails into the wooden fence posts as he sang along with the other slaves.

The young slave looked up and saw the lone white man approaching. He was immediately on alert. The man gave off a scent that smelled like the oil Mister Valentine rubbed on him. But on this stranger, it smelled overpowering; to him, it smelled like trouble.

Thor silently prayed for protection while his fingers continued working. His eyes scanned the field, looking for escape. He sniffed the air once more; the smell of the man was stronger. Sweat ran down Thor's face and he wiped his stinging eyes and scratched his new growth of hair.

The white man stopped a few feet away and looked over the work team. His eyes lighted on Thor. "You, boy. I want you," Slade pointed. "What's your name?"

The boy looked to his fellow workers for help. They avoided his gaze; a sign that they wanted no part in this matter. "Thor."

"What did you say?"

"Thor, Massa."

"Come here."

The boy, stopped what he was doing, affected a sullen attitude, and took several tentative steps forward, head down submissively, but all the time he was on the alert.

"Yes, sir?" he mumbled.

"I'm looking for someone, a boy named George, around your age. I was told he worked on this plantation," Slade said.

"What he look like?"

"I don't know what he looks like."

The boy shrugged and gave a wide grin. "Cain't help you, Massa. Plenty boys 'round my age work here."

"This boy has a sister. She lives several miles away. It's about his sister."

Thor looked at the other slaves who took furtive glances his way. Whatever this man wanted of George, it was not good. "What about the sister, Massa?"

"Never you mind. That's for him to know. Is there a George here who has a sister or not?" Slade said, impatiently.

Thor played dumb; he scratched his stubbly head, shuffled his feet in the grass, and grinned again. "Well Massa, I cain't rightly say. There could be.

Slade was losing patience. He took several steps closer to Thor and hovered over him like a carrion bird. Thor backed off. It was the meanness behind the eyes that startled him.

"You tell him a man named Slade wants to talk with him about his sister. I'll be waiting tonight by the turn, a mile down from here. You tell this George that if he doesn't come, his sister will be in trouble," Slade took a small cameo broach from his pocket.

"And just so he knows I mean business, give him this." He grabbed Thor's hand and dropped the broach into it.

"Tell him he's got to come or else he won't see his sister again." Then Slade shoved Thor back and walked away.

Thor looked at the broach and dropped it in his pocket. He waited until the man disappeared before running to the barn where he knew George was working.

CB

Mercer plantation—night

"It's somethin' not right," Thor insisted. "You gotta tell Massa Mercer 'bout the man. He was jogging behind George, trying to keep up with him.

"What I'm suppose to say? Massa done told me my sister's gone. He say he keepin' an eye on me if she come lookin' to help me run away. She ain't never wanna run away. She too scared. Now you tell me this man say he know somethin' 'bout my sister. That mean she in trouble and I'm gonna find out what."

Thor tugged at him, trying to get him to stop and listen. "If that man got your sister, then he gonna get you too. I'm tellin' you right now, he up to no good. S'pose he only sayin' that 'cause he wanna kill you or somethin'? S'pose she already dead?"

George's heart skipped. He stopped in his tracks and turned to face Thor. Their faces were inches from each other, lighted by the torches that flanked the slave quarters. Thor saw the look of pain in George's face and tried to amend his words. "Look, I ain't sayin' that she dead, but ...but I'm sayin' that somethin' coulda happen to her and maybe you, if'n you meet that man," Thor pleaded.

"But if I don't, I won't know. I ain't seen her and the next thing I know Mercer got me workin' close to the house, sayin' she done gone. He got to know somethin'. This broach belong to my Aunt Sara. She gib it to Leona. So he gotta know somethin'."

"Okay, then but you ain't goin' by yo'self. I be hidin' and watchin'."

George agreed to let Thor tag along.

Before they came to the spot where George was supposed to meet Slade, Thor hid in the underbrush. George stood in the path, whistled and waited for the rendezvous. Time passed and they still waited while George paced, trying to keep warm and Thor hid, shivering. Then George spotted a light up ahead.

"Stay down, someone's comin'," George warned.

George watched as the light grew closer. And then he saw that there were two horsemen. He stood his ground.

"You George?" The man with the light said.

"Yes sir. You come to tell me where my sister gone?"

"Boy, you let me do the talkin'."

The second man spoke up. "We're here to take you to see her."

The voice of the second man sounded familiar, but George couldn't place it. "You lie. My sister ain't run away. She too scared to," George said defiantly.

"Don't sass me, boy," the second man yelled back.

George squinted against the light trying to recognize the men.

"I'll take care of this," said the first. He got down off his horse and approached George, the lantern in his hand.

This the man Thor talked about. George saw what Thor meant when he described the man as stinking evil.

"Can you read, boy?" he demanded

"No sir. I cain't."

Slade thrust a paper in front of George's face. "See this? This here is a advertisement. It says one mulatto girl, comely, long hair in braids, run away from the Mason county jail in Kentucky. Escape aided by the Raven. Owner, Dr. Nathaniel Fowler. Reward if apprehended and brought back safely and unharmed. That your sister?" Slade pointed at the advertisement.

George unconsciously scratched his beard while studying the print on the page, even though he couldn't read. "Yes sir, yes sir, it must be my sister." George was astounded. His sister would never have the courage to run, even though she had always had the opportunity. He looked up at Slade. "You know where she is?" he asked doubtfully.

Slade smiled. "Of course I do. You hear tell 'bout the Raven?"

"Everybody 'round here know 'bout him. Ain't nobody know who he is or what name he go by," George said, cautiously.

"Well, you lookin' at him. I took your sister to safety and now I come back for you. I'm the Raven."

Thor overheard all of this and knew in his heart that something was wrong. Thor stealthily moved among the trees to be in a better position to see.

"Where is she?" George insisted.

"I can take you to her. We'll have to move quickly though. Any minute she could be found out."

Thor shook his head. This was wrong, he thought to himself. He silently pleaded with George not to go.

"How I know you ain't just sayin' this?"

"You saw the broach didn't you, boy?" said the second man, who had dismounted and was standing along side the first.

George had been so engrossed in the runaway advertisement that he'd forgotten about the second man.

The second man stood just beyond the lantern's rim of light, but George was sure that he'd heard the voice before. He stepped boldly forward and recognized him as Dr. Fowler.

George turned to run, but Slade caught him in mid-stride, used the lantern as a weapon and hit George in the head. The blow extinguished the light. Fowler grabbed George and covered his nose with a cloth drenched in chloroform. George struggled futilely to escape. Overcome by the anesthetic, he slumped to the ground helplessly.

Thor heard the scuffle, but couldn't see anything.

"Tie him up and we'll throw him over your horse," Slade said.

"Are you ordering me?" Fowler said, indignantly.

Thor heard the first man growl. "I can leave you to do this yourself," he threatened.

"No," Fowler retracted. "No, just help me lift him."

Thor heard them struggle to get George on the horse then heard the second man laugh. He didn't know what to do. There were two of them; two white men. He knew he'd never be able to fight them so he continued to hide, listening for any clue as to who the men were and where they were taking George. He heard them mount their horses. His first impulse was to run and tell Master Mercer, but then the last time he tried to tell the master something, he got in trouble. After all, he couldn't tell him who the men were, only that they had come asking about George. He thought that maybe it would be better to let Master discover for himself that George was gone.

What I do? Thor anguished over the question and then realized that the disappearance of George would get the entire plantation in an uproar. It would give him a chance to run away in all the confusion. *Nothing.*

Thor whistled to himself as he slowly walked back to the plantation while planning his escape.

ೞ

It was cold and damp down in the cellar, but George was covered with sweat. His scraggly beard was damp from saliva. The smell of excrement and urine permeated the dank room. The cellar had no windows so George couldn't tell whether it was day or night. He had been alternately beaten unconscious, then revived, only to have more pain inflicted on him.

George's eyes—now merely slits after the bruising he had received—followed Fowler's movement as he circled him while holding high a light in order to see the torment he'd inflicted, That included the half-dozen leeches he had placed on George, watching them gorge on his blood. "How interesting," Fowler thought. When the last blood-bloated leech fell to the floor, Fowler squashed it with his boot.

"And that is what I will do to your sister as soon as she returns. But for now, I have patients to attend. I must clean myself up and look presentable. My wife will be awake soon," he said, as he glanced calmly at his pocket watch.

Fowler inhaled into a handkerchief, shook his head and smiled, stupidly. He collected his instruments, unsteadily climbing the stone steps and pushing open the wooden door. A sudden flood of sunlight streamed into the darkness, burning George's eyes. Fowler turned to take one last look at his captive.

"There will be plenty of time for you to imagine the other experiments I have in store for you. Pray that Mr. Jackson finds her soon or there will be nothing left of you for your sister to embrace," he said, Then he blew out the lantern and stepped into the winter sunshine.

George was again swallowed up by darkness. He heard Fowler close the cellar door. He struggled against the chains that bound his hands and feet, but his efforts were useless.

CHAPTER SEVENTEEN

Ripley, Ohio

Valentine had not seen Solomon in several days. He had heard him moving around upstairs packing, but Solomon had not come down to see him nor had Valentine attempted to bridge the gap between them.

He knew he had hurt Solomon deeply. The words just came out before he could think, but between the botched slave-rescue attempt, and Solomon's cavalier attitude, Valentine had let his anger get the better of him. Valentine stood and paced around his dark room. *What if Solomon is serious about abandoning our Raven exploits? Could I do this alone?*

Valentine's thoughts now went to the impending forced march. Grinder had sent word that he was still trying to find out the time and place. After that, it would be up to the rescuers to formulate a plan—a plan that should have included Solomon. Without his partner and his best friend, Valentine felt lost.

He sat in his darkened room, unwilling to light a lamp. *About this time Solomon would be sitting at his desk composing verse.* Valentine thought back on their childhood and how he had spent his early years as Solomon's companion.

The two of them had often huddled backstage among the piles of props and costumes, watching Arabella and the other actors rehearse for the myriad parts they played. The company of stock actors had to learn as many as sixty plays in a season, half of which they would repeat. They rehearsed one play in the morning and performed another at night. The performances ran six days a week and matinees three times a week. Their repertoire included everything from farce to Shakespeare. The pace was grueling, and Valentine enjoyed every minute. He learned how to talk, walk, and act like a gentleman by mimicking the actors' roles. And Solomon was always there to watch and correct him.

Valentine and Solomon had been schooled together, their primers being the plays that the company performed. Valentine occasionally portrayed the lovable, yet impish pickaninny. When he grew older and became more accomplished with his lines, Valentine acted as the prompter, coaching the actors with their lines. He had built sets and fashioned costumes. Whatever job had to be done, Valentine was commandeered for it. He was never bored, always happy to learn, and always eager to help. It was an exciting life and Solomon shared it with him.

Valentine loved the theater, but there was no room for a young black actor in the troupe or, for that matter, any other theater company. Finally, at fifteen, he apprenticed to a barber, a trade where a black man would find acceptance and, even be sought after.

A faint knock on the shop door brought Valentine back to the present. He thought it might be Solomon, with a change of heart. Valentine rushed to the front of the shop with no light to guide him. Once again, he stumbled over chairs and stove to get to the door. He flung open the door in anticipation, and was surprised to see the shape of a woman outlined by the light of a street lamp.

"Sorry, to disturb you sir, but my mas...employer'd like to know if he could buy some of this here lotion." The young woman said, in a hesitant voice, thrusting the empty bottle toward him.

"I... well I was closed. Valentine changed his mind. "Come in...wait. Let me light a lamp so we can see." Valentine rushed around the shop. He came back to the door and opened it wider. "Please come in." He escorted the lady to a chair. "Won't you sit down?"

Leona gathered around her the folds of her new hand-me down wool coat as she had seen the ladies at the Greene's do, and graciously accepted a seat. She looked around at the shop's neatness and then looked at Valentine with curiosity.

"You the owner?"

"Yes, miss. I am. Valentine Kass at your service," he said with a perfunctory bow. He'd never seen such a stunning woman. She had eyes the color of caramel, a lighter shade than her complexion. Wisps of curls peeked from underneath her bonnet, framing her heart-shaped face. Even in comparison to Philadelphia, where free women of color were said to be as beautiful as those in New Orleans, this woman before him was stunning. He continued to stare. "And you, Miss. Your name is...?"

Leona giggled. She immediately hid her smile behind gloved hands. "Mary...Mary George," she mumbled.

"Please, you have a wonderful smile, don't hide it. What's so funny?" he said, amused by her.

She cast her cat-like eyes down to the floor, embarrassed to have looked directly at him so boldly.

"Well, sir I never really saw no colored man who owned his own place. I know colored men who are blacksmiths and carpenters, but I ain't never seen no barber ... no freeman barber before."

"Oh, well I can assure you that there are many of us here in Ohio, and other places, too. You wanted lotion?" he asked, standing over her, unable to take his eyes off her.

She looked up at him and for a moment felt breathless. After she recovered herself, she replied.

"Mr. Greene? The tailor? He asked me to come here and get some lotion for his wife. But he say not to tell her where it come from or else she weren't gonna take it. So, I come with some money to get the lotion 'cause she got a party and she complain about her hands. He done got tired of listenin' to her and sent me here to fetch this lotion."

"Oh, yes. I'll get some right away." But he stood rooted to the spot. "You're Joseph Greene's servant?"

Leona nodded. "Yes, sir."

"You must be new then?"

"Yes, sir. I only been workin' there some days now."

"Where are you from?"

She averted his gaze. "Uh, the nigger town," Leona replied.

"You mean, the Negro settlement, Africa Hill?"

Leona nodded.

"Uhhh ahhhh," he said, rummaging through the cabinet, examining jars, and stalling while he stole glances at her. "And how long have you lived in the settlement?"

"Ah, not long," she said, tentatively.

"What do you do for the Greene's?"

"Cook girl," she replied.

He saw her lean back in the chair and finger the carved serpent-head as she swung the chair toward the mirror and played with her forehead curls. She turned her head one way and then the other as if she were examining her face for the first time.

164

"This here is a real nice shop," she said, standing up to walk around.

"Thank you," Valentine said, pouring lotion from one bottle to another while watching her out of the corner of his eye.

"Are you staying long?"

"What sir?"

He returned and handed her a bottle. "I said are you staying long?"

She frowned. "How come you ask that?" she asked, taking the bottle of lotion and laying it on the table to retrieve money from her coat.

"Well," *Dammit, why did I say that? She's a fugitive.* "It's just that, I...uh...was hoping that you would...would uh...be staying longer."

"Why sir?" she looked at him suspiciously.

"Uh, well, perhaps I could...uh...call, maybe when you're not busy," he mumbled. He pointed to the bottle on the table. "I put rose scent in the lotion and put it in a cut glass bottle similar to the ones that the apothecary uses so your mistress won't know the difference." *I'm rambling. Shut up.*

"This enough?" she said, laying out the coins in a row by size. Valentine took what he needed and she picked up the remaining coins. She looked at her hands and noticing how they were red and cracked, she quickly hid them in the pockets of her coat and said a hasty "thank you" and stood to leave.

Valentine blocked her way. "What I was trying to say was, do you think I might see you, I mean, I pass by the Greene's quite frequently. . ." *Why am I lying?*

Leona smiled. "You mean call on me, like a gentleman?"

Valentine took a breath. "Yes, I guess that's what I'm saying."

Leona giggled. "Well, I don't know. They, Mr. and Mrs. Greene...I mean...I think...well...yes," she beamed. "Mr. Greene, he always workin' at the shop and Mrs. Greene go out and do her callin' in the afternoon. That'd be the best time. That is if Essie, that the cook, don't have nothin' for me to do. I guess you could call on me," she giggled again, shyly.

"Well, fine then. How about tomorrow?" he asked eagerly.

"Tomorrow?" she repeated. "Tomorrow." She gave him a smile then stepped into the darkness outside.

Valentine closed the door and couldn't stop himself from smiling like an idiot. He sang around the shop while tidying the place.

In the years he'd spent carousing with Solomon, Valentine had been attracted to many women and they to him, but he never gave them a serious second thought. He took them as they came, actresses, prostitutes, working women, and daughters of prominent Negro families. They seemed to enjoy his company and he theirs, but there had never been a time he was so completely captivated by any one woman. *My God, I have to tell Solomon.* Then he remembered that Solomon was gone.

He was blowing out the lamps when he saw that she'd left the bottle of lotion on the table. He grabbed the bottle and raced after her calling her name.

"Mary...Mary..."

She was almost back to the Greene's when Valentine caught up with her. He was out of breath. He thrust the bottle of lotion at her. "You forgot this. I've been calling, but you never turned around.

"Oh, uh...Silly me. Thank you," she said, taking the bottle and gingerly putting it in her coat pocket. "You ain't got no coat. It's cold."

"You sure you'll be able to make it back, all right?"

"Yes, sir."

"Valentine..."

"Yes, Mister Valentine..."

"No, call me by my first name, Valentine or Val."

"Yes, Valentine," she said softly.

"Goodbye, Mary."

"Goodbye, Valentine," she said, stringing out the name carefully.

Valentine stood shivering in the cold, watching Mary George walk through the streets of Ripley back to Joseph Greene's home. He recited softly a love poem Solomon had written.

ભ

Joseph Greene's House—same time

Solomon straightened his coat, slicked back his hair and knocked on the door. A plump dark-skinned middle-aged woman with a bright blue head wrap answered the knock. She stood in the doorway, her girth blocking the entrance as she stared at him.

Solomon smiled engagingly.

"How do you do? I'm sorry not to have presented my card beforehand, but I'd like to see Miss Delphine, if she's available."

The black woman stared at him for a moment and with indifference asked. "I'll see if she seein' company this late," she said, pointedly. "Who askin' for her?"

"Mr. Solomon Tucker. Tell her I'm so sorry to call on her so unexpectedly, but I've just recently returned from a business trip and was too impatient to wait a minute longer to make her charming acquaintance again," he said, smiling broadly. The woman gave him a skeptical look and gestured for him to wait on the steps.

Solomon, steadied himself against a wall. He looked down at his boots, noticing their wear. *What I wouldn't give for a good pair of soft leather boots, some decent entertainment, and a meal that doesn't leave me with the trots. I hate this place and every provincial idiot in it. Damn Valentine.*

The inn where he stayed was noisy, loathsome and filthy. There were rats bigger than cats that scuttled underneath his bed at night. Luckily, Solomon had been too drunk over the past several nights to care if the vermin danced a jig on his headboard.

He had worked himself into such an emotional state; he knew he would have to do something to keep from falling into that black hole of melancholia that had swallowed him once before. It had taken every effort on Valentine's part to pull him out the last time. Now they had had a bitter dispute, and while Solomon was not willing to revisit his past demons alone, he was not willing to apologize either. *Let Valentine come to me. I have done nothing wrong. Damn Valentine.*

He mulled over the idea of leaving Ohio after several rounds of ale and cheap wine at a tavern while sitting alone in a dark corner watching the locals. He despised every one of them; the farmers, merchants, boatmen; all of them with their backwoods ways. How he longed for the theater again—the opera and a rousing romp with a beautiful woman. *Damn Valentine.*

Solomon left the tavern and walked aimlessly toward town, reciting poetry, singing, and finally he found himself at the front door of the Greene household. To tell the truth, he was surprised he was even here. He once told Valentine jokingly about pursuing Delphine, for her money, but he had given it little or no thought. In fact, he hadn't even shown an interest in seeing her since he'd come back from their trip to Kentucky. After their fight, he felt that he needed a distraction. Courting a young, homely woman who was rich seemed better than wallowing in self-pity. *I've stooped to this. Damn Valentine.*

The door to the Greene's home opened wider and the plump black servant smiled at him.

"Miss. Delphine will see you now."

"Thank you...uh..."

"Essie," she said turning on her heels.

"Yes, Essie...Thank you." Solomon confidently walked in, leaving in his wake the smell of cheap wine and scented soap. He was ushered into the front parlor where Delphine sat, her skirt of embroidered silk, billowed around her like a delicate fan; she was a study of gentility, which belied the haste in which she had dressed.

"Mr. Tucker, how nice of you to see me. I had thought you'd completely forgotten me." She gave him a crooked grin and held out her hand to Solomon who bowed, turned her hand over, and kissed her open palm.

"My dear love, I had important business to attend to, which is the only reason that I stayed away. Had I not, I would have been here, attending to your every need."

"Well, then I accept your apology. Things have been rather dull around here without you. I had to seek company in the good school teacher who sat for hours reciting the works of dead poets and plying me with candy," she reported, giving him a sly look. "I must say I appreciated the candy much more than the poetry."

"And indeed you should have. Nothing is more tedious than listening to the writings of dead poets when you can have a live one in your midst," he bowed.

Essie, who stood in the doorway listening, rolled her eyes and closed the parlor door. She went back to the kitchen just as Mary was returning.

"I ain't never heard nothin' so full of it, in my life," Essie said to her new cook girl.

"What ma'am?" Mary replied, as she took off her bonnet and coat and hung them up on a hook by the kitchen door.

"Miss Delphine and this man she fond of, Solomon Tucker. If he ain't after her money, I don't know who is. Butter don't melt in his mouth. And Miss Delphine just lappin' up his words like she a cat and he the cream. You get that lotion Mr. Greene asked for?" Essie asked.

"Yes, ma'am." Leona pulled the bottle out from her coat pocket and handed it to her.

"I'm gonna take it up to the missus and put some on her. You stay down here. If you finish cleaning, peak in on them two in the parlor playing love games with each other. Make you wanna bust out laughin'. White people!" Essie spat out and whirled around to go upstairs.

Leona warmed herself near the kitchen stove and nibbled on a leftover biscuit when she heard the sound of the pianoforte and voices raised in laughter. Out of curiosity, she tiptoed to the parlor door and cracked it open...

"Oh, Mr. Tucker how witty you are. Let's try it again," she heard Miss Delphine exclaim.

Leona opened the door wider and saw that Miss Delphine faced the doorway, seated in front of the pianoforte, while Mr. Tucker had his back to the door. He leaned over Miss Delphine, his fingers gently touching her bare neckline.

"Ah, this time, you must play in time to my recitation; the two of us as one," he cooed.

Delphine nodded, struck a chord, and looked up at him as he began to sing:

> *A black bird come into my life and landed on a tree,*
> *He whisper sweet things in my ear and tell me I*
> *should flee.*

Oh, little black bird, why don't you set me free,
'cause I'm leaving' Alabamy and the life of slavery.

They admonished each other for their naughtiness at reciting an abolitionist song.

Leona closed the door to avoid being seen and scurried away. She wondered where she had heard that voice before.

ଔ

CHAPTER EIGHTEEN

Ripley, Ohio

Leona swung her empty basket and hummed the same tune she'd heard Mr. Tucker and Miss Delphine sing. She walked toward the open market to find some interesting trinkets to decorate the Greene's holiday tree; a custom Mrs. Greene began when she visited relatives in Pennsylvania, and which Mr. Greene said he could do without since it created more work for him. But having cut down a tree to Mrs. Greene's liking, the household was obliged to make decorations for it.

Miss Delphine and Mrs. Greene painted eggs and Essie sewed bells on scraps of material. They hung these on the branches of the tree along with candles and decorative bows. Leona was looking for something special as her contribution. As she passed the Razor's Edge, she waved to Valentine who was tending a customer. He saw her and waved back, gesturing for her to come in, but she held up her empty basket to signal that she had errands to run. She was glad it was cold outside so that Valentine couldn't see her blush with pleasure at the sight of him.

True to his word, he came to see her that next day. He smiled and greeted her with both hands behind his back.

"I know this isn't the sort of gift one brings to a young woman on their first ...uh...meeting, but I thought you might like some as well," he said, shyly. "But you must guess which hand," he said.

Leona giggled and touched his right arm. He showed her that there was nothing in his right hand. Disappointed, she pointed to his left. He held his left hand out, but there was nothing there either. Then he reached into his pocket and handed her a glass bottle of lotion tied with a ribbon.

Leona clapped with joy and rubbed some of the lotion on her course red hands. She put her hands up to her nose and inhaled deeply. "It makes my hands smell like roses," she looked at Valentine with admiration. "Thank you, Valentine."

They stood in the kitchen beside the stove, an awkward silence between them. Valentine surveyed the kitchen with its copper pots and iron skillets that hung neatly on hooks against the wall. He smiled. "I didn't know that Joseph was such a gourmet."

"A what?" she answered, puzzled.

"A person who likes good food," he looked down at her.

"Oh, it ain't him, it's the missus that gives Essie the flux. Mrs. Greene's always asking her to whip up a little of this and a little of that and goin' on 'bout some recipe she read in a magazine. And poor Essie, she done fit to be tied. She wait 'til Mrs. Greene walk away, and just makes the food the way she was gonna do it in the first place. Mrs. Greene don't know the difference."

She took his hand. "You wanna see the rest of the house? Essie's upstairs asleep and Mrs. Greene and Miss Delphine are visitin'."

Valentine couldn't resist; he followed her.

She led him into the hallway that divided the two-story house. "This a fine house, better'n the one I..." but she stopped herself. "Better than most I been in," she finished.

A staircase wound toward the second floor. From the back, the kitchen led to the dining area and on the other side of the hall was the library. Leona opened the heavy library door.

"This is where the men go after dinner."

Valentine walked into the library and admired Joseph's taste in oriental rugs and English Regency furniture, particularly an oak and ebony-inlaid library table. Valentine turned and pulled a book from a shelf and opened it.

"You read?" Leona asked, admiringly.

"Yes, quite a bit, actually," he studied the book. "Mmmmm, Joseph has peculiar taste in literature. I'd think Fanny Burney was a bit... forward-thinking for him."

Leona stood on her toes and peeked over his shoulder to look curiously at the book. "Oh, Mr. Joseph don't read those books. He don't even look at 'um. Essie say he buy 'um by the crate and shove 'um up there so's she have more work to do dustin' 'um. What it say? Does it say somethin' bad?" she asked in awe.

Valentine turned to Leona. "Mary, would you like to learn how to read?"

"Me? Oh, no. Thank you," she turned away, shyly. "I don't want to put you out."

"I wouldn't be put out. I have some time on my hands now. You could come to the shop. We could start easy with a newspaper and then move on to books," he looked at her earnestly. "I really wouldn't mind at all."

"Well, if it don't put you out. I'd kinda like to read somethin' from the Bible," she confessed with quiet joy as he covered her hand with his and squeezed.

ᗲ

Life was good, Leona thought as she hummed to herself, remembering his touch. It was much better than she ever imagined while she was in Dr. Fowler's household.

Normally only a few brave souls who could withstand the cold and the chilling wind that blew off the river, visited the open market during winter. Now that it was nearing Christmas, however, people streamed into the market's makeshift aisles, crowding around the stalls set up by the river traders.

The ground was soft and muddy from the parade of people strolling up one row and down the other; a dusting of snow powdered their clothes. The market was dotted with warming fires where people gathered to take off the chill and exchange gossip. Over all the noise, itinerant musicians played for pennies.

The smoke from the fires blended with the smells from the wide variety of foods and spices that were for sale. Leona bought a candy stick and sucked on it as she wandered from one stall to another. She listened to the cacophony of the sellers while they hawked their wares.

It was all very exciting for her—and liberating. She touched the soft fur of animal skins trapped farther west, and smelled the bottles of cologne and perfumes from the East. She admired furniture made in Pennsylvania. She jingled the coins in her purse. She was free.

Mrs. Greene was a bit overbearing and fussy, but nothing in comparison to what she had endured with Dr. Fowler. He always had to know exactly what she was doing and when she was doing it. He controlled every minute of her life, while Mrs. Fowler was more of a human apparition; always present but never seen.

In fact, Mr. and Mrs. Greene, couldn't care less where she went, just as long as she obeyed Essie and did her chores. As a cook girl, she prepared the food, cleaned the kitchen, and did the shopping. Essie also made her help clean the house, build the fires, empty the slop jars, and do the laundry. Essentially, she did the same things as she had done for the Fowlers, except that she wasn't under constant supervision and suspicion.

The best part of it was that she no longer had to dodge Dr. Fowler's unwanted attention. Leona's only regret was that she couldn't see her brother. *But maybe I'll get a message to him telling him where I am.*

She watched a woman making a Christmas wreath. The agility of the woman's fingers so fascinated Leona, that she paid no attention to the man who eased up along side her.

"Le-Le."

Leona turned and smiled in the face of a gaunt white man with predatory eyes. His eyes shone with recognition. "He said you were comely. He wasn't lying."

She immediately realized her mistake. Flustered, she tried to cover her blunder. "I...I... sorry sir, I...thought you was talkin' to me," she said, inching away from him.

"I was, Leona," he pronounced her name with deliberation.

"My name is Mary...Mary George, sir."

The man grabbed her arm and pulled her toward him. "You can stop the pretense, and come with me." He roughly pulled her from the crowded stall as she struggled against him.

"Hey, leave that gal alone. You sir. Stop," a merchant cried and came from behind his stall. Slade stared him down.

"You sir, mind your own damn business or I'll take you in for helping a fugitive," Slade growled. The man stopped in mid-protest, turned away, and walked silently back to his stall. He busied himself straightening his merchandise.

A curious crowd gathered, mumbling and protesting the way Slade was handling the girl. Slade, afraid of creating a scene, dragged Leona away from the market and shoved her in a doorway, blocking her escape.

"Now gal, you won't escape from me."

Leona continued to struggle. "Let go of me. Let go," she cried. "What you want from me?"

"All you need to know is that I'm a slave catcher. And I know who you are. What I want from you is information."

"I don't...I ...," Leona broke down. "Please sir, please let me go. I ain't got no information."

"Oh, but you do. You escaped from the county jail. A man helped you to escape. I want to know who that man is."

Leona blinked back tears. She shook her head. "I don't know. I don't know who he is," she protested.

"Yes, you do. "

"No, sir. It was dark. I... Please sir, I don't know nothin'."

Slade held up the broach and waved it before her. "This broach of yours was our bait to capture your brother."

She stopped struggling.

"We've got him now, Dr. Fowler and I. Fowler wants you. I want a bigger fish. I want the Raven, the man who helped you escape."

Her mind reeled. "Why you got George?"

Slade smiled. "To make sure you get the information I want. Oh, I left him in Fowler's charge where I'm sure you have every right to be concerned. Last time I saw your poor brother, Fowler had him in his cellar chained and bleeding. You know, the man is completely mad. He probably always was, but it seems your escape pushed him over the edge."

Shocked, Leona cried, "He gonna kill him."

"Yes, that's possibly true. He has no use for your brother and after the poor boy couldn't tell him where you were, Fowler decided to experiment on him. Something about...let me see...oh, yes whether a nigger's organs were the same as those of a white person." Slade grinned.

Leona's legs weakened. She slumped against the doorway.

"Now, if you want to save him any more suffering, you'll give me the name of the Raven and make it quick."

"I don't know, I told you. I don't know. We was movin' fast and...and ..." she struggled to remember. "He...was white. He was dark lookin'. Had dark hair like you...and long sideburns, like you." She shook her head. "I seen a little of the captain and the boy on the boat. That's all I know."

"So, there's a whole band of them. A band of abolitionists working with the Raven."

"I...I...yes, I guess so," she said weakly.

"Their names."

"I...I don't remember. Please, take me back so I can save my brother. I promise I won't run away again," she broke down, hysterically.

"I don't want you. If anything, you'll only get in my way. I want the Raven. You give me that information and I'll spare you and your brother."

"Excuse me, is there something wrong?" The voice came from behind them.

Slade turned and saw a constable.

"No sir, just askin' the woman if she wanted to work for me is all."

The constable looked at Leona. "Is this true?"

Leona's face was blank. "Yes...Yes, sir. I...he...was wantin' me to work for him, but I don't know."

"I see. Well, if you have any trouble, I'll be standing right over there," he said, tipping his hat.

They both watched the constable walk away and take a position opposite them. Slade turned back to Leona.

"See, I could have turned you in right then and there, but I didn't. You'll do as I say. You'll give me the name of the Raven. You give me that name and hopefully there will still be something left of your brother to free, you understand?" He let her go.

"How'm I suppose to find out?"

"Put the word out that you need to help your brother escape. The Raven will find you I'm sure." He sneered at her. "Don't worry, I'll be watching you, every minute, every second. If you think about running, you'll lose your life and that of your brother's. Now, go back to your shopping. And don't think that someone will help you. The minute they find out you're a fugitive, they'll turn you over to the authorities." Slade bowed and stepped out of the doorway. "Until then, I would work very hard to get that name," and then he walked away, yelling back at her. "You have until Christmas."

"How will I find you?" she yelled after him.

He turned. "I'll be here every night, waiting," and disappeared into the crowd.

Leona watched him leave. She turned and caught the eye of the constable and forced a smile, then walked away.

She forgot her Christmas errand and walked from one end of town to the other, peaking into shops, wandering through the more notorious parts of town, going from wharf to livery stables all while staring into the faces of men. She stopped several black boys who were hauling cargo up a gangplank; none of them was the dark-skinned boy who had helped her the night of her escape. She was determined to deliver the name of the Raven to the bounty hunter—and free her brother.

ଓ

Slade was very pleased with himself. Luck was with him. Had he come at a different time to the market place, he would have probably missed her. As it was, he marveled at his good fortune.

No sooner had they captured the boy and made him a prisoner in Fowler's cellar, when Slade left, leaving Fowler to deal with the boy alone. *Poor bastard.* Slade had no doubt that there would be little if anything left of George by the time Fowler got through. But that wasn't his concern.

Slade's first thought was to travel to Cincinnati where he was sure Leona would be hidden among the colored community there, in which case she might be almost impossible to find. His instincts then told him to try Ripley since the Raven seemed to operate around the area. The only other place near Ripley she could have crossed was near Portsmouth, but it was much farther east.

Slade posed as a man looking for additional help for his household and for several days he wandered around Ripley's wharf asking discrete questions. Certain that his fugitive already fled north, he was less than optimistic about his prospects, but something told him to linger at the market today. That was when he spotted her.

Fowler had given him a detailed description of Leona. Most importantly, Fowler mimicked her mannerisms: the way she held her head; how she tended to shyly lower her eyes and hide her smile when she was pleased. Fowler had studied Leona for years and so was able to paint a vivid image of her in Slade's mind. When Slade spotted a woman with similar characteristics, he followed her.

While asking around to determine who she was, he kept a constant watch on her. One old woman who was selling scraps of material, cheerfully volunteered that the girl he inquired about was a recent employee in the Greene household. While the woman did not know Leona's name, she boasted that she had heard from Greene himself that he'd gotten her on the cheap.

Armed with this information, Slade closed in. When he called out her brother's pet name for her, and she turned, casting those unusual eyes on him, he knew he had his prey. He was again the finder of lost things; the relentless slave catcher.

Now he walked briskly through the crowd. The town was full of spies. He would go back to his lodgings, soak his hand in water and rub some of the ointment on his aching joints. As Slade rounded the corner, he bumped into a grinder. The slave-catcher pushed his way past the old man, and never gave him a second look.

ɔઝ

Ripley, Ohio—Joseph Greene's home—December 24

It had been three days since she had talked with the slave catcher. Now, on Christmas Eve, Leona walked up and down the wharf, searching the faces of sellers and revelers, looking for anyone familiar. If only she could remember what her rescuer looked like, but it had been dark and rainy that night. Besides, she had been scared out of her mind.

Leona could feel the eyes of the slave catcher on her as she pushed through the Christmas crowds. She knew he was watching her from some hidden recess. She believed he not only knew her every move, but probably her thoughts as well.

She had thought to seek help from the most famous abolitionist in Ripley, and she looked up at the highest hill to where his house stood. *Could I climb the hill without being caught?* she wondered. As she stood with her back to the water, looking up at John Rankin's house, she saw that someone had placed a light in the window—like a beacon. *Could I ask him to help me?* She scanned the crowd and thought she saw the slave catcher. She had only one day left and feared that the slave catcher would reappear to tell her that she had sentenced her brother to death.

It was no use. She had not found any information about the Raven and was now running out of time. Leona walked back toward the Greenes' house, heavy with defeat. She was passing the Razor's Edge when she looked up and saw Valentine smiling in the doorway.

"Come on in. You're shivering," he said, holding out his hand to her.

She took his hand and followed him inside.

"I thought I would see more of you...I mean, you seemed eager to learn to read."

Leona averted her eyes, "I change my mind. I ain't interested, no more."

Valentine was taken aback by her curtness. "I see, well...why don't you take your coat off and sit in the chair nearest the stove while I make tea."

She stared, distracted while Valentine brewed some aromatic herbs. He offered her a steaming cup that she gratefully accepted, alternately blowing and sipping the soothing beverage. He pulled his chair closer to her and asked, "So, how is it that you've been outside; and on Christmas Eve, of all nights?"

She studied her tea, avoiding his gaze. "I must...must a lost track of time," she responded quietly.

"Who would be so important that a young lady like you would risk catching her death over?" he asked cheerfully.

She knew he was teasing, but his kindness pushed her over the edge. The tears streamed down her face.

"Mary? What has happened? Did someone bother you? Are they not treating you well at the Greenes?"

Leona shook her head. "No sir, it ain't that Mr. Valentine."

He leaned back. "Now we're back to Mr. Valentine, is it? Have I done something to offend you?"

She shook her head. "Oh, no sir. No."

"Then what is it?" He was truly concerned.

Leona wanted to tell him; needed to tell him. *What should I do? What can he do?*

She looked up at Valentine, her eyes again filling with tears. "Sir, if I...if I tell you a...a secret, would you...would you...?" Her voice caught in her throat, she chocked on the words.

"Sip your tea," he urged.

She took another swallow and blurted. "I must find the Raven."

Valentine tried to conceal his surprise by standing up and fussing with the hot water on the stove. "The Raven you say? But he is only a myth. Something people have made up."

"Oh no sir, he's real..." she said earnestly. "He's as real as you and me."

"And how do you know this?"

"Because I...." Then she stopped. If she told him that the Raven had rescued her, then he would know she was a fugitive. "Because people seen him," was all she could think to say.

Valentine turned, and forced a smile. "Well, there you have it. Go to those people and ask them who he is."

"I cain't sir, I mean, I don't know 'xactly who knows who he is. He comes at night and steals away the slaves."

"Drink up," he said, pouring more tea in her cup. "And what would you do if you found out his name this... Raven?" He studied her, holding his breath, waiting for her answer.

Her eyes darted from one corner of the shop to the other. She didn't know what to say. She vacillated between telling him the truth and making up a lie. "Why I...I would tell him...I would tell him... Thank you for helpin' the poor slaves."

At this, Valentine burst into laughter. "Thank you. Well, if he does exist, I'm sure he appreciates your sentiment."

"There ain't nothin' to laugh at," she said angrily. "You don't understand. It's...it's...a ...matter of life and death."

"Go on," he leaned closer, "...what is it you want him to do?"

She fumbled with the teacup. It's...it's about my..." Leona cast her eyes downward as she shook her head. "I cain't say." She sighed heavily, then said. "I have to go. It's late and tomorrow the Greenes are having a Christmas dinner." She sat down her unfinished cup of tea and stood wearily. Valentine retrieved her coat and helped her with it. He turned her around to face him.

"Are you in trouble Mary?" He was holding her shoulders and her body trembled as much from her anguish as from his touch. "Because if you are. I can be more help than the Raven can. The Raven is just a story made up by slaves to give themselves hope that one day they'll be free."

Her eyes flashed suddenly with anger. "That's a lie. He *is* real. And I aim to find him."

Valentine scrutinized her closely. "And why do you need to find the Raven?"

"It ain't none of your concern." She averted his eyes.

He took her face in his hands and made her look at him. "Mary what is it? I do want to help."

"You? You a barber. You ain't never seen one day a hard life. You got soft hands and nice clothes," she said bitterly. "You sit and read your books and don't care a fig for people like me...people...people..."

She wrenched from his grasp and bolted. The hollow jingle of the bell above the door echoed in her wake.

CHAPTER NINETEEN

Ripley, Ohio—Christmas Day

Valentine watched the Grinder chew his food around his missing teeth, and looked down at his own mutton that he hadn't touched. He pinched off a piece of bread, soaked it in gravy, and put it in his mouth. *Christmas with the Grinder.*

The Grinder had been to the shop that morning and wanted Valentine to meet him at an inn for Christmas dinner. Valentine had agreed, knowing it was better to be with the Grinder than alone on Christmas.

He and Solomon had always spent Christmas together, wherever they were. They entertained one another, sang songs, and performed snatches of plays. It was always a lively affair.

The Grinder pointed his spoon at Valentine's plate. "You gonna eat dat?" he said, his mouth full.

Valentine pushed his plate across and watched the Grinder spoon gravy over the mutton.

"You gotta eat, dis good." He said.

"I'm not really hungry. "

"Ah, you and Solomon."

Valentine glanced at him sheepishly. "So you heard."

"I hear every ding," he said, pulling off a fistful of bread and sopping it in gravy. "You talk, *ja*?"

Valentine shrugged.

"No. There's nothing to talk about," he said quickly, not meeting the Grinder's gaze. His eyes wandered around the smoky public room. The place was crowded with people passing Christmas Day without loved ones. Some were huddled in corners asleep. A few had found card-playing companions while others sang bawdy songs of love and lust. Even with the noise, the inn had a feeling of loneliness.

The Grinder chewed thoughtfully on the soaked bread. "I come from Kentucky. People upset. Raven got dem runnin' in circles," he said soberly. "I hear tell de brother of de girl Solomon rescued is missing. His owner been lookin' for him. Say Raven done flew over de plantation and sweep him up too. Dey say he run away *mit* his sister. Dey say he help a slave escape and cross at Portsmouth. Den some got him in Covington where three slaves disappear. But, I don't know," he shrugged finally.

"*Der Arzt*, the doctor, dat own de girl, done gone crazy and he holed up in his house. Somethin' not right, *ja*? Dis girl her name Leona, pretty name, *ja*?"

"She's dead," Valentine concluded.

Grinder raised one bushy brow. "You dink? Den why *ist* Slade in town again?"

Valentine started. "Slade's back?"

The Grinder nodded his head. "Saw him *mit* my own eyes. He sneak around here. But I see he come out at night, stay on de wharf...looking for someone. Always looking. Maybe he catch de Raven, *ja*?"

"Well, he won't find him. Not anymore."

"Oh, you dink now, you gonna drop de whole ding?"

Valentine leaned over the table as he spoke, "Look, Solomon and I worked together on this. Solomon has decided to get out. There's nothing I can do."

The Grinder nodded his head. "I see. And you don't ask him to come back?"

"It's not I who needs to apologize."

"Ah, it is apology you vant?"

"Yes...no," Valentine sighed. "I...we've always had a difference of opinion on this thing. It came to a head when he decided to do this rescue on his own," he said, lighting a cheroot.

Grinder coughed and spit phlegm on the floor. He took a sip of water and cleared his throat.

"Well, I have some good news. I found out de place *und* time of de march." Grinder said, eyeing Valentine curiously. "It will take five or six men to do dis job."

Valentine said nothing.

"I was hoping you *und* Solomon, *ja*?

Valentine inhaled and blew a stream of smoke. "It will be just me. Solomon'll get us killed."

Grinder narrowed his eyes and stared at Valentine. "Being a slave gets you killed too, as you should know," the Grinder pronounced pointedly..

Valentine sat smoking in silence while Grinder finished both their dinners.

CЗ

Joseph Greene's home--Christmas Day

The Christmas tree stood in the front parlor by the window, brilliantly aglow with lighted candles and brightly colored decorations. The guests were gathered by the tree. A fire blazed and crackled with the woodsy fragrance of pinecones and evergreen twigs. Evergreen laurels draped the mantle, archways, and the banister leading to the second floor landing.

Joseph Greene, who had fussed and complained for a week about the commotion over the holiday, was flushed and winded, caught up in a lively game of charades. He lumbered among the seated guests, stooped over and swinging one arm in front of him.

"A monkey!" Mrs. Greene cried out.

"No, it's a...a...horse?" the schoolteacher shouted.

Joseph Greene raised his arm over his head, and rotated his hand.

"Oh, oh...I know. A snake," Delphine jumped up and clapped.

Exhausted, Joseph Greene collapsed in a straight back chair, breathing heavily. "An elephant. Elephant. Trunk. Snout. "

"Oh," the guests all chimed in unison.

Greene was flushed. "Where's Essie? Where are our cool drinks?" he said, fanning himself with his open hand. He turned to Solomon. "Solomon, it's your turn. What will you grace us with?"

Solomon stood and bowed to his expectant audience. "I have a song that I wrote especially for the lady who has stolen my heart," and he turned to Delphine, took her hand, and raised it to his lips.

The women sighed, the men glanced knowingly at each other, while the school teacher sat off to the side, his eyes blazing with jealousy.

"If you will accompany me on the pianoforte," he said, as he guided her to the music seat. He bent toward Delphine to confer over the music.

"Just a minute, let's have our drinks before you start," Greene said, sweat beading his forehead. "Where's that girl?" He walked over to the bell pull and jerked on it vigorously as he glanced at the mantle clock.

"Give Essie some time," Mrs. Greene walked over to her husband and put her arm around him. "Sit by the window away from the fire. It's cooler over there, dear." She guided her husband to a chair by the window where he could lean his head on the cool pane. She nuzzled his ear.

"Stop fussing. This is a wonderful Christmas and you made a splendid elephant," she said, patting his balding head affectionately. "Now be quiet and let Mr. Tucker sing." She sat on the arm of the winged back chair and pulled out her fan to cool her husband. "Mr. Tucker, would you begin?"

Solomon nodded to Delphine who struck a chord. His rich tenor echoed throughout the parlor:

> *I love you dear, I truly do*
> *You are my world and heaven too*
> *Your sunshine dried my every tear;*
> *Oh, doubt me not, I love you dear.*

> *I love you dear, I love your eyes;*
> *They promise me love's Paradise,*
> *But should their pledge be insincere*
> *Still be my theme, I love you dear.*

Leona heard the music emanating from the closed parlor door as she cautiously balanced the punch and glasses on a heavy silver tray. She turned the doorknob and put her back to the door to prop it open while she slipped in quietly so as not to disturb the merry-making. She walked carefully toward the guests, her eyes intent on the glasses so as not to spill a drop. No one paid any attention to her. They were enjoying Solomon's song:

I love you dear, if you but knew
My faith, my hope, my all are you;

Solomon launched into the last lines of his song; his arm flung outward and he turned from Delphine to the guests:

All joys are mine when you are near
Unchanged always, I love you dear.

He held the last note and made a dramatic gesture with his arms, catching the attention of Leona who, at that very moment, looked up. Solomon and Leona's eyes locked. Her hand slipped, the punch bowl tilted, the glasses slid, and the tray fell. The clatter of breaking glass reverberated throughout the parlor. The ladies all screamed. Men jumped up from their chairs, afraid of getting red punch on their fine attire. Everyone was in a frenzy of motion except Solomon and Leona who stood, staring at each other, frozen in shock.

"My God girl," Joseph Greene shouted. "What's wrong with you? Where's Essie? Why isn't she serving?" streamed the questions.

"Look what you've done. My dress…" one woman exclaimed.

"You clumsy nigger," cried the merchant from Red Oak as he brushed red punch off his best suit.

Mrs. Greene shouted orders. "Get a towel. Get something. Don't just stand there like a tree. Do you hear me?"

Leona blinked. She looked around her, stunned. Her mouth opened in surprise, then she looked down at the mess on the floor. She looked at Solomon and then at the Greenes. Horror-stricken, she bolted from the room.

Solomon stood with one arm still open, the last note dying from his lips.

All the guests scooted back their chairs to avoid the stream of red punch flowing like a river along the wooden planks.

Solomon's mind was reeling. *Where had she come from? What was she doing here? Think fast.* He took a deep breath and in an imploring, soothing voice, he took command of the scene. "Ladies, gentlemen, my gracious host and hostess, I am so sorry for causing such a commotion."

The voices in the room immediately hushed.

"I take full responsibility for this disturbance, I obviously scared the poor wretch with my voice," he said laughing. "Whether because of its beauty or its dissonance, it makes no difference. Allow me to make my apologies to the girl."

Delphine half rising, took his hand to stop him. "Oh, Solomon it was not your fault. You were perfectly wonderful. Your words...your words..." she had tears in her eyes, overwhelmed. "My heart was so full with the words you sang."

Solomon bowed graciously to Delphine. "You are a kind lady," he said, taking her hand and lightly brushing it against his lips. "But nevertheless, I feel responsible."

"Nonsense, dear man. The girl is obviously inept. What I'd like to know is, where is Essie?" Joseph Greene bellowed beside him.

Solomon smiled indulgently. "You are most kind Joseph. But I can do nothing less than make my sincerity felt. Point me to the kitchen and I'll have this matter disposed of in no time." He dramatically swept out of the room before anyone else had a chance to stop him.

Once the parlor door closed, he raced to the kitchen where he found it piled high with waiting, unwashed dishes. Steaming pots and pans of food simmered on the iron stove. The kitchen, which had been immaculate that Christmas morning, now looked as if an artillery shell had discharged in its midst. He found the girl trembling behind a table.

"What are you doing here?" he demanded of Leona who backed away.

"Please, don't hurt me," she cried out, hysterical.

"Hush, before you alarm the entire household," he told her, inching closer. "Silly girl, I'm not going to hurt you. How did you got here? You were supposed to be on your way to Cincinnati. You're suppose to be free, you imbecile. Why aren't you in Canada or Detroit or some other place?"

"I...I...thought that...I well, I thought ab'litions was gonna eat me and...and...so I jumped and...then this Indian woman...she helped me...and then Massa...I mean, Mister Greene he brought me here."

"You're the Mary that the Greenes refer too?"

Leona nodded.

"Oh my God, the joke's on me." Arms akimbo, he stood watching Leona. "Well, it looks like we both have a secret that needs keeping. I'll keep yours, if you'll keep mine."

Leona hesitantly stood and faced Solomon. "Then you are the Raven?" she said.

His expression changed slightly. "Love, don't ever mention that name and me in the same breath."

She came around the table. "But you *are*, the Raven?"

Solomon saw the look in her eyes and mistook it for awe; he confessed. "Well, if you must know yes; yes I am. But love, you are sworn to secrecy; lives will be lost, governments will topple. This is a secret of utmost importance that must be kept between the two of us," he teasingly exaggerated. He cupped his hand around her face. "My but you are a pretty thing. But enough of this. Where's the other one? The older servant?"

A voice rang out from the end of the hallway. "Oh, Mr. Tucker. Mr. Tucker are you all right?"

"Oh, you mean Essie," Leona wiped her eyes. "Well, she...uh, she had too much of the Christmas cheer, sir. Done fell down drunk. I put her to bed, that's why I was servin'."

"Well, mmmmm, okay. Go in there and clean up that mess and we'll call it a day." He was about to turn and leave when she grabbed his sleeve, and whispered earnestly. "Mr. Tucker, please you got to help me. It's about my brother, sir. You got to help him escape."

"Oh, Mr. Tuuuuuuukkkkkkkeeeerrrr are you coming back?" Delphine's cry came closer.

"What?" He turned back startled.

Leona's eyes shone brightly. "You have to help him escape. He..."

"Not here, not now," he whispered back. "Get whatever you get to clean that mess up. Don't let on you know me and don't say another word."

He looked into those pleading cat-like brown eyes of Leona's and saw only desperation. "Now look. I'm not in the rescue business anymore."

She trembled and clung to his sleeve.

He sighed. "All right. When I leave, I'll sneak back around to see you and you can tell me what your problem is."

"Oh thank you, sir," tears streamed down her face. She still had a death grip on him.

He struggled to pull away. "Stop groveling, and act natural," he whispered.

"Oh, Mister Tucker, there you are," Delphine cried petulantly bursting in. She stood in the kitchen, hands on hips, looking from Solomon to Leona and sensed something between them. Her territorial instincts were aroused and she stepped closer to Solomon and laid her hand on his arm. "I feared you'd gotten lost or worse, been entrapped by the pleadings for mercy of this wretched kitchen help."

"Just reassuring her that no punishment will come her way. Solomon laughed. It seems your other woman, Essie was..."

"She done took sick, ma'am," Leona blurted out. "That's why I serve the punch. I ain't never served punch before and I ...I," she held her head down. "I just be scared, ma'am."

Relieved, Delphine relaxed. "Well, I see. I guess we shouldn't punish you for something you didn't know how to do. But come quick before the floor and rug are ruined." Delphine shifted her attention back to Solomon. "Mr. Tucker won't you join us in the library while she's cleaning up? We'd love to hear your poetry," then in a lower tone, "But not the Raven poems. The Greenes' company aren't predisposed to such radical thinking. Perhaps tomorrow you will grace me with more abolitionist verse," she giggled taking him by the arm and guiding him out of the kitchen.

"Tomorrow then." He took one backward glance at Leona and put a finger to his lips.

She nodded in reply. After they were gone, Leona looked heavenward. "Thank you," she whispered.

 C3

Later that night

Solomon listlessly went through his armoire picking out an outfit. His head ached from the brandy he'd consumed after he'd spoken to the girl and agreed to rescue her brother. "God, what's wrong with me? How could I be so foolish," he said as he rummaged around for a suitable disguise.

Clothes were strewn over the bed, on the floor. Bottles of wine lay on the desk, underneath the bed, and in every corner of the room. *Valentine is right. I'm such a reprobate.*

Whenever he had too much to drink, he could always count on Valentine to give him some concoction to remedy his ailment. Valentine was better than a chemist.

Solomon rubbed his face, "I can't think." He threw the clothes down in frustration.

Why did I say I would help?

But he knew why. He wanted to prove he could set things right between himself and Valentine.

Valentine had always accused him of taking the Raven's exploits lightly, of using them as an amusing way to past the time, of viewing them as a form of backwoods theatre. But he wanted to prove that he could do a rescue alone. He wanted to prove to Valentine that he could operate on his own and carry off a successful mission. Pride and ego had made him confess his identity to the girl, but respect from Valentine was his reason for attempting the dangerous mission alone.

Ever since they were boys, Valentine had watched over him like an over protective governess. When Solomon got in trouble, Valentine got him out of it. Valentine was the responsible one. Valentine was the mature one. Valentine was his best friend, his brother, and yet, Solomon wanted more; he wanted to show Valentine that he could be a man, not the silly, spoiled child whose mother had doted on him.

And so when Leona, told him about her brother being held captive by the doctor, he'd agreed to cross over with her and try and get him back safely.

But what's the plan?

Solomon slumped in a chair. A blond curl fell across his face. He couldn't think. He needed Valentine to help him. They used each other as a sounding board for ideas until one of them would come up with something plausible. He held his head in his hand while he scanned the papers that littered his desk. Last night in a burst of creativity fueled by brandy, he had started a new poem based on this mission.

> *A girl of dark and lustrous hue,*
> *Whose eyes did shine like morning dew,*
> *And smile so bright could blind the sun,*
> *So sweet was she, the birds did come,*
> *To sing with her of joy and bliss.*
>
> *But then a storm of trouble brewed*
> *And stole her light and airy mood...*

"And on and on it goes," he said, tossing the poem aside. He wondered how he should end it. Of course, in order to end the damn poem, he had to have a plan. Raven, raven, raven. *I am the Raven, what do I do?*

CHAPTER TWENTY

Ripley, Ohio—December 26—morning

The bell over Valentine's shop signaled him. He wasn't expecting any customers the day after Christmas especially not this early. He looked up from the book he was reading and saw Solomon standing awkwardly in the doorway.

"I came for a haircut, sir. I trust you're open and ready for business."

Valentine laid down his book and rose stiffly.

Solomon looked around the shop as if seeing it for the first time. He glanced at the newspaper that served as insulation; the hardback chairs that lined one wall; the mirror and barber chair, which were the only elaborate pieces in the entire place. The barber shop was neat, uncluttered and provincial, not at all like the barbershops in Philadelphia. Yet, in spite of its shabby appearance, it was Valentine's pride.

Solomon walked inside and hung up his topcoat. He put on the airs of an English gentleman, teasing Valentine. "I think you could afford to spruce the place up a bit. A little color on the walls might help. Certainly more comfortable chairs."

Valentine bantered back in his own affected accent. "And scare away my clientele? The river traders and boatmen don't want elegance. They want a good shave and haircut. Gentlemen of your ilk patronize the barber down the street where they can lounge in style, but they will look just as bad when they leave as when they arrived."

"What? You would take ruffians, river rats, and Kentucky keel haulers, and make them fashionable, but not me? I've never known you to turn down a client, especially one with money," he said, flopping in the barber chair that Valentine had vacated. "The works my good man. And make it quick. I have work to do."

"And when did you ever do an honest day's work?" Valentine teased.

"Oh, did I say honest?" Solomon countered.

"Well, whatever work you're planning, you do need a haircut and a shave unless you plan to kiss the fair and beauteous Miss Delphine with stubble on your chin."

Solomon waved, dismissively. "She will take me anyway I come."

"Ah, so you have won her heart?"

"And with it her purse, I hope."

Valentine snapped open the barber's cloth and tied it around Solomon's neck. "And is there something special that you would like?"

Solomon somberly looked at Valentine and dropped all pretense. "I...I..." He didn't know how to begin. "I am at your mercy," he said, leaning his head back.

"You'll have to wait while I heat water."

"Mmmmmm."

Valentine set to work, boiling water and sharpening his razors. "So, tell me, how do you like your new lodgings?" He beat out a rhythmic pattern on the strap.

"They're comfortable enough. The food is horrendous. The other boarders are a bore, but I get to pinch the fat buttock of the inn's servant girl who gives me an extra sweet. Life could be better, but I'm not complaining."

"Well, that's a change. You never stopped complaining all the time you were here." He beat a more percussive rhythm.

198

"If I complained, it was only because of the disagreeable company that I was keeping," Solomon said, dropping the affectation.

"As I remember it was you who refused to seek the company of others," Valentine countered.

"I was inconsolable. My life as I knew it had ended," Solomon's voice rose.

"You had no life, if you call lying in bed day and night and drinking yourself into a stupor a life," Valentine shot back.

Solomon yanked the cloth from his neck and stood up. "I came here to make amends. I wanted us to be friends again, but I see now that it is hopeless. You will always think of me as that little boy that you had to take care of. You will never see me as a man who is capable of guiding his own affairs."

Valentine slammed the sharpened razor on the table. "No, because you still want to play in the theater. You see the whole world as a stage and you are the main character. Your entire life is a play where others take secondary roles. You are still play-acting. And if I have done one thing, it is to drag you into the world of reality where you can be of some use."

The words stung. Solomon blinked and took a deep breath. "Well, I see that my attempt at reconciliation has been aborted by your inability to see me for the man I truly am. And so sir, I shall leave and trouble you no longer. I have a mission to accomplish." Solomon snatched his coat off the rack and walked to the door. He grabbed the knob, then turned back briefly.

"Belated Merry Christmas," the bell jangled stridently as the door banged shut behind him.

03

Northern Kentucky woods–afternoon

"I'm thinkin' roast pig, potatoes, a little cider and baked apples. Now *that's* what I call a good dinner," Harry said to Jack as they tramped through the damp woods, the result of a sudden warm spell, their senses primed for any movement around them.

"Right 'bout now I'd just be thankful for a plump rabbit. I'd even take a squirrel," Jack said, then added. "You sure we ain't lost?"

Harry and Jack were now foraging for game in the forest after the sheriff fired them from their deputy positions. They could thank Dr. Fowler for that. After Leona was rescued by the Raven, Fowler complained long and loud that Harry and Jack let the Raven take his property. He called them illiterate and incompetent, and threatened that if they weren't fired, he would sue the sheriff and the county. Harry and Jack found themselves out of a job the next day with no money and no prospects. They were leaving Maysville, Kentucky as they had come.

Only four months before, the two young men had been Virginia coalminers who had gotten fed up spending their time down in a hole. Then one of them, neither one could remember who, decided it was time to do something else besides digging coal for the rest of their lives. Harry and Jack wanted adventure and excitement and they struck out on their own to find it.

They had packed all that they had between them on two horses and set out for Kentucky eventually to make their way to the Mississippi and the Western regions. They had heard stories about adventures on the Mississippi and about the western lands beyond the river. They even had heard about the gold rush in California and thought that digging for gold had to be better than digging for coal. Between them they had two rifles and shared a keen sense of adventure, although the adventure seemed to be failing them. The only prospect facing them now was starvation.

The rifles they had slung over their shoulders were loaded and ready to fire, if they saw game. Over the past two hours, they had spotted a deer but before they could aim, the deer dashed deeper into the woods.

"Come on Harry, let's give it up. Maybe we can beg fer food at a farm."

Harry shook his head. "I'm tellin' ya, we'll find somethin'. I ain't gonna eat no raw turnips or beg for bread today. I'm catchin' me somethin' if'n it's just a damn squirrel."

Their feet sunk in the soft carpet of wet leaves and mud underfoot as they moved deeper into the woods with Jack trailing Harry.

"This part of the country suppose to be full of game," Harry said.

"Well, why'nt you tell that to the game, 'cause they ain't cooperatin'," Jack complained.

Harry stopped short. He turned and put his finger to his lips and gestured to his far right. "Somethin' moved."

Jack looked to the spot where Harry was pointing sure that the light was playing tricks on his friend. They stood frozen, waiting for more movement. "I don't see nothin'," he whispered back.

Harry shook his head and raised his rifle to his shoulder. He sighted along the barrel. "We're gonna eat fer sure." He cautiously got down on one knee to steady his aim, and waited.

Jack stood still, listening to his stomach growl and hoped that his friend was right. He was so hungry that raw turnips sounded good to him. Then he too saw something move. He squinted. The bushes swayed twenty yards in front of them. Harry's shot reverberated through the woods and clipped a branch above the target. They waited, hoping the shot would flush out their prey.

"Come on, let's move forward," Harry whispered

The bushes moved violently and out crawled, two hands, a torso, and finally a figure that raised up, ready to run.

"By God, it's a nigger!" Harry exclaimed. "Hey nigger, stop or I'll shoot." He fumbled with his rifle and let off a wild shot. The figure raised his hands and stood still. Both men ran toward him and stopped short. The three stood several feet apart staring at each other.

"Jack, I think we got us a runaway," Harry gloated, aiming his rifle at the boy's midsection.

"Ask him if he got some food," Jack whispered.

"He better than food. Now, take this rope from my pocket and tie his hands."

"Why me?" Jack protested.

"Cause I got the rifle trained on him and you standing there bald-faced with nothin' to do, that's why."

Jack took the rope from Harry's pocket and approached the slave as if he were a wild animal. Caught runaways were as dangerous as wild boars and just as unpredictable, he'd heard.

As Jack crept closer, he could see the boy was half starved himself. His wrist bones protruded from the sleeves of the too-small coat he wore. There were scratches and bruises on his face and the new growth of hair on his head was compacted with dirt and leaves.

"Now you just stand still or my friend'll put a bullet through you," he said, grabbing the quaking boy's wrists and tying them securely with the rope. "What's your name?"

The boy starred wild-eyed at Jack. Even in the cool of the afternoon, he was sweating profusely.

"What he say his name was?" Harry shouted.

"He didn't," Jack shouted back. "I think he one of them nigger boys Mercer's lookin' for. What's your name boy?" he poked the boy in the stomach.

"Thor," the young boy cried out. "Thor."

"He *is* one of them nigger runaways. Mercer own you?"

Thor said nothing, just bowed his head.

"Boy, look at me when I talk to you. You Mercer's?"

"Yes'm," Thor said softly.

"Drag him along and we'll tie him to the saddle," Harry ordered.

Jack jerked the boy forward on the rope like a stubborn mule. And like a stubborn mule, the boy dug in his heels.

"Harry, he ain't movin'."

"He'll move all right." Harry rushed toward the boy and shoved the rifle into the boy's chest. "Now listen," Harry snarled, "...me and my friend here ain't ate good for some time—and we're mighty hungry. You look pretty good to us right now. We can kill you here and feast on your skinny black ass, or take you in and see what we can get fer ya. It's up to you."

Thor looked from one to the other and then he stepped forward.

Harry and Jack, the young adventurers, dragged the boy behind them as they trekked out of the woods back to their horses. Jack leaned over to Harry and whispered, "That was a good 'un. Eat 'um," Jack chuckled.

Harry positioned his rifle snuggly in the crook of his arm as he leaned toward Jack. "You ever tasted nigger meat? They say it taste like chicken." He hooted when he saw the expression on his friend's face. "Come on, we gonna take this boy back to Mercer."

"I'm hungry now," Jack whined.

"We gonna find somethin'. When we get there, betcha we get ourselves a good meal and a big reward. Anyway you cut it, we gonna get some money outta this."

ᴄʒ

Ripley, Ohio—same time

Down below Valentine could hear the muffled laughter and shouts from the patrons in the inn. He continued walking up the creaking stairway to the second floor. When he came to the landing, he looked down the dimly lighted hallway. The inn accommodated five rooms.

Solomon had been living in one of them ever since he had moved out. It was the second door on the left, the innkeeper told him. Valentine walked down the hall and stopped at the door. He was about to knock then hesitated, trying to decide how he would apologize. It wasn't easy for him. Since having escaped slavery, he made it a point not to apologize to anyone for anything because his life as a slave had been a continuous apology for being born black. He realized, however, that Solomon was right. He had too much pride, and because of that Valentine had lost his best friend—his only friend.

Valentine knocked and waited for a summons, but there was none. He knocked again. "Solomon, are you in there? Are you asleep?" Valentine turned to walk away, but decided to try the doorknob. It turned and he opened it.

The room was dark, there were no windows, only the dim light from the hallway guided him. Valentine felt his way toward a lamp on the desk and lit it. He held the oil lamp high to survey the room. Just as he suspected, Solomon was as much of an indolent housekeeper here as he was in the room over the shop. The armoire door stood open. Clothes were everywhere. Wigs and mustaches lay scattered on the bed like dead rodents. There were papers piled on the desk and strewn all over the floor. Valentine looked through everything and compulsively straightened up. It was during this process that he found one of Solomon's unfinished poems:

> *A girl of dark and lustrous hue,*
> *Whose eyes did shine like morning dew,*
> *And smile so bright could blind the sun,*
> *So sweet was she, the birds did come,*
> *To sing with her of joy and bliss.*
>
> *But then a storm of trouble brewed,*
> *And stole her light and airy mood,*
> *And left her with a sorrow great,*
> *A brother George had met his fate,*
> *A hostage he'd become.*
>
> *She begged for George to be let go,*
> *But captor did not want it so,*
> *"I'll trade a life for his," he said.*
> *"If you resist then he'll be dead.*
> *And so, to her, she had no choice.*

Valentine studied the poem, puzzled. "What is he writing?" he said out loud; his voice sounded hollow and forsaken in Solomon's room. "Where have you gone?" He walked to the armoire and looked at the costumes. Everything was in such disarray; he could not tell what was missing, if anything. He searched through the clothes. Each one reminded him of a role that Solomon had played: the forlorn lover in a romantic comedy, a ship's captain in a melodrama. His hand stopped. Something was missing. Valentine tried remembering other roles Solomon played and then realized that the costume of an upper class gentleman in an English farce was missing. "For Christsake, not that old theatrical role, again."

Valentine went back to the desk and rummaged around. He found the two pistols and stuffed them in his pants. He remembered Solomon's heated words: *I have a mission to accomplish.*

"What mission would have you dressed as an Englishman?" he pondered. Valentine blew out the light and closed the door behind him.

☃

Ripley wharf –evening

When the cold spell broke and the weather turned warm, fog blanketed the ground so thick it was hard to see beyond a few yards. The thaw left slush underfoot. The wharf was now muddy and slippery. The mud caked Solomon's polished boots as he paced back and forth. Mud spotted the hem of his finery: his thinly lined, wool topcoat, and checkered silk waistcoat and shirt.

He had chosen his appearance carefully. A flowing mustache blended with his closely trimmed beard, and a dark-brown wig matched them. Then he purposely added a touch of powder to his short sideburns to give him the appearance of age. He then walked from one end of Ripley to the other, testing out his new appearance. The affect was worth the effort. He was a mature, upper class Englishman who was touring the backcountry of

America. Of course he admitted to himself, the fog helped conceal his youthfulness.

The ferry captain, whose face was a criss-cross of deep wrinkles from sun and wind, released thick plumes of pipe smoke that mingled with the haze of fog drifting up from the river. Solomon unfurled a scented handkerchief and delicately placed it over his nose to lessen the offending smells that wafted from the nearby animal pens and the noxious aroma of the ferry captain's pipe. He continued to pace the dock impatiently, waiting for Leona to appear. Captain Julius and Tom were probably on the river, unavailable. Solomon was lucky to find a ferry to take him to Kentucky.

"How long we gonna wait?" the ferry captain said, watching Solomon fan his handkerchief beneath his nose.

"Not, long...uh...could you, please smoke down wind?" Solomon coughed.

The ferry captain, sighed, got up from his stool, and moved farther from Solomon. "Ain't use ta good tobacco. Where you from?"

"On the contrary I am used to good tobacco," Solomon countered. "In England we sell some of the finest in the world."

"That a fact." The ferry captain said, noncommittally. "Sorry you don't appreciate ours."

"I'm sure it suits your needs," Solomon retorted, continuing to pace. He began reciting a few lines of poetry aloud to keep his mind off the problem of the rescue:

> *Most wonderful things are we planning to do*
> *Tomorrow,*
> *Clouds dark will give place to a sky filled with blue*
> *Tomorrow,*
> *And hopeful we drift on life's turbulent sea,*

> *Unmindful the while that the fates may decree,*
> *That for us in this world never more will there be*
> *A Tomorrow.*

The captain coughed and spit over board. "That was kinda sad, son. You got anything a little livelier. Sorta take the dark out of the soul, you might say."

"No," Solomon said. He took a silver flask from his pocket and downed the brandy, hoping it would inspire him. He was no closer to figuring out how he would execute the rescue than he was yesterday when he first promised to help the girl.

Where is she?

Solomon and the girl were to meet at eight o'clock on the docks where she was to give him last minute directions to Fowler's house. He had thought of creating a ruse to get into the house, feigning medical assistance because of a wagon accident, or perhaps an attack by marauders—depending on which was most plausible at the time. He would distract the doctor by asking him for assistance.

Then what?

His fingers played with the watch chain on his waistcoat, a habit he had acquired for calming his nerves. He remembered how Valentine had teased him about buying a fob to play with to ease his nervousness. Then Valentine had given him a miniature portrait of his mother as a birthday present to wear on his chain.

Solomon pulled the chain from his pocket and peered into the delicate face of his mother. Even through the dull light from the wharf torches, he could see Arabella's enigmatic smile. Solomon smiled back at her; then remembered his last conversation with Valentine. *He will never let me be the man I truly know I can be.* He shoved the fob back in his pocket. What a fool he had been to think he would hear an apology from Valentine's lips.

"The man thinks he's never wrong. And I can never be right. And therein lies our dilemma," Solomon concluded.

"Ya say somethin'?"

Solomon had forgotten he wasn't alone. "No, my good man. Have you nothing better to do than to watch me?" he said irritably.

"Well...no. Just waitin' for ya ta board, is all."

"In good time, sir, in good time." And Solomon waved the man off with his handkerchief.

The captain squinted through the darkness, "It's just that I seen you somewhere's is all. You sure you ain't from around here?"

"Absolutely not. I've recently arrived in your country," accentuating his English accent. "Having spent time in your eastern states, I'm traveling south to see what lies there," Solomon replied nonchalantly.

The ferry captain scratched his stomach reflectively. "Same thing that lies here I guess. Now me, I go across the river and back. Ain't nothin' on either side worth seeing."

"Well I intend to explore the nether reaches of your world and write my adventures once I return home. Your land has infinite possibilities and vast reaches where no white man has set foot. That, my dear sir, is the land that I wish to see."

"And get your head cut clean from your body by them injun savages? Not me. It's enough of an adventure just to steer this boat to the other side and come out safe and sound without patrollers shootin' you or thieves takin' your cargo. Safe at home with the wife and kids, is what I seek every night. Good meal. Warm bed. Little ones runnin' 'round. That to me is a life," the ferry captain said, puffing reflectively on his pipe.

"And that's all you want?" Solomon persisted.

The ferry captain took another drag from the pipe and watched the smoke intermingle with the fog. "What more is there, other than the love of a good woman? I see all these young men carousing, wantin' adventure, wealth, fame. Ya ask me, ain't nothin' like comin' home to a warm fire and a woman who thinks ya the center of her world."

The captain stretched and stood up. "Well, I'm headin' into the cabin. Take the chill off. You welcome to come in with me."

"I shall stay here, sir. It won't be long." Solomon watched the captain retire and saw a light glow from the cabin.

The love of a good woman. He thought of Delphine. She had a mischievous sense of humor, and enjoyed poetry and literature. In fact, he knew that she was an avid reader. They discussed the works of American and European authors. She was plain, that much was true. Yet when she smiled those bucked and crooked teeth at him, it made him feel as if he were the center of her world.

Delphine was rich, and that was an asset. *Could I love her? Would it be so difficult?* He stood on the dock in the misty air, watched the fog swirl around him, and pondered those questions.

CHAPTER TWENTY-ONE

Outside Maysville, Kentucky— Dr. Fowler's home—same time

𝓢lade had pulled up a chair and was sitting in the corner of the cellar with a handkerchief over his nostrils. The stench from the boy and the smell from the chloroform was overpowering in the closed space. He hoped the smell wouldn't permeate his clothes. He would give anything for a smoke just to mask the smell.

Fowler didn't seem to notice the stench of excrement and urine coming from the boy as he took his pulse.

"How much did you give him?" Slade asked.

"Enough to keep him quiet. Just checking to see if his pulse is steady." Fowler let go of the boy's wrist and it dropped limply.

Slade saw where the chains around the boy's naked ankles had cut into his flesh. "How long do you think it'll take them?" Fowler asked as he surveyed his instruments on the table.

Slade did not tell Fowler that Leona was not coming. She would have only complicated the situation and been witness to murder, since he did not intend to keep the brother alive. "I give them an hour or two," he lied. "I've asked the authorities to come 'round in the morning."

"What if they don't come?...Leona...I mean." Fowler asked anxiously.

Slade shrugged. "Well, we get rid of the boy. I told her that either she brings the Raven, or else her brother dies. I doubt if she'll risk that. And if the authorities come and don't find anything, we'll just say, it was a false alarm."

Fowler clapped his hands together gleefully, while mumbling incoherently under his breath. If the boy was the worst for wear, so was Fowler. His eyes were sunken, his face ghostly white.

"Might I suggest you go back to your office and prepare?" Slade added.

Fowler whirled around. "You will not harm her. She is mine."

"Yes, sir. No harm will come to her. "Once I capture the Raven, we'll chain him and wait for the authorities.

"And what of the boy? Can I keep the boy?" Fowler asked, eagerly.

"We'll get rid of him before the authorities come tomorrow. If they know we kidnapped another man's property, we'll be guilty of slave stealing. There should be no evidence of him at all."

"Yes, yes. I understand perfectly. Yesterday Mercer rode over with a few men and knocked on my door. He asked me if I'd seen George. I told him that the boy was probably lured by his sister into running. He said that might be, but there were two of 'um missing, George and another fellow. He figures the other musta followed."

"Then that's good. They'll be on the look-out for two boys."

Fowler rubbed his hands together and walked around the unconscious George as if he were appraising a prize horse. "Do you think their organs function like ours?"

"Frankly, I don't know and don't care. That's your profession, not mine."

"Their brain capacity must be smaller than ours. I wonder what their brain looks like. You know, I read somewhere that…"

"Dr. Fowler, it's getting late and we need to be prepared."

"Yes, you're right, Mr. Jackson. Absolutely right. I shall go now," he said, clutching the lantern and moving toward Slade who squinted from the glare.

"You're blinding me."

"I'd like to take a look at that hand sometime."

Slade reflexively, slid his hand away. "Not now."

"Yes, yes some other time then. I will go now and prepare."

With that, Fowler climbed the stairs and opened the cellar door, letting in the cold, clean air. He shut it and left Slade in the dark to suffocate from the stench of George.

Slade wondered, not for the first time, if Fowler would be capable of pulling off the trap. Fowler's mind was so gone from the constant use of chloroform, that one wrong word or movement could foul up their whole plan. Fowler might be more of a liability than an asset. *And what will he do when he finds out the slave girl is not part of the package?* Slade vowed that if Fowler spoiled his chances for revenge, he'd kill the man.

⊗

Riley, Ohio—same time

Valentine squinted in the fog to see whether there were others on the street. This was a desolate part of town even without the enveloping fog. Foot and horse traffic was minimal here unless you had business with the local coffin maker. Yet, Valentine was still careful. He stood in the doorway and waited, looking around to see if anyone saw him. In Ripley, everyone was a possible spy for the southern sympathizers.

He rapped twice on the door then paused and rapped again. He heard the shuffle of feet from the inside. The door opened a slit to reveal, by lantern light, the sun burnt countenance of Captain Julius. When the captain saw Valentine, he opened the heavy wooden door all the way and ushered Valentine into the dimly-lit room of the coffin maker's shop.

The men huddled around a light set atop one of the plain wooden coffins that occupied the shop floor. Grinder was in the center of them hunched over a map; his gnarled fingers tracing the contours of the banks of the Ohio River.

In Valentine's memory, this was the first time that all the abolitionists had gathered as a group, and the first time Valentine revealed himself as one of them. He glanced at the men, who returned his gaze, then quickly looked away. Besides Captain Julius and Tom, who were seated in the corner, there was Tom Collins, the coffin maker, and the apothecary, John Dunst. Everyone in Ripley knew Congregationalist minister, John Rankin; and, Valentine believed that the young men standing next to Rankin were two of his sons.

The only colored man besides himself was John Parker. Parker was a free man and worked in the iron foundry. His home was on the banks of the river—an advantageous spot for fugitive slaves to hide. Parker nodded, acknowledging Valentine, and looked back at the map. These men volunteered to rescue slaves and risk their lives in the process. Now they all were working together.

"Everyone *ist* here, now," Grinder said, looking around. He coughed to clear his throat. "Ve know de slaves vill be taken to a place five miles east of Maysville. De *Annabelle ist* due there in four days. Captain Julius will take us across. Right, captain?"

The captain nodded.

Rankin spoke up. "What do we do once we come to the encampment?"

"When de men asleep. Den you free de slaves, *ja*?"

"But where will the slaves go? There's nothing but river, woods, and the town. They'll just get caught again unless they can cross over," one of Rankin's sons protested.

Grinder shrugged. "Maybe dey get away. Dis de best ve can do. There're too many of dem to get across safely. Ve free dem. Once da slaves free, Captain Julius and Tom will pick all of you up."

"If there's a problem?" Parker spoke in a low baritone.

Grinder looked at all of them. "You got weapons? You use dem."

"Grinder, where did you get this information about the place and time? We were led to believe it would be a much longer march. This is less than a few miles out of town," Tom Collins questioned.

Grinder smiled, showing yellow crooked teeth. "Ephraim Mercer likes his liquor. I made sure he had plenty. He say dey too risky to walk slaves farther. Dey picked dis spot." Grinder emphasized his point by jabbing his finger in the map. Rankin looked up, frowning.

"If we get caught, that'll be the end of us."

"Den don't get caught," Grinder retorted.

The men agreed to meet back in three days to cross over to Kentucky near Maysville where they would lay low. Then on the fourth day, they would invade the encampment.

Everyone disbursed, leaving Grinder and Valentine alone in the room. Grinder was folding up his map when he asked. "Vere *ist* da boy?"

Valentine shook his head.

"I don't know. I saw him earlier today when he came to the shop. We had another argument. I went to his room before coming here, but he wasn't there. So, I took his pistols. I'm doing this alone." Valentine said, laying the pistols on the table. "There is no more Raven."

ⱳ

The uproar in the Greene household had delayed Leona, who now raced to the dock. That morning Essie woke up in a foul mood, most likely because she had an awful headache and a bad stomach from consuming too much Christmas punch. Mrs. Greene chastised Essie about being sick on the most important occasion of the season. Essie then lashed out at Leona and gave her additional chores, having conveniently forgotten that the reason Leona served the punch was that Essie had gotten drunk.

Then Miss Delphine, who had been waiting all afternoon for Mr. Tucker to appear, realized he was not going to show and took to her room. Mr. and Mrs. Greene fussed over their distraught niece. Tea had to be made. A special dinner had to be served. A cold compress had to be administered; and Essie, who wasn't about to put herself out, had Leona do the work. Only after all of them had retired was Leona able to sneak out, knowing that she would never return.

When she told Solomon Tucker about her brother's capture, he told her that as the Raven, it was his duty to set her brother free. He had been so confident, so reassuring and yet she knew she was sending him into a trap.

She raced through town and stopped only once in front of the Razor's Edge, but the lights were out and she saw no sign of Valentine. What would she have said anyway? He was a man who seemed so far above her that she could not conceive of him ever understanding her plight. She was saving her brother's life and sending another man to his death. How could someone like Valentine Kass, a free black man, understand her peril?

Leona lingered a moment in front of the shop, her hand resting on the doorknob. She wanted to see him again, to tell him everything. She wished he would hold her in his arms and make her believe that things would work out. Instead, she released her grip on the knob and headed onward. Her shoes squished in the mud as she skirted the open market area to the wharf. She saw the figure of Solomon Tucker through the veil of fog.

"Mr. Tucker, sir. Mr. Tucker." Her voice carried on the wind. He turned around as she breathlessly ran to him.

"I'm sorry I'm late."

He took her aside and whispered. "I'm traveling under the name of Edwin Fitzhugh."

"Yes, sir."

"I will rent a wagon from a Maysville livery and proceed to the Fowler place. I'll need directions."

Leona bit her lip in concentration. "It about two miles out of town. The cut is to the left. I think you follow that around and...uh...you gonna see a white house and behind it a barn. "How will you get my brother?" she asked nervously.

"I plan to knock on the door," he quipped.

"That it?" Leona fidgeted nervously.

"You have a better plan?" he countered, irritably.

"I...no..." Leona lowered her head with a sense of dejection.

Solomon softened his tone. "All right then. You say your brother was being held in the cellar?"

"Yes, sir."

"Where'd you get your information?"

She nervously averted her eyes. "I heard from...someone who...who come from Maysville."

"But who?" Solomon insisted.

"Uh, just some men talkin'. One of 'um was braggin' on the fact he caught him a coupla slave boys. One said it was my brother. He..he...was tellin' the other about...about how they looked. It was my brother. "

Solomon was becoming apprehensive. The success of his plan depended on Leona supplying him with accurate information. *Suppose, it wasn't true? Suppose they didn't have her brother?* His stomach tightened and he felt lightheaded. He twirled the watch fob. *If he could have only told Valentine his plan. Valentine would know what to do.*

The ferry captain emerged from the cabin. He scowled at Leona. "This who you been waitin' for all this time?"

"Yes, my housekeeper."

"Ahh uh, she got papers saying she's free?"

"She's not going with us. Only me. She...she came to give me information."

"Where're your bags?"

"Bags sir?"

"Yeah...clothes...things you put on? You doin' all this travelin' around, don't ya need clothes?"

"They was stolen sir," Leona piped up. "We's taken the railroad and those folks done lost all we had. That's why I'm late. Was gonna buy some things, but don't seem like none of the stores open."

"Quite so," Solomon added. "The scoundrels had the nerve to tell us that we'd misplaced them. And all along we had entrusted our worldly possessions in their care. Your system of transportation is inadequate. Now I shall have to buy what I need."

The captain sucked on his cold pipe. "Well, ain't that curious," he said, untying the rope from the dock.

Solomon steered Leona out of earshot of the captain. "Continue, tell me where everyone is in the house."

Leona sensed Solomon's anxiety. "Fowler don't go to bed 'til late sometimes. He probably in his office with his medicine that he takes that makes him crazy."

"What kind of medicine?"

"I don't know. It's in a bottle. He use it to put the patients to sleep. But he take it too and talk and act funny afterwards. Missus always up in her room, upstairs and to the right. The cellar is on the side where the barn is, near the field. That's where he said my brother is."

"I thought you said that you overheard a conversation."

"Yes, no..I..." In that moment she knew she couldn't let him go further. She had trusted that the slave catcher had her brother and would set him free, but that could be a lie. If her brother was with Fowler, he'd more than likely be dead and she'd be sending Solomon to his death. She grabbed Solomon's sleeve.

"Don't go," she whispered urgently.

"What?"

"It's a trap. He made me do it."

Solomon thrust her out of earshot. "Tell me what you know," he whispered urgently. The whole story tumbled out at one time.

"He...he say he make sure Dr. Fowler don't hurt my brother no more if I get him the Raven. He say if I don't, my brother's a dead man. I told him I knew who the Raven was, but I don't say your name. I figured he cain't kill you 'fore I could get you over there."

"Well, that's awfully considerate of you," Solomon said sarcastically.

She looked away. "You go to Dr. Fowler's, they gonna capture you or...kill you and maybe kill my brother too," she added weakly.

Solomon grabbed her by her shoulders and shook her. "Who told you?" He demanded.

She gasped at Solomon's abruptness. Leona recovered herself and continued. "He don't give me his name, but he a slave catcher. He got dark hair and thin. Like you looked when..when...you come to the jail to get me. He look like that. Look like when he look at you, he can see right through you. He wear this hat to the side ...and ...and ...he got this funny smell. This medicine smell, like you smelled when you got me from the jail."

"Slade! Damn!"

Leona cried. "He say he don't want me. Once I get you to Kentucky, he don't need me, but say if I double cross him, he gonna make sure my brother dies and he gonna hunt me down."

"Do you know if your brother is even *in* that house?"

"I..." she stopped crying and thought. "No, sir. He just say Fowler got him in the cellar. That's what he told me."

Solomon snapped the chain on his watch fob. "Now what?" he puzzled aloud. He pulled on his broken watch chain and handed it and the fob to her. "If I don't come back by tomorrow then find an old man, a grinder and tell him what I did, you hear? He's an old German man with a beard."

"But...but, what if I cain't find him? What if he ain't here?"

Solomon thought. "Then give the fob to Mr. Valentine Kass. Do you know him? He is the barber at the Razor's Edge."

"Yes sir," Leona took the fob in bewilderment. "Yes, I know Va...Mr. Kass."

"If you can't find Grinder, tell Valentine what has transpired. He will have connections."

Leona looked up at Solomon, puzzled. "Mr. Kass?"

Solomon put his hands on her shoulders. "This is information that I am giving you in secret. You must never reveal what I've said—to anyone."

"Yes, sir. I understand, sir."

"Once you've delivered the message you must leave Ripley and go to Cincinnati. There may be a chance that Slade will come back for you. He'll then be searching all the routes around here. In Cincinnati find a Quaker by the name of Levi Coffin who will help you. You will find his shop and ask to board passage out of the city to the next station. Do you understand?"

Leona nodded her head.

"And who is the man you are to ask for?"

"Levi Coffin, a Quaker."

"Good, well..." Solomon took a deep breath and let it out slowly. "I suppose it's time." He stepped onto the ferry and looked back at Leona who stood forlornly on the dock. "Anything else you need to tell me?"

Leona shook her head. "No sir, good luck sir. And thank you."

"By the way, how is Miss Delphine?"

"Miss Delphine fit to be tied when you didn't show up. Upset herself mightily."

"She was?"

"Yes, sir. She take a great store in you."

"She was that upset, really?" He smiled, flattered.

"Yes, sir. I tells her you musta gone on a business trip in a hurry, like. Couldn't get no word to her. That kinda stopped her from cryin'."

"Really?"

"Says she rather spend time with the school teacher if she gonna have someone always comin' and goin' like, not leavin' word where he is or what he doin'."

"The school teacher? That ignorant buffoon. The man can't cite a decent line of poetry."

"Yes, sir. That's what I tell her. I tell her that Mr. Tucker know mor'n the school teacher. And he nicer lookin'."

"Well, thank you for your good taste," Solomon preened.

"But she say if the cats away the mice will play."

"Why that...that...that...brazen little vixen."

છ

CHAPTER TWENTY-TWO

Maysville, Kentucky—later that evening

When Solomon alighted from the ferry he saw that the Kentucky wharf was abuzz with activity at that late hour. Men carried torches as they searched among the cargo and boarded the boats. Solomon watched as they methodically made their way from one boat to another. They were looking for someone, possibly a runaway since they usually hid near the wharf on the chance they could jump on a boat.

"We got another one," a patroller shouted, then grabbed a black boy and pulled him from a boat.

"You get over there with the others," he ordered.

Every boy who was a certain height and age was asked to line up on the wharf. Several men on horseback watched the process as one by one the sleeping black boys were awakened from their berths and made to stand in the cold. A huge black man carrying a torch ran up to a white man on horseback.

"I think we got them all, Massa," the huge black man said, in deference to the young white one on horseback. Solomon recognized his Underground compatriot.

"Good job, Jubba," the rider said, as he took the torch and road toward the line of boys. "The Raven may have brought them here."

"Yes, Massa," Jubba said, then he too road off.

At the word "Raven," Solomon concentrated on Ephraim Mercer who was holding a torch outward to examine the boys. Mercer slowly rode down the line. Several boys were visibly nervous. Solomon could see them quaking.

"You know a nigger boy named George?" Mercer asked. He was greeted with silence. "What about a boy named Thor?"

Again only silence and foot shoveling.

"They are my slaves and I believe they were either kidnapped or ran away. I have reason to believe they are trying to cross," Mercer shouted.

None of the boys answered, but Mercer caught a movement and ordered one boy to step out of line.

"You, what's your name?"

"John, Massa," he mumbled, lowering his head to avoid eye contact.

"All right, John. You seem to be bright. You know a boy named George or one named Thor?"

John shook his head, "No sir, don't know nobody by them names."

"Who do you belong to?"

The boy pointed to his right toward a pirogue. "That my boss' boat.

"George is taller than you. He has a stubbly beard. Thor is tall and thin with a shaven head."

"No sir, we just come from upriver, sir."

"Step back in line," Mercer ordered and continued moving down the line. Mercer pulled several more boys out of the line and questioned them, but none of them gave him the information he wanted. He was almost to the end of the line when one boy looked around and gauged the distance between him and the cut in the road that led from the dock. Before Mercer could get to him, he bolted, dashed passed Solomon, scurried around crates and bales, and headed toward the woods. As if on cue and of one mind, the rest of the boys scattered, causing a diversion and confusion. The patrollers chased boys in all directions.

"That one's not mine. Catch him if you must, but I'll not pay for him," Mercer shouted after the pursuing patrollers.

Solomon caught Mercer's eye and nodded. "I say sir, you lost your slaves?"

Mercer reined in his horse. "Yes, sir I did. And when I find them, they'll be sold off with the rest of the lying, thieving lot. And you sir, what is your business? "

"Adventure. I'm an adventurer from England."

"Well, welcome to our fair land."

"I could not help but overhear that a bird has taken your slaves?" Solomon said innocently.

"No sir, a damned abolitionist who calls himself the Raven."

"And when you catch them, you plan to sell them?"

Mercer impatiently steadied his horse. "You English don't hold to slavery. I'd advise you to keep your opinions to yourself around here," Mercer snapped.

Solomon bowed. "I am not here to cause trouble."

"Make sure that you don't. We don't like people interfering with our business."

Mercer was about to leave when Solomon shouted after him. "Sir, I'm looking for a horse and wagon. Can you point me to a livery?"

Mercer pointed straight ahead. "Over there, but the pickings are slim. A group of men are using every conveyance to get to Gibbon's Farm."

"Thank you." Solomon bowed again and walked toward the livery where he found a sleepy stable boy who rented him a horse and wagon.

 લુ

Fowler's Home—later

Slade was dozing in the cellar when he was awakened abruptly by a noise. His eyes adjusted to the dim light from the lantern. His fingers tightened on the trigger of his gun. But all he heard was the pitiful moaning of the boy, George.

Upstairs in his office, Fowler also heard a noise, but he assumed it was the clock in the front parlor ticking off the seconds. He had nodded off after another whiff of the chloroform, and was now slumped over his desk. The house was quiet except for the field mice scurrying across the floor. He could even hear his own uneven breathing as he struggled to control his excitement.

When the clock struck the hour, Fowler jumped and let out a gasp. He tried to keep his mind from racing. He slowed his breathing and willed his muscles to relax, but he kept wondering if something had gone wrong. *She should be here by now. Why hasn't she come?*

Fowler got up and walked around the desk. He dared to peak out the window at the darkness beyond and saw nothing, not even a hint of movement. Then, out of the corner of his eye, he saw a flicker and peered more intently in the darkness until his mind was able to register what he was seeing. He forgot about the trap, flung open his office door and screamed: "Fire!"

 લુ

Slade heard Fowler's scream and heaved the wooden cellar door open with his shoulder. He saw Fowler racing, arms waving, trying to halt the stampeding horses. Then he saw the barn burning and watched as Fowler stopped and veered to the right where the water pump stood. Fowler frantically pumped and raced toward the barn with a bucket of water, splashing most of it on the ground.

Already a third of the building was in flames, and the horses, including his own, were racing at breakneck speed through the woods. Slade ran to help Fowler as he pumped more water into the bucket. It was only after three trips to the pump that he realized they had been duped. The fire was only a distraction to get them away from the cellar.

Slade doubled back to the cellar and found the door closed. He whipped out his pistol and pointed it blindly in the dark as he stumbled down the wooden stairs. He heard a scratching sound and saw a flicker of light.

Solomon Tucker sat with his legs crossed opposite George in the chair where Slade had been sitting. He was holding a Lucifer that illuminated his smile like a jack-o-lantern. "What took you so long?"

Slade was speechless.

"Seriously, I would have thought you wouldn't have fallen for a common trick like that. Well, I suppose there's always the first time." Solomon uncrossed his legs. "I don't know what you did to this poor boy, but he's unconscious and smells like wallowing hogs. I'd ask you to come and join me, but really the stench is overpowering in here. Why don't we move outside where we can have fun watching the good doctor save his barn although I think he will not be amused," Solomon gazed at the Lucifer as it burned down to the tips of his fingers then he blew it out. Both men were plunged back into darkness.

"You wouldn't by any chance have another light, would you? This place is rather dreary and I'm sure young George would appreciate it. Once he comes to."

"Get up and step slow and careful toward the boy," Slade ordered.

Solomon groped in the darkness and stumbled and crashed into a chair. "Damn, I'm having a devil of a time maneuvering. A light please would be most helpful."

Slade felt along the earthen wall and carefully stepped down to search for a lantern. When he found it, he realized he'd put himself in an awkward position. In order to light the lantern, he had to put down his gun.

"Here allow me," Solomon said, his voice close enough that it startled Slade.

Solomon struck another Lucifer. He took the lantern away from Slade to light it. A pale yellow circle of light bloomed in the dark. "There now, that's much better. I presume that the doctor will be joining us shortly. Why don't we make ourselves comfortable," he said, stepping toward the table and resting the lantern on it.

Slade followed Solomon deeper into the cellar. "Who are you?"

Solomon bowed with a flourish. "The Raven, at your service."

Slade's eyes narrowed to slits. "I swear I'll kill you if you make fun of me."

"Oh love, didn't know you were so sensitive. I swear to you, I am the Raven. That's who you were expecting, wasn't it?"

"You're lying. You're a foreigner," Slade said, looking around again as if to find someone else lurking in the cellar.

Solomon rolled his eyes. "How many times must I tell you, I *am* the Raven. What more do you need? I am the dark knight that rescues slaves...a spirit sent to lead them home and so on...and so on..." Solomon reached into his pocket, then halted, as he saw Slade's gun focused on him, and then slowly pulled out his flask. He held it up so Slade could see. "Brandy, sir. I'm dying of thirst. I'd offer you some," he said as he took a swallow. "But I'm not inclined to be generous to a man who has a gun on me."

"Your name?"

"The Raven."

"Your real name before I shoot you and end this game."

Just then Fowler came stumbling down the stairs breathless, and covered in soot. "Why are you just standing here? My barn. My buggy. My horses." Fowler stopped and looked at Slade and Solomon illuminated in the circle of light. "Who is he?"

"That's what I'm trying to find out, if you'll let me," Slade barked.

Solomon turned to Fowler. "How do you do. I'm the man who burned your barn. I am the Ra..."

But before Solomon uttered the last syllable, Fowler ignited like gunpowder and exploded toward him. Slade aimed his gun and fired off a shot that echoed dully off the earthen walls, stopping Fowler in mid-stride.

"Leave him alone until we can get down to the bottom of this. Slade moved toward Solomon. "Who helps you?"

"I work alone."

"I'll teach you to toy with me," Slade raised the gun again. Solomon braced himself for another gun blast.

"For God sakes, what do I care whether he is or isn't the Raven," Fowler ranted. "I want the girl. Have him tell us where the girl is."

"Don't you see?" Slade said. "He is an imposter. Look at his clothes, his manner. He hasn't seen a good days work in ages. Look at his hands. They're like a woman's. This man is not the Raven."

"I don't care!" Fowler shouted. "You think I'm going to pay you money for him?" He moved between Slade and Solomon. "Where's the girl?" he demanded.

Slade forcefully pushed him out of the way.

Fowler pitched forward and caught himself before he fell. "You've stolen my money," he whimpered.

"Why don't you go upstairs to your wife," Slade coaxed.

"To my wife?" Fowler emitted a high pitched laugh. "That ugly sow? Where's Leona?"

"Maybe someone saw Leona in Maysville," Slade said nonchalantly.

"You will look for her won't you?" Fowler's eyes pleaded.

"When I go into town, tomorrow."

"She's not in town," Solomon interjected.

Fowler turned on Solomon. "How would you know? Where is she then?" He looked from one man to the other.

Solomon smiled. "Why don't you ask Mr. Slade again?"

Slade kept his eyes on Solomon.

Solomon taunted, "Go on, tell him the girl wasn't part of the deal. You wanted the Raven and for that you bargained with the girl. So..." Solomon raised his arms, "...here I am, at your service."

Fowler flew into another rage. "Not here? What do you mean she's not here?"

"I hate repeating myself, Solomon replied, feigning boredom. "The girl, Leona, did not come with me. I came alone on a mission of mercy to save poor George here from the hands of kidnapping slave stealers," he looked from one to the other, "...which I presume are the two of you."

"She was part of our agreement. You promised me Leona." Fowler swung wildly at Slade. Slade backhanded him with the gun, knocking Fowler sideways into the table. Fowler grabbed a scalpel before he went down.

"My dear Slade, your reputation as a violent man is well-earned."

Fowler looked up at Solomon. "What did you call him?"

"Slade, that's his name," Solomon repeated.

What color there was in Fowler's face drained as he sprang to his feet, clutching the scalpel in his hand. Spittle flew from his mouth as he attacked. "You! The same man who kidnapped her from the jail? You are the one who helped her escape? What have you done to dear Leona? What have you done to her?"

Fowler slashed at Slade's face, leaving a red slit across his temple, and stepped back to attack again when Slade fired four shots into Fowler, sending his body ricocheting off the table and onto the floor. In the aftermath, the silence was deafening. Both Solomon and Slade watched Fowler's body twitch then slip into death.

Slade turned the gun on Solomon. "Now, about you and that nigger."

Solomon backed up and shoved his hand into his top coat pocket. He grasped a wet handkerchief and pulled it out, dabbing it on his face and then waving it in front of Slade's. "Love, look at me. I'm positively sweating like a peasant."

"I'll get rid of the boy then wait till the authorities come and take you away."

"I wouldn't do that if I were you."

"And why not?

"Well love, George here is the way you got the Raven...I mean trapped me. If you get rid of the boy, then what reason would the Raven have had for attempting a rescue?" Solomon let that sink in, then added waving the handkerchief. "On the other hand, if you don't get rid of the boy, then you'll be accused of kidnapping. Of course, the dead doctor would have been your witness, but now that he's gone, well, that just leaves my word against yours."

"The reward for the Raven is alive...or dead."

"Yes, that's true. But who is to say that I am the Raven? I mean, after all, you don't even believe me. And if you don't, then why should the authorities? No, I'm afraid, you're in a quandary."

Slade moved forward holding the gun inches from Solomon's chest. "Whoever you are, you will be dead before the sun rises. I will get rid of the boy and I will tell the authorities that you tried to rescue him and in the process, burned the barn and killed Dr. Fowler."

They heard a bump above them. Slade looked up and inadvertently lowered his gun. This was Solomon's chance. He leaped forward and grabbed Slade's gun hand. With his other hand, he thrusts a chloroform-drenched handkerchief over Slade's nose. Solomon pressed harder while Slade struggled to get free.

While Fowler and Slade had been distracted by the fire, Solomon entered the cellar and realized that he would not be able to unshackle George without a key. He looked around the table and found Dr. Fowler's chloroform. It was the medicine that Leona referred to that made Fowler "act funny." Solomon knew the medicine well. He had been invited to enough sniffing parties in Philadelphia. Solomon soaked his handkerchief in the anesthesia and waited for his chance to use it.

Now, he felt Slade's body go slack and at the same time heard more noises upstairs. *Could the authorities be here?*

Solomon dragged the unconscious Slade to a chair and dumped him in it. He rifled Slade's pockets but found nothing. Solomon turned his attention to Fowler. He took a deep breath then knelt down beside the dead doctor's body. Blood was still oozing from Fowler's wounds. Solomon searched the doctor's pockets and found a set of keys. One of them had to unlock George's chains, he hoped. More noises came from upstairs. Solomon hurried over to George and fumbled with the keys until he found the right one. He unlocked the chains from around George and shackled the unconscious Slade.

"The slave catcher becomes the slave. The irony," he said picking up Slade's gun and shoving it in his pocket.

CHAPTER TWENTY-THREE

Fowler's Home—December 27

Solomon cocked his head to one side and heard George's uneven breathing. "Wake up. Wake up,"

But the boy did not respond.

"Come on, love. Don't let them get you. Show them what you've got."

Still George did not respond.

"We've got to get out of here." Solomon gently slapped George's face to revive him. He heard George mumble something and let out a sigh. "Well at least you're not dead. That's a mark for our side. Now let's get you to your feet and out of here," Solomon said, as he hauled George up, but the boy was dead weight.

"Leave me alone," George murmured. "Let me die," he said, struggling weakly.

"You're not going to die; but I need you to move. Put one foot in front of the other."

George could only sob.

"Look, don't give up," Solomon said, desperate to calm the boy for fear his own doubts would get the better of him. "All we have to do is get out of this cellar before we get caught. I've got a horse and wagon in the woods." The boy moved one foot forward, then the other.

"Can you stand on your own?" George wavered a moment, but then stood his ground. Solomon turned back, retrieved Slade's gun, and stuffed it in his pocket. He grabbed George, half-walking, half-carrying him.

The barn was still in flames as they stumbled out of the cellar and onto the ground. Solomon heaved George up. They struggled blindly through the woods in search of the wagon and horse that Solomon had left tied to a tree. They had gone a half mile from Fowler's when Solomon heard the horse whinnying, and headed in the direction of the sound. By now, Solomon's eyes were adjusting to the dark. He was able to distinguish the outlines of trees, stumps, and branches before he and George tripped face first on the muddy ground.

"Just a few steps more and we'll be there. There's the horse and wagon I came in," he said, lurching forward.

George was breathing heavily. "I...I...cain't....go..."

"Yes you can," Solomon said forcibly. "We've got to make headway."

They made their way forward in the darkness. Once Solomon found the wagon, he removed his coat, wrapped it around George, and fairly dumped the boy in the back. Solomon untied the reins and climbed on top of the seat. He ripped off the brown wig and threw it in the underbrush. Then he closed his eyes, grabbed the false beard and mustache he had glued on and ripped them from his face. The searing pain made his eyes water and he gasped.

"My God!" he cried out. His chin and cheeks felt raw and he could swear he tasted blood from his peeling lips. He called over his shoulder. "How are you?" while wiping the tears from his eyes. George moaned underneath the coat.

"Have heart love, we'll be safely across in no time," he said with as much enthusiasm as he could muster.

Solomon lashed the reins so the horse could maneuver the wagon around and back down the trail. He looked at the brightening sky and hoped they could put distance between Slade and themselves before the sun rose. They would have to abandon the wagon eventually and take to the woods on foot.

ଓଃ

Ripley, Ohio—same time

Streaks of pink colored the sky as if someone had scratched the night. It was almost dawn, but still dark enough for the workers to carry torches as they loaded cargo.

The night before, Leona watched as Solomon's ferry disappeared across the water to Kentucky. She then left the wharf and huddled among the bales of hay in a livery stable. The sounds of the horses and livestock lulled her into a light, fitful sleep until she heard the stable boy arrive. Then she snuck out and wandered the wharf.

Leona briefly thought about finding the man called the Grinder, but it was much too early. Solomon and George still had many hours left to cross over before she sounded the alarm. They had until evening to return, but she was anxious.

By now Essie had awakened and found her missing. She wondered if the Greenes would look for her. She would have to hide soon before the sun was fully up. It wouldn't do for her to be caught. How would she explain why she left without giving away the fact that she was a runaway? No, it would not do for her to be caught. She stood bundled in her shawl on the wharf, and absentmindedly played with Solomon's watch fob.

ଓଃ

Farther down the wharf Valentine was also gazing across the languid Ohio River at Kentucky. The smoke from his cheroot blew back in his face as he contemplated his fate and those of his fellow rescuers. In three days, they would be mounting their largest rescue, as far as he knew. He was thinking what all of them had been thinking—that someone was surely going to die. Images of the bodies, black and white, lying on the ground invaded his mind. He could almost hear the screams of slaves as they dashed back and forth in their attempts to escape the mayhem. He saw chaos.

Valentine drew deeply on his cheroot and closed his eyes to will the images from his mind. Suddenly an image of Mary George appeared. He saw her sensuous smile, the tilt of her head, and the wisps of hair that framed her face. He felt the light cool touch of her hands, and the way she hid them because she was ashamed of their roughness. He held out his own hands; hands that she said were too soft and smooth to be of use.

The streaks of pink in the sky bloomed into crimson. Agitated, Valentine crushed his cheroot underfoot and wandered down the wharf, hoping to release some of the pent up anxiety he was feeling. He did not see Mary George until he was several feet from her. He watched her gazing across the river; but, he hesitated, not knowing how to approach her. He almost turned away when she turned around, startled to see him. Valentine smiled and stepped forward.

"What are you doing out so early?" he managed to blurt. She looked down, saying nothing.

He rushed on. "Uh, I assumed you'd be cleaning up after the festivities.

She averted her eyes.

Valentine stepped closer. "This is no place for a woman," he said, taking her elbow good-naturedly.

She pulled away from him. "I...I...have to...uh wait for...someone."

"Well, not here, unless you're looking for thieves and scoundrels. Come, let's go back to the shop. I'll make you some tea or coffee and you can get warm," he insisted.

"No, please...I..."

"Oh, I see. You're having a secret liaison," he teased. "Well, whoever he is, he needs to be horsewhipped for deserting you like this. Come on, you're shivering," he said, holding her hand in his. He felt the warmth flood through his body.

"No, sir. I...I must be going." She dashed off without a glance back. Valentine frowned, puzzled by her curt response. He watched as she disappeared around the corner. He turned around and walked back to his shop to have a cup of coffee and mull over Mary George's reaction. *Did I say something wrong?* he wondered as he opened the door to see a nervous Joseph Greene.

"Where have you been, Val?" Greene said, petulantly. "I've been waiting." Valentine shrugged out of his coat and hung it up. "Been down by the river getting some fresh air."

"Humph, you call that fowl stench that blows off the river, fresh?"

Valentine was in no mood, "What can I do for you, Joseph?" he said wearily, lining up his razors.

"I need to ask you a favor," Joseph said, blinking behind his glasses. "It's about my niece. You see, she's rather upset and I thought that you might...well, you might be the person to intercede."

"Intercede?"

Joseph fidgeted with his clothes, looked out the window, then back at Valentine. "It's about Solomon. Apparently, my niece has taken a liking to him."

"Isn't that what you hoped?" Valentine said, bemused while pouring himself coffee. He offered a cup to Joseph. Joseph shook his head, declining.

"I just want to get to the bottom of this."

Valentine sat in his barber chair, legs stretched out and sipped the steaming liquid from his tin cup. "Go on; your niece and Solomon."

"It was going quite well, actually. And he seemed interested in her."

Valentine made no comment.

"Well, he was supposed to come over and he never made an appearance."

"That sounds like Solomon," Valentine said, sarcastically and then added. "He tends to be forgetful at times, especially when he's in the middle of writing something." He blew on his coffee. "I saw Solomon briefly yesterday or maybe it was the day before," Valentine frowned, remembering the painful confrontation between them.

Joseph glanced at Valentine, sheepishly. "I don't suppose you could, I mean, go over to the inn and well, sort of ask around…"

"Joseph, I'll not interfere in his personal life."

"I know the two of you had a disagreement," Joseph confessed, holding his hand up to stop Valentine from interrupting. "But after what happened—and then my girl ups and disappears as well…"

Valentine's hand shook. He spilled coffee in his lap. "What are you talking about? Mary George?" Valentine stood up and grabbed a towel to wipe the wet stain from his pants.

"She's gone. Early this morning or maybe late last night. And then when Solomon..."

"You think that Solomon and your cook girl...?"

Joseph hesitated. "Well, yes. I mean it was the strangest thing. We were listening to him sing. She comes in with punch, takes one look at him, he looks at her, and she spills everything on the floor. What a mess! Punch was over everybody. The guests had to leave the room so she could clean." Joseph continued.

"Then he goes back to the kitchen to talk to her, and when Delphine went back to get him...Delphine told us that they were deep in a discussion. The next thing you know, Solomon doesn't show up. Then Mary George ups and leaves. And she is quite comely, that girl..." his voice trailed off.

"We, the wife and I, have grown quite fond of Delphine and, well it would break her heart to know that she'd been jilted because of a nigger gal and so unseemly..."

Valentine had heard enough. He threw the towel down. "I see. You're not worried about Solomon, just worried whether your niece would be embarrassed. I can assure you that wherever Solomon is, he's not with Mary George or any other *nigger*." He spat out the last word. "And now, if you'll excuse me, I have some work to do."

"But Valentine..." Joseph whined.

Valentine repeated firmly. "Joseph, leave."

Joseph blinked in astonishment. "Well, you needn't get upset over...I mean...he is an *actor*."

Valentine walked to the door and opened it. He waited for Joseph.

"I'm sorry if I...ah...offended you," Joseph mumbled as he walked through the door. Valentine watched Joseph cross the street and head toward his shop. Then Valentine slammed the door and locked it. He grabbed his coat and raced out the back in search of Mary George.

಄

Kentucky Woods—dawn

When the sun came up, Solomon and George had abandoned the horse and wagon to make their way on foot. Their breaths burst in clouds of vapor in the damp, crisp air. With George weighing him down, Solomon's leg muscles ached. He pushed ahead anyway beyond weariness; beyond his self-doubt. The soft ground was sucking at his shoes and the bottom of his pants legs were heavy with caked mud. Even though he wore the thinnest of wool, he was still sweating and was moving on pure adrenaline.

They took to the underbrush and beat back the low-hanging branches and scrub brush to make a path by a stream. There, George collapsed saying he couldn't go on any more and tried as best he could to clean himself in the icy water. Both bedded down a few feet from the road, exhausted.

While they rested, Solomon was alert to every sound, every snap of a branch or rustle in the trees. When they heard the sound of men's voices in the distance, they scrambled deeper in the brush and waited for the men to pass. George breathed heavily beside him.

"How long, you think?" George whispered. Solomon didn't answer; he put his hand to his lips and waited as the men drew closer.

"...ain't no horse can go that far in one day," he heard one man say.

"How much you wanna bet? How much? I done trained enough horses to know I can spot me a racer when I sees it and that horse look to me to be a winner," the second man challenged.

"You thinkin' 'bout askin' the owner if you can be her trainer, Jesse?"

"Thinkin' 'bout it, Russell. Soon's he can think straight. Losin' two slaves done got him all riled up."

"Seem to me, that were a smart move on his part. Lettin' people think we goin' one way, and we headin' in the opposite direction to Dover."

"Yeah, he brung in more armed men to guard the river. Let people believe we gonna board the slaves there."

Solomon heard one of the men groan.

"Hold up a minute. I got to take a shit."

"Again?"

Solomon heard the sound of the man dismounting and coming toward him. Solomon and George buried themselves deeper in the underbrush. Solomon felt for Slade's gun.

The man called Russell yelled back as he scrambled through the brush. "I cain't help it. I been got the trots."

Solomon could see the man in front of him. His back was turned as he lowered his pants. "Oh, God," Solomon whispered.

Russell squatted, groaned and grunted, and let out a stench that was paralyzing.

"Russell, if you like this, you ain't fit to ride," Jesse yelled from the road. Russell moaned and grunted, more stench.

"Sick as I am, I ain't gonna turn down good money. I'm takin' these niggers to Gibbon's Farm. Whew!"

The stench wafted Solomon's way and he loosened his grip on Slade's gun to cover his nose with his hands.

Jesse yelled out. "You just gonna slow us down"

"What's got into you? So what if we kinda late. They gonna wait for us."

"Just that I wanna get this over with. Ain't no tellin' what gonna happen. Suppose we run into trouble, you know," he lowered his voice, "the Raven?"

"I can always shit all over him," Russell shouted back.

They both laughed.

"I'm feelin' better now. Let's go get these niggers to the camp so's I can rest. You stay up front, I'll ride in the rear."

"Good, 'cause I don't have to smell ya." Jesse retorted.

Solomon listened as the voices and the shuffle of feet faded in the distance. His sweat had dried and he was now chilled. His muscles were stiff and aching. He stretched and rubbed his legs.

"Guess we can get up now," he whispered to George.

George didn't move.

"George, what is it?"

George lay on the ground. "Mister...George said, choking back tears...we goin' the wrong way."

CHAPTER TWENTY-FOUR

Fowler's Home—December 27—morning

𝓢lade moaned and regained consciousness. The side of his face was burning and he tried lifting his hand to the pain. That was when he found his hands chained to his side. He looked around to orient himself, but there was nothing but darkness. He wiggled and squirmed in the chair, but there was no give in the chains. His right hand throbbed so badly that his fist had become nothing more than a claw. He painfully unclenched his hand to get the circulation back.

Slade opened his mouth to yell, and felt a searing pain down the right side of his face. He remembered that Fowler had slashed him with a scalpel He was a wounded animal. He had made his living tracking; now, he was nothing more than prey, humiliated by his adversary, his face scarred; his name ruined.

As his eyes finally became accustomed to the darkness, he could see the outline of the table, and beside it lying on the floor, was the body of Dr. Fowler. He tried to remember the last thing that happened. He had had a gun on the man who called himself the Raven and the next thing he knew, he was out cold. The man had escaped along with the slave George. Now he was trapped in the cellar and with the stench of death permeating his lungs.

He did not know how long he had been out. He gritted his teeth from anger and pain as he stomped his feet, rocked the chair from side to side, strained and stretched his body. He tried scooting his chair forward. *Maybe there's something on the table—the keys—to help me escape.* Finally, out of frustration, he threw his head back and let out a noise so primordial it sounded inhuman. He coughed up phlegm. Then he heard a sound. It was coming from the cellar door. A soft tread of footsteps approached.

"Down here, I'm down here," he yelled.

Silence answered him.

He yelled again. "I'm chained. They chained me," he yelled into the darkness, but still there was no answer. "For God sake, you'll let the murderers get away. Help me!"

Still silence.

"There's a man been killed here. And I'm chained. I need help." He heard a scraping sound and waited. He heard the cellar door open and a stream of fresh air flooded the stifling cellar. A flickering light appeared at the top of the stairs.

"Help me. I'm chained. Who's there?"

A light floated down the stairs. When it hit his eyes, he was blinded and turned away. The figure slowly glided toward him. He heard the rustle of a skirt and a beam of light glinted off a scalpel in her hand.

"Mrs. Fowler?" he whispered incredulously. She did not say a word, but stepped toward him so he could see her in full view and he was startled by how young she was. She may have been a year or two older than the slave Leona. Dr. Fowler had to be twenty years her senior.

Even young, Annie Fowler's thin, pale face was lined and blotched. Her huge blue eyes were sunken and unfocused. Her wrists were no larger than a child's. She tilted her head as if attempting to understand the havoc that had taken place.

"He's dead, isn't he?" There was an otherworldly quality to her voice.

"Yes, he is. A man killed him and tied me up. I…"

But Annie Fowler wasn't listening to him.

He watched as she held up the scalpel and examined it as if seeing it for the first time.

"He never loved me, you know. He told my father that he would take care of me. But he never loved me. Not like a man should a woman."

"Yes, please find the keys and unchain me," Slade said, impatiently rattling the chains to show he was bound.

"He took me as his bride when I was thirteen. Papa was dying and he wanted to make sure that I would be taken care of. Papa told Dr. Fowler that I would inherit all his money."

"Mrs. Fowler, we have no time. Those men who murdered your husband are escaping. I don't know how long it will take the authorities to get here, but the longer we wait, the farther they'll get. Unchain me," he demanded.

Instead, the young woman moved closer to her husband's body, using the lantern to examine him.

"…but I think he just wanted my money…" she continued, oblivious to Slade's demands. "Louisville is such a lively place. My father and I would go to the theater, the opera. Oh, we had such a wonderful time. But Dr. Fowler never took me any place," her voice hardened. She stepped over her husband's body and shone the light in Slade's face.

"He brought me here to this place and all he cared about were his patients and his experiments. He used to experiment with animals in the cellar, did you know that?"

Slade coxed her gently. "Mrs. Fowler, you should put the scalpel down. You might hurt yourself."

"Poor little things. I would come down here and try to comfort them. Poor little things. I gave them a proper funeral. I shall do the same for Nathaniel when the authorities get here. I will bury him where I buried the animals." She walked toward Slade and held out the scalpel inches from his face.

She shook her head. "He took me at thirteen. He kept me here like a prisoner," her voice quivered. "But he was my husband, you see. And I am always to obey my husband. That's what Papa told me."

"Mrs. Fowler, I have to get out of here and find the men who killed him. This is my job. This is what I do. You want that, don't you? Are there keys?" he asked, desperately afraid that one wrong word would set her off. Her lips twisted and her eyes narrowed.

"He didn't pay any attention to me after *she* grew up," she spat out. "He would just stay in his office and sniff those chemicals and all he could talk about was his dear sweet Leona," she drew the name out in eerie singsong.

"Leeeeooonnnaaaa, Leeeooonnnaaaa."

She's as mad as her husband. "Mrs. Fowler, listen to me. Find the keys and get me out," he said, emphatically. She bent over him, the lantern in one hand, and the scalpel in another. She was so close that he could smell her fetid breath.

"You're hurt, you poor thing." She set the scalpel and lantern on the table and pulled out a set of keys from her skirt pocket and held them up. "Let me unchain you." She knelt down and unlocked the chains. When they fell away, Slade stood and grabbed hold of the chair to steady himself. He rubbed his legs.

"Do you know what time it is?" he asked Mrs. Fowler who had been drawn back to her husband's body and was staring at it curiously.

"I need to cover him," she said to herself. "I don't like all this mess. I told him so. I don't want any blood in my parlor. It's my house, too," she whimpered. Her thin body shook. She turned and squinted up at him, her head cocked coquettishly to one side. "And who are you?"

Slade blinked, surprised at the question. More surprised that he had no answer. He could not use his real name. His reputation was ruined. *Who was he?*

He turned his back on Mrs. Fowler and without another word, climbed the cellar stairs to daylight. When she called out to him, he ignored her. His only response was to slam the cellar door in his wake.

CHAPTER TWENTY-FIVE

Ripley, Ohio—morning

Valentine scoured the wharf, searched the warehouses, and questioned the dock workers to see if they'd seen a young brown skin woman with a shawl. Frustrated, he ran up and down the main street, searching the crowd, and then he headed toward the open-air market. He wandered the aisles until, out of the corner of his eye, he saw a woman standing in a doorway. The shawl covered most of her face, but he knew it was Mary George. He ran to her and grabbed her by the arm before she had a chance to run.

"Tell me where Solomon is, Mary."

She tried to pull away. "I don't...don't."

Valentine gripped her harder. All the passion he had for her— the desire, the intimacy turned in on itself and exploded into rage. He shook her. "Don't lie to me. Joseph Greene said you and Solomon were talking last night. Now Solomon's gone and Greene thinks you've gone with him."

"I ain't workin' there no more," she said defiantly and looked away.

Valentine grabbed her face and held it. "You'll tell me the truth," he demanded. "What have you done with him?"

"I ain't done nothin'. He was...was gonna rescue my brother and...and he told me to come get you if...if...he don't make it back." She held her head down, avoiding his eyes. "But it ain't time yet. He still got 'til tonight," she insisted.

Valentine looked at her stunned. "You're the girl in his poem? The one who...who...has a brother?"

"Yes, sir Mr. Valentine. This...this slave catcher he told me he was gonna kill my brother if'n I didn't get the Raven to him." She looked away.

"And you told Solomon and he decided to help you?" he said, sharply.

Leona nodded

"And then what happened?" he demanded.

She fidgeted and lowered her gaze. "He took hisself a ferry over last night. I...told him...where...to find Dr. Fowler's house," and then she added softly, "...but then I tells him that it was a trap 'cause I figure I don't want him dead. When I told him, he tells me he goin' anyways. He say if he don't come back to tell this man called the Grinder...and if...if I cain't find him to come to you."

"Look at me," he shouted. "You led him into a trap?"

Her head jerked up. "I was scared they was gonna kill my brother." She began crying softly.

Valentine swiftly raised his fist and smashed it against the wooden door. Leona screeched and ducked, crouching in a ball.

"You sent him to his death," he bellowed.

She covered her face.

"Get up," he demanded.

She still cowered.

Valentine looked around and realized he was drawing a crowd. He willed himself to be calm, and bent down to enfold her in his arms. "I'm sorry, let's go back to my shop where we can talk," he said gently. He held out his hand and she hesitantly took it. He pushed his way through the crowd until he got to the shop. He unlocked the door, pulled her inside and closed it behind them. "Now, tell me the whole story. How did you meet Solomon,

Mary?" Leona looked at him briefly, then down at the floor.

"It's Leona...My name is Leona..." she began. And she told him how she had been put in jail, how Solomon got her out, how she'd jumped overboard because she thought they were going to skin her alive or eat her.

She told Valentine how Greene thought she was from Africa Hill and hired her for his household. That's where she met Solomon who said he could help rescue her brother George.

"The slave catcher say he gonna kill my brother if I don't give him the Raven."

"What's his name?"

Leona shook her head, "He don't tell me his name. But Mr. Solomon think his name Slade."

Valentine recoiled at the name.

"Please Mr. Valentine, I'm tellin' the truth. He told me to fetch you if somethin' went wrong, but its not time."

"Mary...Leona...How do I know this isn't another trap?"

"I swear to God...on my brother's life...I'm tellin' the truth." Then she reached into her skirt pocket and pulled out the watch fob. "He gib me this for you. And he say once I do, you would know what to do. He say make sure I get outta town to Cincinnati to a mister...mister..." she closed her eyes trying to remember. "Lee...Lee"

"Coffin, Levi Coffin," Valentine finished. He stared at her, weighing whether to believe her. "So, you're that runaway."

"Yes, sir. I...I think so."

He nodded his understanding.

"Do you regret it?. I mean, leaving? "

"Oh, no sir. I...I...was real scared 'cause I been told that the abolitions eat slaves like me. But...but...I know better now. Dr. Fowler tells me that so's I wouldn't run away. My brother George, he was right about Dr. Fowler. I know better now. I been free and...and...I like it...I meets nice people. Nice people like you," she said, giving Valentine a lingering look.

"Well, you must be hungry," he said abruptly and then he walked out of the room.

Leona did not know what to think. She was so tired from worry and guilt that her legs shook and her hands sweated. She brushed her palms down on her skirt and leaned against the door, surveying the austere surroundings. There was one chair near a bed and a table. There were no decorations, nothing to hint at who Valentine was. It was as bare as a slave's quarter. She heard Valentine as he entered the room carrying a plate.

"Come and sit down and have something to eat, bread and cheese," he gestured, setting the plate down. He saw her looking at his room and smiled. "Most of what I have is in the barber shop, he said, pouring her a steaming cup of strong coffee. The lines in his face softened as he watched her sip the strong brew then shovel the cheese in her mouth.

Valentine sat across from her with his hands folded tightly, waiting patiently for her to eat her fill. When she was done picking breadcrumbs from her plate, he slid the plate aside.

"I need you to do something."

"Yes, Mister Valentine."

"I need you to go to Grinder and tell him your whole story. Also tell him that I must find Solomon."

"But...it ain't evenin' yet. He said to wait until it get dark," Leona protested.

Valentine ignored her. "How long do you think it would take to go back to Dr. Fowler's?"

She shrugged, "Maybe a hour...that is, if you got a good horse. He don't live that far out of town, but it set back off the road a piece. He don't live near nobody except the Mercer plantation. That's where my brother was."

"Would patrollers be in that area?"

"They don't go that far in...but one did, that's how I was caught," she folded her hands in her lap and looked down. "Mister Valentine, I...I...didn't want nothin' ta happen to Mister Solomon. But that man, he...he said that if I don't give him the Raven, he gonna kill George and come back for me," she looked up. "I don't want nobody to get hurt," she shook uncontrollably.

Valentine looked at her as she sobbed. Part of him wanted to rush to her, soothe and comfort her. The other part hesitated because he didn't know who he was dealing with. This woman who had so captured his heart, this woman who had been the cause of his arguments with Solomon, this woman who had admonished him because she felt he could not relate to being a slave, this woman who still smelled of his rose lotion, stirred feelings in him so violent he didn't know whether to hit her or kiss her. And yet, this woman had set a trap for his friend that could get him killed

Then she said something that was so unexpected, it took his breath away. Leona looked at him and through her tears, she took his hand and whispered, "Mr. Valentine, I...I can go back, if you think it'll save my brother and Mr. Solomon. I'll go back."

"You would go back into slavery?" he choked.

She nodded.

Valentine rushed over, pulled her to her feet, and impulsively kissed her. She returned the kiss, and for one moment they forgot where they were. Valentine was the first to come to his senses. He pulled away and stared into her eyes.

"Leona," he said softly, allowing her name to roll off his lips. "If they are alive, I will free them," he said, his lips brushing her hair. "You'll never be a slave again, I promise."

CHAPTER TWENTY-SIX

Maysville, Kentucky—afternoon

Valentine had taken several hours to prepare. He had scrambled to get supplies he thought he could use: extra clothing, knife, rope, wine he laced with laudanum, chloroform, and food. Now the sun was high overhead as he kept his horse at a steady pace, guiding the animal around the stacked bales and barrels ready to be loaded onto boats. He pulled his battered hat over his face and scratched where the heavy workman's woolen pants were biting into his skin. He felt for the fake pass in his shirt. His freedom papers were lodged in his boot. Solomon's pistols were stuffed in the band of his workman's pants, but he wished he could keep his heart from racing.

Every beat of his heart reminded him that he was alive and free, but his freedom was a temporary illusion. That was because anyone could point a finger at him at any time, and accuse him of being a fugitive. Then he would be back in slavery. He pushed this out of his mind by trying to think about something else. Immediately, Leona's face appeared.

Valentine remembered how Leona looked when he last saw her. She stood in the doorway before she went to find Grinder. Her eyes were gleaming with excitement as she held his hand and whispered softly. "I'll pray for you." Their lips touched lightly. He clung to her knowing that this might be the last time they would see one another.

"Hey, watch it nigger." Shaken from his thoughts, Valentine pulled up the reins abruptly before he ran down a worker who was carrying a barrel on his shoulders.

Valentine tipped his hat. "Sorry sir. 'xcuse me, sir." Valentine watched after the man and fought the urge to turn around and look toward the floor of the wagon where he had hidden the supplies in the false bottom.

Valentine had gotten the wagon from Jubba. The same Jubba that young Thor had complained to Valentine about. What Thor didn't know, but the Raven did, was that Jubba, a big, seemingly slow slave, used his hire-out status to help runaways escape.

Jubba had hidden fugitives on the plantation and in nearby buildings. He also transported them to the river, or sometimes found other ways for them to cross. Jubba himself did not want to escape. He said he was more useful to the cause if he remained a slave. Jubba had deliberately broken Mercer's wagon in order to build another with a false bottom so he could transport his human cargo more effectively.

Valentine bumped along in the wagon and snuggled down in his tattered coat. He tried his best to clear his mind of any doubt about the mission, and to look like a dull-witted "darky" to match his disguise. He glanced at the activity around the wharf. It looked as chaotic as usual; yet something about it that was not quite right.

He turned to see some of the slaves loading cargo on wagons. On the other side, a few passengers boarded a steamer up land toward Virginia. Then he noticed a number of men smoking and lounging among the crates, barrels, and luggage piled along the dock. He avoided staring, but as he passed in his wagon laden with lumber, he saw that these men were carrying rifles and guns. *Patrollers.*

They mingled in groups of twos and threes scattered around the wharf. A shiver of apprehension went up his spine. Where were the captured slaves? He kept his eyes lowered and pulled his hat down.

"You with the wagon, move out of the way." He heard someone yell. Valentine did not respond, but kept driving.

"Did you hear what I said? Move your wagon and let the other one pass."

Valentine looked in front of him. Another wagon was coming toward him at a fast clip with a woman standing up and gesturing madly. She was spooking the horses and the driver was trying to gain control.

Valentine maneuvered his wagon to the far right to let the other wagon pass. As he did so, the people around him stopped and stared at the woman who was exposing her petticoats as she mindlessly sang.

> *In fancy I am back again in my old Southern home,*
> *Where summer lingers all the year around,*
> *Down on the old plantation, never more again to roam,*
> *Where dear to me is every foot of ground.*
> *Again at Mammy's cabin door I linger still as death,*
> *Or 'neath the open window softly creep,*
> *Fearing e'en to lose a note, I almost hold my breath,*
> *When Mammy rocks her little one to sleep.*

Valentine stopped his wagon to let the oncoming wagon pass and watched the young woman dip and twirl.

"Mrs. Fowler, please sit down before you get hurt," he heard the driver yell.

She stared at the driver and then she collapsed onto the seat.

"He's dead," she wailed. "Won't somebody help me? My husband is dead," she cried as the wagon passed Valentine.

Valentine looked at the back of the wagon and saw a body draped in a sheet. *If Fowler is dead, where are Solomon and George? And where is Slade?*

ଓଃ

Northern Kentucky Woods—same time

"This was my plan all along," Solomon assured George, as he ate wood sorrel, a wild plant that tasted like potato. "At night, we follow the road," Solomon said, spitting out most of his. George looked at him skeptically as he chomped on the stalk of a Sow thistle plant and sucked the milky substance from its stem.

"But we ain't goin' toward the river. We goin' in the opposite direction," George said, handing Solomon a piece of stalk. Solomon took the Sow thistle stalk and bit into it. The milky juice oozed out of the plant. He chewed part of the stalk and forced himself to swallow a mouthful then threw away the rest.

Solomon leaned back on a tree trunk and gave George a reassuring grin. George smiled back and curled up in a ball to sleep. Solomon's face sagged the minute George closed his eyes. George was no more than fourteen or fifteen, Solomon surmised, and he was looking to Solomon to get them to safety. "Trust me on this George, we'll wait here, and at night we'll travel. We'll be fine." Solomon had told him. *If only that were true.*

Solomon slumped down and closed his eyes. He too needed sleep badly. But he could only conjure memories of his youthful stage career. He saw himself as a young actor getting thunderous applause from the audience. He saw his mother Arabella hugging him affectionately backstage, and smelled her perfume and tasted the make-up she wore as he kissed her cheek triumphantly. It had been a good life. He had been a good actor; he could have been a great one, if he had pursued it.

Nonetheless, being part of the Raven had given him opportunity for stellar performances on a world stage. A montage of faces danced before him: faces of despair, hopelessness, anguish, and defiance. He heard himself say, "I've come to rescue you." And he remembered the pride he had felt at his and Valentine's heroic deeds. How many fugitives had they guided, he and Valentine? *Valentine. He doesn't even know I'm in trouble. He doesn't even know I'm sorry.* He chocked back tears.

Now Solomon waited for the final curtain call on the tragedy that was his life. He had no idea where he was or where he was going. If they didn't do something soon, both of them would die from exposure. *No one will come. We are here alone. We will die.*

&

Valentine smelled the acrid odor of smoke as he passed the cut to the left that led to the Fowler house. His instincts told him to keep straight on the road. If Fowler was dead and his wife taken to Maysville, he surely wouldn't find Solomon or George still at the house. He followed the road straight for a mile until he saw an old mare grazing on the stubbly grass along the side of the road. She had been tied to a tree still hitched to the wagon. The horse was a sorry specimen, sway backed and mottled with fly bites.

Valentine jumped down from his own wagon and untied the old mare and inspected the wagon. He found a clump of hair in the back, picked it up and smelled the scent of glue. *This is the wagon Solomon used.* Valentine climbed back on his own wagon and proceeded down the road.

He had no reason to believe that Solomon went west. It made more sense to go north to the river, but then maybe he knew that the river was heavily guarded. Or maybe he had just gotten lost. Either way, Valentine followed the road, looking right and left along the tree line to see if he was able to spot anyone.

He noticed that the road was heavily traveled. Imprints from several wagons were visible in the mud. There also were footprints, one after another, as if in a line. *This couldn't be the forced march,* he thought to himself, *it was too early and they were heading in the wrong direction.* Again, Valentine felt anxiety as a physical pain. His stomach knotted. Something was wrong. He glanced up, and saw some noisy crows circling overhead— scavengers. This was not starting out well at all.

He had no idea where Solomon would be, and the farther he got from town, the more dangerous it became for him. His stomach fluttered and his hands sweated. He wanted to turn back, but his gut told him to keep heading west. There was only one thing to do.

Valentine cleared his throat and in a shaky baritone, he sang out the two stanzas of a song that Solomon had written. He hoped that those who heard him would think he was just another contented darky passing the time. The one person he hoped would hear it would know he was on his way.

> *His soul is black, as black as night,*
> *A good luck omen to those in flight,*
> *For he has come to set them free.*
>
> *And in the darkness he does roam,*
> *A spirit sent to lead them home,*
> *Where freedom waits for them.*

He continued to sing as he approached a slow moving line of slaves ahead of him. Men and women chained together, shuffled along as best they could on cut and swollen feet, their ankles chained, their hands tied behind their backs. The chain on their necks connected them to one another. The only way they could move was in single file. Their clothing was threadbare and Valentine could see the whip marks on some backs. These were the ones too mean to keep, but too valuable to kill. The women, some of whom had had birthed their master's bastards, were now expendable and could be sold for profit. A guard rode in the rear and another in front. The one in the front had a whip slung over his shoulder. Valentine tipped his hat to the rear guard, as he maneuvered his wagon around the column.

"How'd do, Massa. Just passin' through," Valentine said with deference.

"Hey, nigger got a pass?" the rear guard yelled at him.

"Yes, sir. Yes sir, I surely do. Gonna take dis here lumber down de road a piece." Valentine slipped his hand in his ragged coat pocket and pulled out a crumpled piece of paper and leaned over to hand it to the guard. The man looked at it and then yelled to the front of the line.

"Hey, this here nigger say he got a pass," the man waved the pass in the air.

"Well, let him pass by then," the front guard yelled back. The rear guard handed the paper back to Valentine who bowed repeatedly and averted his eyes.

"Thank you, sir. Thank you, thank you. Much obliged." Then as an afterthought he added. "Dis here road lead where, Massa?"

"You lost, nigger? Your master gonna whip you good. This the road to Gibbon's Farm and better get where you goin' for we take you to be sold," the guard roared with laughter.

CrossMark ∞

"Shhhhhh, you hear something?" Solomon said over George's snoring. George whimpered softly. Solomon strained to listen and he heard the Raven's song; a song that he had written.

"Good God, he's audacious not to mention off key. Get up," he turned his attention to George, "It's my friend here to save us. Let's head toward the road."

Solomon raced through the underbrush, beating back bushes and low hanging limbs. He stumbled on a rock and steadied himself, hurrying to catch up to the sound before it disappeared. He heard George straggling behind him. Solomon bolted toward a clearing and ran out into the dirt road, almost colliding with Valentine's wagon and spooking the horse.

"God it's good to see you," he yelled.

Valentine reined in the startled horse and yelled. "Get back. Guards behind."

Solomon disappeared again into the bush. Valentine jumped down from the wagon to calm the horse, and then went around to the back of the wagon. He looked down the road behind him to see how far away the patrollers were. They were too far to see what he was doing, so he opened the false bottom of the wagon, and grabbed two bundles of clothes and tossed them into the bushes.

"Put these on. And give those to George," Valentine said hurriedly, pretending to tighten the ropes that secured the lumber on the wagon. "Don't come out until I tell you it's clear." Valentine walked to the front and bent down to examine the horse's hind leg. He was like that when the column of slaves and the two guards caught up with him.

"Nigger, get out of the way," the lead guard shouted.

"Cain't, sir. My horse. I think he done got a pebble in his shoe. He was limpin' and I stops the wagon to see."

The guard did not answer, but unfurled the whip and let it fly across Valentine's head. The crack of the whip just missed the side of Valentine's face. He stood still, barely breathing until the column of slaves shuffled by, their eyes averted. The rear guard passed and sneered down at him.

"Told you, you better get goin' 'fore you one dead nigger out here, boy." He laughed and swayed jauntily. It was only after the column had disappeared down the road that Valentine was able to take a full breath.

Solomon ventured outside of the brush towards Valentine.

"Are you all right?

"Fine, just my pride bruised."

"Well," Solomon said, staring at Valentine and holding up his arms. "What the devil am I supposed to be?" Solomon turned around to show Valentine how the black narrow coat, double-breasted vest, and narrow-legged trousers fit. "An undertaker?" Solomon looked down at his feet. His pants legs came above his ankles, showing the top of the black leather, well-worn boots on his feet.

"Actually, you're the body." Valentine replied.

"What! Oh, you've gone too far. How did you think of this?"

"I wouldn't have thought of it at all had I not cornered the girl, Leona, who told me everything about your wild-eyed scheme," Valentine said tersely, while he pulled the bit roughly out of the horse's mouth. The horse protested, snapping at Valentine's hand.

Solomon stood on the other side of the horse.

"I rescued *him* didn't I?" He turned and yelled. "George come out here and meet my friend," Solomon turned to Valentine. "I saved his life, *by myself*," he said emphasizing the words.

Before Valentine could speak, George appeared out of the bushes, dressed in working trousers and a loose work shirt that was too large. He sported a sea cap that he took off when he bowed to Valentine,

"Yes, sir. Mr. Solomon here rescued me." He said, clutching his hat.

"How are you doing? Are you hurt?" Valentine asked.

"Beat up some and real tired," George said softly, scratching absentmindedly on his patchy bearded face. "Sure would like a bath and some food, though. Wouldn't mind that. And…and…to see my sister. Where's my sister?"

"She's all right. Scared for you. She's on her way to Cincinnati," Valentine said. "There's some bread, cheese, and dried beef in the bottom of the wagon. You eat whatever you want. Let the horse wander while Solomon and I talk," Valentine said, turning deliberately to Solomon, "…about a lot of things."

They did not say another word but stalked across the road and plunged into the woods until they were out of earshot of George. Using the dense foliage to deaden their voices, they circled each other, ranting.

"What possessed you to do this? I wouldn't have known anything about this until it was too late. You could have been killed. George could have been killed. And it looks like Dr. Fowler has been killed, and please tell me you didn't have anything to do with that." Valentine's words cascaded over each other in a torrent of accusations.

Solomon gestured wildly, "The girl needed help; and for the first time I didn't have to weigh every move and every consideration. I just did it because it was the right thing to do. And as for you, I didn't need your help. You saw that I could save someone without you and if you think that you're going to stand here and accuse me of being childish and immature, you've got another thing coming. And no, I didn't kill Fowler. Slade did." Solomon lobbed back.

Valentine was the first to break the stare. He rushed to his friend. He grabbed him by his shoulders and hugged him fiercely.

"I thought you might be dead. I'd forgotten how resourceful you are."

"I almost was. And I was so scared. Christ, what was I thinking? You should have seen Fowler and Slade. They were like nightmares come true. And where the hell are we, by the way? We're supposed to be going to the river and I've been going in the opposite direction." They both drew back and laughed.

Solomon scratched the rough wool pants that were biting into his skin. "What'll we do?"

"The river is out of the question. Valentine said. "There are too many patrollers. I saw them when I came in."

"Well, we can't go any farther. They're taking those slaves to Gibbon's Farm." Solomon said, recalling the conversation between the two patrollers.

Valentine kicked a rock and sent it flying deeper into the woods.

"I don't understand. Grinder assured us that the forced march would be sometime around the 30th of December, and the meeting place was east of Maysville."

"From what I overheard they're gathering near Dover. The only thing our friends will find near Maysville is an empty field," Solomon said, now using two hands to scratch the cloth. Did this dead man have lice? I think something's crawling over me."

Valentine wasn't paying attention. "That means that our friends will be walking into a trap. And there's no way to warn them." He was looking overhead at the sun. "It'll be dusk soon. We might as well bed down and get a fresh start tomorrow." He turned to Solomon. "With that suit, they may not recognize you."

Solomon shook his head. "What? Who wouldn't recognize me?"

Valentine walked over to Solomon. He put his hand on his shoulder. "Why the other slave catchers and the guards."

"And who, pray tell, am I supposed to have caught?"

"Me. Tomorrow, I become the fugitive slave. You're going to be the slave catcher. George is going to hide in the false bottom and when the opportunity presents itself, you'll cause a distraction, and George and I will free the slaves."

"You mean the two...three of us are going to attempt to free the slaves? Just like that?"

"You have a better idea?"

"And those men who damn near ran you down; I suppose they won't recognize you?"

Valentine gave him a knowing look. "When did a slave ever look a white man in the face? Those men wouldn't know me from any other slave in chains. Playing a slave is the ultimate disguise because you become invisible. I'll change clothes to make sure they don't recognize the clothes."

Solomon looked at his friend, doubtfully. "What's gotten into you? You this...this...isn't a plan. It's a suicide mission. The guards are heavily armed and you just propose to waltz in there and," he gestured with a wide sweep of his hands, "...unchain them and set them free. And you think I'm reckless and foolhardy. This is the most inadequate scheme we've ever done."

"And because it is made up at the spur of the moment and because I have brought several bottles of wine laced with the apothecary's sleeping potion, I think it'll work. So, let's get a good night's sleep. Valentine saw the look of astonishment on Solomon's face. He smiled. "Besides, I'm working with one of the bravest men I've ever known. The fact that you were so willing to rescue that boy is a testament to your bravery. You should be proud of that."

Solomon beamed in reply. "Oh, you should have seen the look on Slade's face when he saw me sitting there waiting for him. I thought he was going to have a seizure. And Fowler was spitting, cursing, and wailing. The man was definitely not all there."

"What happened to Slade?" Valentine asked.

"I have no idea and don't care. I left him chained."

"Well, I'm just glad Leona will be safe. She should be on her way to Cincinnati by now," Valentine said somberly. "That poor girl. What she's been through."

Something about the way Valentine said the last words made Solomon look intently into his face. "You plan to find her when all this is over?"

"I hadn't...I mean, I wasn't..." Valentine stammered.

"Val, if slave catchers can find fugitives hundreds of miles from home, why can't you find one girl? I can tell by the way you say her name that you've taken a liking to her."

"I...well...I..." Valentine was flustered. "I never thought to..."

"My advice to you is to find her and when you do, don't let her go. I think you're in love."

"Love?" Valentine repeated the word as if it were some mysterious ailment.

Solomon shook his head. "Val, you have many excellent qualities, but understanding a woman's wants and needs is not one of them. They practically throw themselves at you and you sit there like a stone statue. Remember that young woman...what was her name? The one in Philadelphia who kept plying you with cakes and cookies? All you could say was what a great cook she was. The woman was feeding you scones so you could appreciate more than her culinary arts. Now, take my Delphine for instance..."

"Your Delphine? When did she become yours?"

Solomon flashed back to the moment when he stole a kiss from Delphine in a corner of the parlor when they were alone. Kisses she was eager to confer. He smiled slyly at Valentine and recited:

Pluck from the fairest flower that grows in the heart,
Of fallen dews ere daylight glows add part;
Bid Cupid fair, then brew o'er lovers' flame—
This nectar that the very Gods would claim—a kiss, a kiss.

"Nevermore," he sighed and stood. "I have stolen her heart. That is what happens when you recite poetry in the ear of a young woman in a darkened corner of a room."

"And so you want to settle down with her?" Valentine asked.

Solomon just shrugged. "Maybe. We'll see, after this. If there is an after..." He looked at their surroundings and sighed. "I suppose another night of sleeping on the cold, hard ground won't kill me. Let's break the news to George that he's not a free man, yet."

CHAPTER TWENTY-SEVEN

Near Dover, Kentucky—Gibbon's Farm—December 28

For several days the captors had marched the recalcitrants, runaways, and saboteurs to Gibbon's Farm. The male slaves were being shipped to New Orleans to work in the sugar plantations until they died. Some of the women were being sold as prostitutes.

The slaves came mostly from small family farms, although a few were from large hemp and tobacco plantations like Ephraim Mercer's. Whether they worked in the house, or in the fields all had displeased their masters in some way, and were now being sold.

Slaves were being herded in from hamlets and towns like Germantown, Mays Lick, Augusta, Washington, and Maysville. By late afternoon twenty-one slaves had been rounded up, guarded by seven armed agents. This idea between two drunken men— one, a steamer captain desperate for money, and the other a young Kentucky planter needing to unload one or two unwanted slaves was a mirror of other transactions.

Slave owners in the upper south rid themselves of problem slaves and met the demand of slave holders in the lower south who needed slave labor in the mosquito-infested sugar, cotton, and rice fields there. Everyone benefited—except, that is, the slave.

Solomon and Valentine approached Gibbon's Farm, which was a thirty-eight acre stretch of land near Dover, Kentucky.

Interestingly, no one could remember how Gibbon's Farm got its name. There had never been anyone named Gibbon, and it was certainly not a farm. In fact, it was nothing but a clearing surrounded on three sides by woods. The fourth side jutted out into the Ohio River at a spot called Gibbon's Landing, making it an ideal place to load and unload passengers and cargo.

Solomon walked to the back of the wagon and knocked three times on the false bottom, the signal for George to crawl out and hide among the trees. Once George was out of sight, Solomon tied Valentine's wrists with a rope. When Valentine and Solomon entered the clearing, they saw agents wrestling with a slave who had been brought in from Maysville. The slave stood six feet tall and was built like a bull. Even with his hands shackled, the hulking slave resisted. He flung two agents to the ground, and then held one agent in a headlock.

Finally, another agent crept up from behind the resisting slave and hit him over the head with a piece of wood that split on impact. The slave sank to his knees, and guards dragged him by his arms to a tree and chained him securely.

The men and women were kept separate. The men sat chained, nearest the fire where they could be easily watched, and the women were placed farther away.

"Just play along," Solomon whispered to Valentine as he dragged him down from the wagon and pulled him along.

"Git over there, nigger. Go on," Solomon shouted, pushing Valentine in front of him. Valentine stumbled and was shoved by Solomon to a tree set apart from the rest of the male slaves. As Valentine pretended to struggle against his ropes, he spotted Thor down the line among the other slaves. Thor did not see him.

Once Valentine was tied, Solomon took his place with the other agents in a circle around the fire. All the agents then pooled their food and ate while the slaves sat on the periphery, cold and hungry.

Solomon nodded acknowledgements to Jesse Frye and Russell Caudill. Russell, the ailing guard, sat away from the rest of the group.

"Well fellas looks like we all made it." Jesse said, biting into a piece of dried meat. All we do now is wait for the steamer signal."

Solomon watched the others shovel their food in their mouth, using their hands to wipe, and belch their satisfaction. The two ne'er-do-wells, Harry and Jack, had brought in Thor and the female cook from the Mercer plantation. Solomon recognized them as the two men he had fooled helping rescue Leona. Then there were the two guards that had harassed Valentine—Jimmie Lee and Collins.

Jimmie Lee and Collins used to work the river, Solomon found out. They now were paid bounty hunters. Jimmie Lee was a tall, thin man in his thirties, Solomon guessed. Collins was much older and balding. Apparently, they both were good at their job because they had marched thirteen slaves; nine men and four women to Gibbon's farm. The last guard was a man named Monroe who brought in the giant of a slave from Maysville. The guard was a short, stocky man who had a hard face to match his disagreeable temper. He was the son of a plantation owner.

With his blond curly hair, smooth skin, and blue eyes, Solomon seemed out of place among the roughneck bunch. His dead-man's black suit made his already pale skin look translucent, a fact that did not go unnoticed among the group.

"Solomon, you say you from Maysville? Me, Harry and Jack worked with the sheriff's office. Harry and Jack moved on," Jesse laughed knowingly. "Don't recall ever runnin' into you. Do you boys?"

Harry and Jack nodded and mumbled.

Solomon smiled. "Did I say Maysville? I've been through Maysville been through many towns—but, I live around Murrayville in Virginia. Anyone been there?" He looked around. Everyone shook their heads. "Nice little town, Murrayville. Right on the Ohio border. Have a hard time stopping slaves from slipping over. Keeps me busy."

"How'd you get this job?" Jack asked.

Solomon was at a loss. "Well...uh...I...was...uh...it's a long story."

Harry shrugged. "We ain't got nothin' else to do. I don't mind listenin'. Do you fellas?"

They mumbled.

Harry smiled at Solomon, "Go on, Solomon tell us a story."

"You know, I'm pretty tired." Solomon yawned and stretched.

"Oh, come on. It ain't that late," Russell pleaded. "Take my mind off my innards," he said, his stomach growling.

Solomon wasn't prepared with a story. Neither Valentine nor he had anticipated that he'd have to come up with a reason why he was there.

"Them slaves ain't goin' no place and we ain't neither," piped in Jack.

"Not unless that Mercer gal wanna play," Harry laughed.

"She not the only one. We got plenty to go around," Jack added.

"Hey, nigger gals, you wanna play wit us?" Jimmie Lee yelled at the group of women slaves. Collins stood and ambled over to a female slave. He teasingly pulled and poked her.

"You know, I might as well fess up," Solomon blurted. "It was the Raven that brought me here," he said, hoping to distract Collins. Collins stopped teasing the girl and walked back to the fire.

"The Raven? What you got to do with the Raven?"

"Ah, well. I heard stories and thought I'd just take my chances at trying to track him down."

"No shit?"

"Did you have any luck?"

"Did you see him?"

"What he look like?"

"I know he operates in these parts," Solomon said.

Jack spoke up. "Me, Harry, and Jesse here had our run in with the Raven, didn't we boys?" Jack laughed.

Jesse, embarrassed, mumbled. "You ain't never gonna let me live that down, is you?"

"Oh, come on Jesse, tell 'um," Jack persisted. The attention turned to Jesse.

"Well, I been this close to the Raven." He pinched his forefinger and thumb together. "I seen him with my own eyes."

"Do tell," Jimmie Lee urged.

"Yes sir. And for a nigger, he done outsmarted me. I got to admit. I was shamed," Jesse admitted.

"He ain't no nigger. No nigger is that smart," Monroe grimaced, hacked, and spit.

"This one is. He were dressed as a old black woman carryin' coffins in a wagon. I was 'bout to open one of 'um and he told me it were cholera that done killed them people. Well, I took off like the devil was on my tail. Didn't look back, neither."

"No shit? But how you know it were him?" Monroe's voice cracked with excitement.

"They told me he left his mark. A black feather on them empty coffins that they found by the road near the river. Lucky for me that same night I caught me a runaway gal and took her to jail. Otherwise they'd a kicked me off patrol, and I need the money." And then he added slyly. "At least I didn't let a slave escape under my nose."

"Yep, that Raven a tricky nigger-lovin' bastard," Harry nodded, feigning innocence.

"You dumb peckerwood," Jesse piped up, turning to the others. "He ain't gonna tell you he and Jack is the ones who got tricked too. The Raven come straight to the jail and took that gal I brought in right from under Jack and Harry's nose. And you said he was a white man," Jesse said.

Jack bristled. "Maybe he was and maybe he wasn't. He coulda been a nigger, coulda been real light, like them colored bucks over yonder," he said pointing to a couple of light-skinned slaves.

"And you was drunk..." Jesse countered.

"And it was dark," Harry said, defensively. "He come in dressed like a agent with papers and everything. Had on this hat pulled down so far, couldn't see his face. But he done stink and the smell done opened up my nose. He say he gonna take that gal to Virginia and next thing we know, we got a rescue on our hands," Jack continued. Solomon held his breath, waiting to see if they recognized him.

Harry added, "Jack's right. He trick us good. Said his name was Slade and..."

"I don't care what you say. Ain't no nigger that smart ever. Look at 'um," the balding Collins turned toward the gang of slaves who sat huddled together in the cold. "They 'bout as smart as my mule. Ain't none of 'um can out smart the likes of us. Musta been a white man." Collins stood and stretched.

Monroe scratched his ample stomach. "Still, maybe we better take turns on a watch, just in case. They ain't gonna catch this weasel asleep."

"What for? The steamer gonna be here shortly," Collins protested. Besides we made sure that whoever ask us about the march, we tell 'um the pick up east of Maysville, so's whoever gonna try and rescue them, gonna find theyselves in a trap, that includes that damn Raven."

Jimmie Lee held up the keys to the locks. He placed the keys in a saddlebag.

"I better check my boy," Solomon said, standing. "All this talk of the Raven is givin' me a conniption fit," he said as he walked toward Valentine.

"Did you hear what they said about the Raven?" Solomon whispered to Valentine.

"Uhuhhhhhhh."

"They still don't know who they're lookin' for," he laughed. "These guys are unbelievable. My God, my performance must have been superb," he gloated.

"Make sure you don't start shooting off your mouth." Valentine cautioned.

"Hey, why are you bein' so out of sorts?"

"What do you think? I'm cold, the ground's hard, and my legs are asleep." Valentine snapped. "Just give them the wine," he said as the other slaves stared at the two of them.

Solomon walked leisurely to the wagon. He spotted George in the bushes and Solomon signaled for him to stand by. Then he rummaged in the false bottom to find the bottles of laced wine. He also discovered that Valentine had a bottle of chloroform.

"Mmmmm, great minds think alike," he said smiling. Solomon held the bottles up as he approached the campfire.

"Hey boys, we done a hard day's work. We need to celebrate," he said handing the bottles to the men. Drink up," he said, standing in front of Russell. "Russell, what about you?" Solomon asked.

"I still got a poor stomach," Russell complained.

"Oh, come on, just one drink with the rest of the boys," Solomon shoved the bottle in his face."

Russell shook his head, "Na, I still got the trots."

"In that case, you need this. Nothin' like takin' your mind off your ailments," he grinned at Russell.

Russell reluctantly took the bottle and held it up, then shrugged. "You might be right."

"Course I am." Solomon sat down and watched as the men passed the bottles of wine around and drank liberally. Solomon pretended to take a swig from his own bottle while listening to the men's exploits.

After awhile Jack stood up. "I think I'm gonna see 'bout the little gal we brought in. What you think Harry?" he said, staggering slightly. Harry looked up at his partner.

"Yeah, you do that," Harry laughed and lay down on the hard ground with the bottle propped up on his stomach. He turned to look at Solomon. "This here some good wine," he yawned.

"Where's your friend going?" Solomon asked, pretending to take another drink while watching Jack disappear beyond the circle of the campfire light.

"Lookin' at the niggers," Harry said, matter-of-factly. Harry stretched and yawned again. "I think I'm gonna get me some shut eye," he said to no one in particular. He rolled over on his stomach, and laid his head on his folded arms. The half-empty bottled rolled on the ground, spilling what was left.

Monroe turned to Solomon, rubbing his eyes. "Where'd you get this wine, boy?" he said, slurring his words.

"Brought it with me," Solomon answered.

Monroe squinted at Solomon suspiciously. "You know, you funny lookin' and talkin'," he sneered. "Maybe you thinkin' you the biggest toad in this pond with your fancy talk and manners, but I'm here to tell you, you just another cussin' poor white cracker. Maybe he..."

"Maybe you need to shut up," Jesse slurred back.

"Who the hell you talkin' 'bout shutin' up, sonny? I just sayin' don't seem like the type to get his hands dirty."

"You a plantation owner's son. How would you know? Us here gotta make our livin'. We don't have no rich daddies to give us things."

"What I got I earned, boy."

"Don't call me boy."

"Why not? You is, ain't you? Cain't even grow a decent beard. Straight out of your momma's womb, you is," Monroe teased. "That is if you call a Kentucky whore your momma," he derided.

Jesse lunged at Monroe, knocking him to the ground. Jimmie Lee tried to stop Jesse, but Monroe jumped up and took a swing at Jimmy Lee; now, those two were brawling. Both hit the ground and Jesse jumped on top of them.

All three kicked, screamed, pulled hair, and pinched noses while they tumbled on the ground and then as if they were tin wind-up toys, they wound down and stuttered to a halt. They passed out on top of each other.

Solomon surveyed the heap of bodies. "I'll be damn. It worked." He stood over them and kicked each one. The sound of snoring was his only response. Solomon rifled through the saddle bag and retrieved the keys and shouted for George.

"Over yonder," George yelled back.

Solomon ran to the spot and found George standing over Jack with a tree branch in his hand. Jack's pants were down around his ankles and he lay unconscious beside a female slave.

"What happened?"

"He was tryin' to do her. So I hit him 'fore he could," George said matter-of-factly.

"Good for you. Drag him over there and we'll tie them all up."

∽

"That's the last of them," Valentine said, shoving a piece of torn shirt in Harry's mouth and stepping back to see the scene; seven white men sound asleep gagged and chained to each other. "I've never seen such a beautiful sight in all my life." Valentine said, turning to Thor. The skinny boy smiled broadly.

"I was wonderin' if that was you, Mister Valentine. I says to myself they done kidnapped the freeman, ain't no hope for me. Then I sees George comin' out of the bushes, givin' that white boy a poundin' and I knows I was gonna be all right," Thor laughed.

"How'd you get caught?"

Thor grimaced, "When I run from Mercer plantation, I did what you told me, I tryin' to find Cap'n Julius, but I got lost in the woods and was hidin' when them two crazy boys," Thor pointed a finger at Harry and Jack who were asleep against each other, "...found me and tied me up."

"Now for the hard part," Valentine said as he placed a hand on Thor's shoulder. "You were brave to try running alone."

Thor just shrugged. "You gib me the way. I just ain't made it yet."

"Are you willing to try again?" Valentine looked intently into the boy's eyes in the waning sunlight.

Thor grinned broadly now. "I ain't scared, if that's what you mean."

"It could be dangerous. There's no guarantee you'll get to the other side safe."

277

"Ain't no guarantee as a slave neither."

Valentine let out a heavy sigh, knowing that what he was going to ask the boy to do would put him in danger, maybe even cost him his life, but he had to ask anyway.

Valentine looked at Solomon who had been listening to the conversation.

Solomon pulled out Slade's gun from his waistband. "Here give this to the boy." And Solomon handed Valentine the gun.

Valentine took the gun and made sure it was loaded before handing it to Thor, then he continued, "A group of men from Ripley, Ohio are outside Maysville, Kentucky. They think they are going to rescue slaves, but they have been led astray into a trap. They will be ambushed if they continue. I need you to go back to Maysville and find Captain Julius. He knows where the men are hiding. Tell him that I sent you. Tell Captain Julius that they're headed for a trap, and he's got to warn the men not to try anything. Then have him take you across."

Thor studied Valentine. "What you gonna do?" he asked.

Valentine turned to look at the group of slaves who were untied and huddled around the fire.

"We're going to get on that boat and take it to Cincinnati. We'll leave these men here," he said, tossing his head toward the sleeping agents. "Someone will find them."

Thor looked at the group of slaves who were now talking loudly among themselves. He saw two of the men fighting over some food. He watched as the big slave from Maysville picked up a gun and pointed it at the group of white men. George was trying to stop him.

Thor looked back at Valentine. "You gonna try to get all them on the boat?"

Valentine nodded.

"They ain't gonna wanna go. They gonna wanna kill these white boys."

"I'm going to try not to let that happen," Valentine said matter-of-factly.

Thor nodded. "No offense, Mister Valentine, but I'm gonna take my chances in Maysville and help your friends. I figure if I don't make it this time, it's my own stupid fault. But if you don't make it, it'll be them dumb niggers' fault."

"You're a good man, Thor. Take one of the horses."

Thor shook his head.

"They see me ridin' a horse, they know I'm a runaway. I go on foot. I can run fast." And with a wave, he headed back toward Maysville while Valentine and Solomon walked toward the unruly group of slaves.

"I wanna go home," complained one slave.

"Why didn't you kill them?" protested another

"We ain't gonna leave our families."

George was trying to calm them while Solomon stood apart from the group. He knew his white skin would not be of any use to Valentine now.

Valentine shouted over the mob. "Look, this is the only way that all of us can get to safety and freedom. If one or more of you try to run and get caught, they'll know that we've escaped."

"So, we don't get caught," shouted one slave.

"No, the steamboat will be here shortly. The same boat that was going to take you to New Orleans. We need to get on that boat and we need to take over the crew."

"It don't make no difference. We gonna be captured anyway. If'n we gets on that boat, them guards and crew gonna kill us," a coffee colored slave shouted. "If'n we gonna die, might as well take some of them with us."

Several of the men got up and rushed the unconscious guards, punching and kicking them. George was trying to fend them off, but the others overpowered him and threw him to the ground. Valentine reached for one of the pearl handled pistols he had kept hidden. He raised it and fired. All the men stood still.

"You'll leave those men alone or die." He pointed the gun at the slaves who were hovering over the guards' bodies. My friend and I," and he turned to Solomon, "...have a plan. Listen to what it is. If you don't want to join us, fine; but those who do will leave with us."

Valentine's plan was risky, and five of the twenty-one slaves chose to stay behind, including the Maysville giant. Those five promised not to run until they heard the signal—two blasts of the boat whistle—that everyone was safe on board the boat. They also promised not to harm the guards, but Valentine wasn't gullible enough to believe they would honor the second condition.

ဆ

Gibbon's Farm—December 29

They heard the whistle from the *Annabelle*. It was just before sun up when shadow and light played to their advantage. The slaves were expected to be marched to the landing where they would board. Valentine walked toward the slaves and stopped in front of several light-skinned men. He whispered something to them. They all nodded. Valentine looked at Solomon and George. "You know what to do," he said. George got in the middle of the group. Solomon gathered up some provisions and fell to the rear. Valentine watched them file by and he held up a pistol for all to see.

"If any one of you cries out, tries to run or warn the crew, I'll kill you myself." He glanced back at the five slaves who were staying behind, and wondered if the guards had a fighting chance of surviving.

℃

A light-skinned deckhand with mud-caked feet cautiously entered the saloon where Captain Thaddeus Moxley was pouring himself another celebratory drink. The captain was smiling as he counted the money from the Louisville Bank for the shipment of the slaves. With this first payment, he figured he could pay on his loan and pay his crew. The agents would divide the rest.

Once he delivered the slaves and they were inspected, he'd receive the rest of his money. Then he would own the *Annabelle* free and clear. He looked around, trying to decide how to refurbish the saloon once he became sole owner.

"Whaddaya think about skylights?" Moxley asked as he walked around his saloon.

"Huh?"

"You know, I could raise the ceilin' above the hurricane deck and put in skylights. Instead of plain glass, get one of them nigger arte-sans to make stained glass for the skylights. I'd put mirrors on one wall to make the place look larger. Seen that in one of the bigger steamers," Moxley said, smoking contentedly as he pointed to furniture.

"Velvet furniture. Some of them old style paintings along the wall." Moxley swept his hand around the room. Make it into a fancy passenger liner. Place where people'd know this was a class steamer." He stuffed the cigar in his mouth.

The deckhand shuffled from one foot to the other uncertain as to whether he should say something.

"Ah, Cap'n?"

"Crimson for the carpet and some chandeliers," Moxley offered.

The deckhand looked at the shabbiness of the saloon, at its peeling wallpaper, faded carpet, and flaking lattice work.

"Yes, Mas...boss. That'd be real pretty. Uh Cap'n, them slaves down in the cargo hold sir. One of the agents wants to speak to you."

"All of them accounted for?" Moxley turned.

"Yes, boss. We got seventeen."

"Seventeen, you said?" Moxley frowned.

"Yes, boss, uh, sir." The slave nervously fidgeted with his clothes.

"There's supposed to be twenty-one."

"Yes, sir, one of the agents wants to speak to you," he said hurriedly.

"Send him in."

The deckhand turned to leave.

"Wait."

The deckhand froze.

"Turn around," Moxley ordered. The deckhand turned cautiously.

"You're new, right?

The deckhand opened his mouth, but only a squeak came out. He closed it and licked his lips then tried again.

"Yes, sir boss...I...I...just, uh come on de boat."

Moxley pointed at the man's feet. "Where'd you get that mud?"

The deckhand looked down at his feet."Uh, sir. We had to drag some of 'um on board, boss...sir"

"Next time, you clean your feet or wear shoes. I don't want you ruining the carpet."

"Yes sir. Boss, sir." And the deckhand rushed out as Solomon came sauntering in.

"Cap'n, Solomon Tucker's the name. Agent for Mercer." Solomon held out his hand.

Moxley shook it and gestured for Solomon to take a seat. "Let's get down to the bottom of this."

"Hope your trip was without problems," Solomon said.

"It was as smooth as could be," Moxley said, sitting back in his chair. Break in the weather put us a day ahead. Now, have a seat and pour yourself a drink, son. And tell me how it is I'm carryin' seventeen slaves instead of the twenty-one I was promised?" he smiled sardonically.

Solomon poured himself an ample drink. "We had fewer than expected."

Moxley frowned. "I expect to get paid the same regardless. The deal was for twenty-one slaves," Moxley said, playing with his drink.

"Oh, don't worry sir. You'll be paid, all right."

Moxley stood. "I need to inspect 'um."

Solomon removed the pistol from his coat. "I think you should stay here with me captain," he smiled. "It's better that way."

Moxley let out a roar, and upended the table knocking Solomon over. Just as Moxley was reaching for the gun, Solomon flung it away. Moxley penned Solomon to the floor with his massive hulk and grabbed him by the throat.

Solomon flailed his arms, pounded his fists against the man's head, but he was slowly loosing the battle for air. Moxley and the room spun and grew dim. The next thing he knew, Valentine was slapping his face.

"What happened?" Solomon gasped.

Solomon looked over and saw Captain Thaddeus Moxley who lay on his back, open-mouthed, arms flung out wide. He resembled a beached whale.

Valentine held up a chloroformed soaked cloth.

"I see you've cut it close again, "Solomon said as Valentine helped him to his feet.

CHAPTER TWENTY-EIGHT

Cincinnati, Ohio—December 30, 1850

The Annabelle made an unscheduled stop in Cincinnati, and the crew members unloaded cargo. From there the crew fanned out from the wharf where, it seemed, they scattered and vanished in a matter of moments—at least that's what witnesses remembered.

Valentine, George, and Solomon found the Quaker abolitionist sorting through dry goods.

"Levi Coffin," Valentine called out, though slightly winded. Coffin turned. His deep-set eyes narrowed as he appraised the three strangers.

"Yes? He said, pressing his thin lips together. "Mr. Coffin, my name is Valentine Kass. This is Solomon Tucker, and our friend George. We've come to ask you to hide us and seventeen others."

"I see," Levi said, setting aside the clothing.

"We are rescuers," Valentine answered, "... soon to be hunted."

"Then by all means, I must help you." The abolitionist smiled for the first time. He then turned his attention to George who was standing in the background.

Valentine pushed George forward. "George is Leona's brother. I trust you have met her?"

Levi studied the young man. "Yes, she told me all about you. You are very brave. Your sister was worried about you." He looked at all of them. "All of you."

"Is she...is she here?" George asked eagerly, as he looked around the warehouse.

"Come with me. I'll take you to a safe house and then we can talk."

Valentine hesitated. "Wait, there's so much you need to know. And the others...they need to be hidden..." but he didn't finish the sentence. Levi gestured for them to follow him.

"They can hide in a secret room off the warehouse until I come for them, but we must get the three of you hidden," he urged them.

They scurried out the side door, down an alley, around a corner and entered a nondescript building. Levi Coffin finally listened to Valentine's explanation as they climbed two flights of stairs. Only after they walked over the threshold of the bedroom and closed the door did he speak again.

"They can't stay in the colored section too long. It will be the first place the authorities will check. Then they will need suitable clothing and will have to be fed. But rest for now and I'll have someone bring food. Tomorrow we'll come up with a plan," he said, walking to the door. "Leave everything to me."

George called out. "My sister, is she all right?"

Levi said somberly, "Your sister is fine." Then he closed the door after him.

After Levi had gone, Solomon turned to Valentine. "Well, we might as well make ourselves comfortable. Anyone want the bed, because I sure do," he said plopping down on the bed and stretching out. "George, Valentine, I'm sure those chairs are adequate. If you don't mind, I'm going to get some sleep."

George and Valentine took the chairs and tried to make themselves comfortable. Finally, George got up and lay down on the floor. Valentine slid down on the seat and propped his feet on the small table. Valentine was drifting into sleep when Solomon spoke.

"You know, we'll not be able to go back to Ripley."

"Yes, I know," Valentine replied.

"Then what will we do?"

"Find another place, I suppose. It's safe for us in the North."

"Valentine, what would you say if I chose not to go with you."

Valentine sat erect and turned toward Solomon. "Why?"

"I thought perhaps I might do something on my own. Perhaps pursue the stage again."

Valentine thought about this. *Solomon, on his own.* "It's your life my friend. Live it the best way you know how."

Solomon smiled to himself, "Thank you." He then rolled over and went to sleep.

Valentine too fell into a dreamless sleep, so he did not hear the door open several hours later. By now, the room was dark; and, a figure moved stealthily across the floor without any attempt to light a lamp.

Valentine's eyes shot open. He could see nothing more than a form in front of him. Alarmed, he grabbed the figure.

"It's me," Leona whispered.

"I...I...thought you were on your way to..."

She put a hand over his lips. "Don't wake the others. I couldn't go. I...I...had to stay...to know...if you or...or my brother or Mr. Solomon was alive." And she kissed him.

ଓ

Cincinnati, Ohio—December 31, 1850

The next day the authorities found the crew of the *Annabelle,* including its blustering captain, tied naked in the cargo hold. A cluster of black feathers lay on the boat deck. The authorities searched the wharf and the colored district of Cincinnati for the runaways, but the fugitives were nowhere to be found. The authorities sounded the alarm.

At the same time, and several miles outside of the Cincinnati city limits, a funeral procession of colored, wailing mourners walked behind a horse-drawn hearse to the graveyard of the African Methodist Episcopal Church.

When they reached the grave site, they buried the contents of several bags of clothes in an open grave. They then regrouped in twos and threes and with the assistance of buggies, wagons, and horses, headed north, using several different routes. On the other side of town a black couple along with a young man drove a wagonload of free labor goods to the Friends community in Indiana.

There was also one passenger on a steamer heading back toward Pittsburgh, an English gentleman who "...had just come from touring the Western regions of America." His name was Edwin Fitzhugh. He pronounced his adventures in America. "Splendid, love. Simply splendid."

The news in the papers reported on the event as one of the few slave revolts on a United States river. The *Annabelle's* captain was mocked. The owners of the fugitives threatened to sue him over the loss of their property due to his laxness. There were seven armed guards found badly beaten and still tied to trees. Their assailants had disappeared in the woods, and according to the reports, for months terrorized slave owners in two Kentucky counties.

Near Maysville, hired bounty hunters, and patrollers waited in the clearing to trap expected rescuers. It was evident after two days, however, that no one was coming and the ambush was foiled. However, they did find and arrest an old German man who, when questioned, said he had gotten lost. They took him to jail for questioning and found him dead the next morning. Mercer, who had plotted the trap, cursed his bad luck at losing his slaves and his money.

Patrols were stepped up along the Ohio and Mississippi and every cargo and passenger ship was searched. Northern papers hailed the Raven as a national hero. And the price on the Raven's head tripled.

ဢ

Ripley, Ohio—March 1851

"People just come and go. Come and go," Joseph mumbled to himself as he stood in the doorway of his shop, huddled against the cold and watched as three men loaded Valentine's beautiful green velvet barber chair onto a wagon. He bemoaned the fate of his friend Valentine who met his demise in a wagon accident, according to rumor.

It was a sign of the times Joseph Greene thought. Nothing stayed constant. Servants vanished, friends died, ministers left. *I shall miss him.* He blinked behind his spectacles.

"I say sir," Joseph yelled as he ambled across the street, bundled against the frigid cold, "Where might those things be bound?"

"Don't know sir. My orders was to pack 'um up and close down the business."

Joseph walked back across to his shop and watched as the workmen finished loading the furniture. He pulled out a letter he'd received several days before. The postmark was from Philadelphia. It was from Solomon Tucker who had written to inquire about Delphine.

Joseph glanced at the letter and refolded it. How things change, he thought once more as he entered his shop and closed the door against the chill. Three months ago his niece Delphine would have given anything to see Solomon Tucker again. Then Mr. Tucker had simply vanished without a trace, and with no word as to his whereabouts.

Delphine consented to marry the schoolteacher, and in a hasty ceremony less than two weeks before, the Greenes had seen their niece married. The young couple moved back to Tennessee where the schoolteacher was learning how to run a plantation.

Everyone was in such a hurry, Joseph thought, shaking his head. It was now up to him to write and break the news to Mr. Tucker. He wiped his glasses with a handkerchief and examined the seam on a pair of pants.

ଔ

Detroit, Michigan; April 1851

Valentine wrapped a steaming cloth around the stumpy neck of the out-of-town gentleman who casually sat reading a paper. His new barbershop was established on Congress Street. Competition was fierce. It seemed to him there were more barbers in Detroit than in all of Ohio, but he hoped to hold his own thanks to the help of Leona and George who provided "additional services" to clients. George peddled Valentine's lotions and herbal remedies on the streets of Detroit. And Leona provided sweets and cold meat sandwiches to clients who wanted a delicate snack while they waited for a shave or hair cut.

When Valentine wasn't busy establishing his business, he was working with Detroit's Colored Vigilant Committee who was involved in resettling the fugitive population that poured into Detroit daily. The committee provided food, clothing and if needed, resettlement in Canada. But Valentine was hoping to do more and made it apparent to Mitchell Scott. Scott was a light-skinned black man who often passed himself off as white in order to gain information about slave catchers who roamed the streets of Detroit.

Scott scoured the taverns and bars where slave catchers and bounty hunters frequented. He passed on the information he gleaned from those conversations to a clandestine organization whose members played a proactive role in helping slaves escape to Canada. Valentine heard rumors that these men, all of whom were prominent black leaders in the city, had formed a covert group whose agents were dispersed throughout the country and infiltrated the slavery system, putting men in strategic positions on plantations and farms in order to spirit slaves to freedom and, some say, plan revolts. Valentine wanted to be a part of this group, but first he had to gain their trust.

Valentine had changed his appearance. He now wore his hair long and sported a mustache and beard, which took some getting used to. He took to wearing more formal attire like the more prosperous African American men in the community. Leona chided him constantly about his "uppity" appearance.

"You look like an undertaker," she would say to him.

"Better an undertaker than a corpse," he teased. But inwardly he knew that it was better for him to look like the men with whom he wanted to bond. And so, he affected the outward appearance of a man of means as opposed to the fugitive that he was.

Valentine found himself scratching at his beard endlessly, and now that it was getting warmer, the beard and mustache were unbearable. He wiped his brow of sweat before he sharpened his razors. The bell rang over the shop and George ran in.

"George, get out your shine box for the customer."

"Yes sir, Valentine," George said, bending over the man's shoes.

"Did you help Mr. Smith get his cargo loaded safely?"

"Yes sir. And he was truly grateful." George glanced at Valentine with a hint of conspiracy.

"Good," Valentine said, knowing that George's "cargo" was a man who had recently run from a Kentucky plantation and was safely hidden in Finney's barn with other fugitives. They were waiting until it was safe to cross the Detroit River to a fugitive settlement outside of Windsor.

Valentine leaned over his customer and glanced at a section of news in the *Detroit Daily Advertiser* devoted to the growing contention between the North and South over seceding from the union. One particular long poem caught his attention:

> *One Raven's call is heard no more.*
> *He lies on a cold Kentucky shore.*
> *Dead, he fought to end the laws*
> *That enslaved men, true to the cause.*
>
> *Trapped, he did not beg or cry.*
> *Instead, by his own hand he did died.*
> *Proud, of years he toiled for good*
> *Of Freedom's song he understood.*
>
> *No man owns another's soul,*
> *Or heart, or hands, or body whole*
> *And grind him down until he's dust*
> *In God, not man, our fallen trusts.*
>
> *But there are more to take his place.*
> *Conspiracy of Ravens face*
> *The evil that men do*
> *To fellow brethren of darker hue.*

And like the train that rides the rails.
Stopping at hill, river, dale,
Picking up at creek and sound,
Passing village, hamlet, town...

Freedom's train is how they go.
Underground so no one knows.
Who they are or where they've been,
Breaking bondage is their end.

So, if you hear a Raven's caw,
Know that no one does it all.
Men and women, black and white,
Pledge to carry on the fight.
                    The Raven

Valentine re-read the first two stanzas and knew that Solomon was sending him and others a message that someone in the Underground had died. He silently prayed for that person's soul and knew he would be welcomed, with open arms, in heaven.

His customer, sensing Valentine's curiosity, looked up. "This Raven fellow has proven to be an embarrassment to those slavers. Mind you, I think slavery is an abomination. However, I don't hold to civil disobedience either, but this Raven is entertaining."

"Yes sir, he is that."

Valentine gently positioned the man's head.

"But then some say, he don't even exist. That it's the work of a radical faction of abolitionists bent on goading the southerners."

"Ahhhhuhhhh," Valentine said, lathering his customer's face.

"If he did exist, you'd think someone would give him up for the price on his head."

"Sir, I'll need you to close your mouth while I shave you," Valentine said, holding the straight edge near the man's throat.

"Of course, of course," his customer sighed and closed his eyes.

Valentine Kass angled the straight edge along the man's jaw line. This was his last customer of the day. He would straighten up the shop and meet Leona.

 times

Somewhere in the wilderness—April 1851

A lone equestrian, dressed in black, wearing a cream felt hat cocked to one side that hid a jagged scar on his temple, rubbed his disfigured right hand that curled into a claw. Slade transferred the reins of the horse to his left hand and rode purposefully east where he hoped to find the things he'd lost— his gun, his name, his purpose...and the Raven.

THE END

About the Author

Ann E. Eskridge has been involved with media for her adult life, first, as a television reporter, then as a freelance writer. She made a transition into screenwriting then playwriting. Her movie credit includes the award winning television movie, Brother Future. This movie appeared as part of the Wonderworks PBS series.

She has a passion for African American history and culture. This led her to explore subjects like the Underground Railroad, all-black towns in Oklahoma, New Orleans' free people of color, and the Gullah community on the Sea Islands.

Her writing on the Underground Railroad include the non-fiction book: *Slave Uprisings and Runaways: Fighting for Freedom and the Underground Railroad*, published by Enslow Press for a series on African American slavery; *American Profile Magazine* "The Light of Freedom: Uncovering the Underground Railroad", January 27, 2002; *American Visions Magazine*, "The Underground Railroad" February/March 1999

She holds a BA in Journalism from the University of Oklahoma, an MA in Telecommunications from Michigan State University, and an MFA in Creative Writing at Spalding University in Kentucky.

Made in the USA
Charleston, SC
11 October 2012